The Vacationing Wife

T. A. Malone

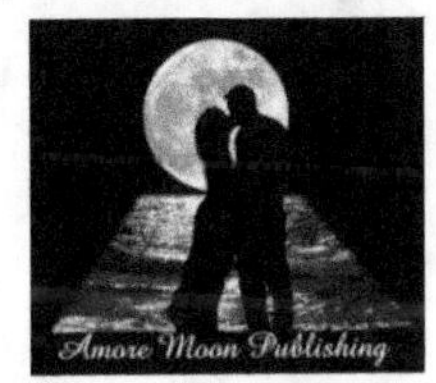

2016, Amore Moon Publishing
www.twbpress.com/amoremoonpublishing

The Vacationing Wife

Edited by Terry Wright

Published by Amore Moon Publishing, an imprint of TWB Press

ISBN: 978-1-944045-27-2

Chapter One

COLD WATER SLAPPED HER in the face, shocking Maya into consciousness. She cried out in terror. Her eyes snapped open, but a swath of cloth impaired her vision. She felt woozy from a drug-induced stupor.

"He-he-hello," she croaked, blindfolded and dripping wet.

No answer.

She tried to move her arms, but they were bound behind her, tight against the back of a metal folding chair. Her bare feet were tied, as well, and touched a cold hard floor. She could hear her own panicked breaths coupled with someone else's breathing and the occasional sounds of footsteps. She pivoted her head, tried to get her bearings, to sense something, anything familiar. But one fact could not be ignored.

The air didn't smell like the freshly laid linen of the Presidential Suite, where Nick had fucked her brains out, but reeked of sweat and reefer.

"Re-Re-Rebecca?" she called out. "N-N-Nick?"

She heard the echoing sound of sneakered feet moving swiftly across the hard floor, and then a stinging blow struck her left cheek, forcing a scream from her dry throat. Another second later, a harsher blow hit her right cheek and snatched the air from her lungs.

"Be quiet, you spoiled American bitch." Another slap fell on her left cheek.

She gasped as tears stung her eyes. "Please, no mo—"

The man grabbed her by the hair and wrenched her head backward. His mouth was inches from her ear, and his hot, foul breath filled her nose. “Speak again...” he hissed. “Utter another fucking sound and I will cut your fuckin’ throat. Nod your head if you understand now, huh?”

She nodded rapidly as tears streamed down her face.

He let her hair loose and smacked the back of her head.

The blow compelled her to sit up straight. She felt pee pool around her thighs and she began to shake.

“Look, mon,” another voice, filled with laughter, came from behind her. “She don pissed on herself now.”

The first man stopped walking. She heard his shoes twist on the floor followed by complete silence in the room, causing her to shake more. She heard him say something faintly.

Then she heard the click of a gun being cocked and held her breath as her life flashed before her blindfolded eyes. The unseen man fired a couple shots, and Maya forced her lips shut to stifle a scream. She rocked back and forth in the chair as fear and confusion ran rampant in her mind. Was she shot? Was she wounded? Was she going to die?

“She a smart one, no?” the first one said, his remark full of villainous mirth. “Smart and scared.”

She shook so hard her teeth and her body trembled on the verge of convulsions.

“She gon have a heart attack, mon.” The second man laughed. “She so scared.”

The first man grabbed her by the face, but his voice was soft, gentle. “Okay now, we’s got to find a medium. You listen, and you obey, no problem, mon. You make noise, you don’t follow directions, you die. Easy to comprehend, right, mon? Nod your head.”

She nodded.

“Good now.” He let go of her face. “But now I need you to relax. Breathe nice and easy now. In deep and out.”

She took a deep breath, held it, then let it out slowly

as if she were at the gym in yoga class.

"Again."

She breathed in deep then her mouth reacted before her brain could intervene. "Who...who are you?" she managed in a quivering whisper. "What did I do? What did I do?"

"Shh now, deary, all will be told when the time comes, ya hear? Now I need you to be quiet and relax. I'll have some of the girls clean this piss off ya when we get to your new home." He paused to rub her left thigh, causing her to jump. "You a pretty little thang." His hand rested halfway up her thigh. "Don't make me hurt you no more." He squeezed her thigh while smacking his lips. Then, abruptly, his grip released and his footfalls walked away.

She breathed a little easier, having learned from the short conversation that killing her was not her captor's plan. *Just be cool.* She kept breathing deep. *Be cool. Help will come. I'm the wife of a billionaire. How long could I possibly go missing before my husband notices*?

"Now stay quiet, deary," the second man said. "Get relaxed. After all, you got the rest of your new life ahead of you." He walked away.

Maya held her breath as she mulled his words around in her brain. *The rest of my new life? What was that supposed to mean?*

She heard a door open and the sound of a man coughing then the door closed. The sound of a lock sliding in place made her heart thump. She swallowed hard and breathed in deep then heard the same cough again. "Who's there?"

"A quiet man," a voice said. "Now you be a quiet woman."

She bit her lower lip to keep from screaming. Her tremors had subsided but her mind was still baffled. *Just what the fuck was going on?*

Chapter Two

MAYA STROLLED OUT of her office building. She wore a breathtaking powder blue Versace gown, a white Sable stole draped over her supple shoulders, and designer heels. Pedestrians stared in awe and cleared a path for her to the waiting limo at the curb.

Her husband poked his head out the back passenger window. "If I knew that gown was going to be so revealing, I wouldn't have let you wear it."

"Baby, why are you snapping at me? You brought the dress to my office. No, no, correction, Nikki, your ever-ready assistant, brought me the dress. Well, at least *she* knows my tastes. Besides, I don't see anything wrong with it. It fits perfectly."

The driver opened the door for her.

"Now slide your sexy ass over so I can get in."

"You know I always sit on the right side."

Maya pouted. "Baby, don't make me walk around the car and into the street."

He motioned across his lap. "Crawl over me."

She smiled and climbed over him, being sure to drag her chest across his face and rub his cock through his tuxedo pants. "Thank you, baby," she whispered in his ear.

He moaned then slapped her ass. "Fuck, woman, you stepped on my shoe."

The limo driver shut the door.

"Oh, my love," she replied sweetly as the driver got in behind the wheel and slid the car into drive. "I am so sorry. Your toes okay?"

"You did that on purpose."

"Really?" She glared at him. "Of all the things I just did to you on purpose, you focus on the fact I accidently stepped on your foot?"

He grunted and turned to look out the window.

Maya scowled at him briefly and wondered if Nikki was the reason he was fucking his wife less and less lately. However, Maya refused to be sad and allowed the passing city streets to provide her comfort. The streetlights relaxed her mind. She mused about the people passing by on foot, or in their cars or on bikes. Who were they? Where were they going? She used to share her musings with her husband who was rarely a source of conversation when they rode in the limo together. Often he was conducting business, and as Maya turned to talk to him, she found him in his usual place: on the damn phone, ruling his mighty empire.

"Oh, they want to play hardball on our bid? Let them know we'll retract our offer in one hour. When they call back, and they always do, charge them ten percent more for not choosing us in the first place. Hide it in the taxes and fees like we always do." He inhaled. "Tell that heartless bitch I'll see her when I feel like it...and send flowers to my mother..."

When Maya first met her husband he was so damn sexy, handsomely clad in a dark gray tailored suit. His handsome face, weathered mildly by age, was framed in a well-cut yet premature silver head of hair. And yes, the first time they fucked, he gave her an orgasm, a fact he brought up to this day. Turned out, the back-arching climax he created came more from skill than love.

Then he bought her gifts. Lots and lots of gifts. Lavish gifts, and he invested in her business. One day he had an idea and shared it with her. Then he had some more ideas, which he referred to as suggestions that quadrupled her business while cutting the hours she had to work. He followed all that up with one hell of an engagement ring, party, and a new car. It was easy for her to say yes. After all, she'd fallen in love with him, probably more than he loved her.

They arrived at the country club, barely a word passing between them since she got in the car. Still, Maya refused to be sad as she started to wrap the soft Sable stole around her. Then she felt his hands on hers, helping her put the stole around her neck and bare shoulders.

"Thank you for joining me tonight." He kissed her on the cheek. "You are truly my better half."

Maya gushed at the compliment and brushed aside all his earlier transgressions in that lone moment of praise.

He helped her out of the car and flaunted her as they walked inside. The host stood by the door and greeted partygoers at the entryway with genial smiles and a gift bag for all. As usual, Maya smiled radiantly and relished the compliments from men and women alike.

"Beautiful dress."

"I love your hair."

Maya Valdis was often the most beautiful woman in the room. Tonight was no different. Even the hostess bestowed that title upon the younger woman. An hour later, drunk and burdened with a horrible marriage of her own, the hostess called Maya a bitch and other unflattering nouns, though all preceded by the word *beautiful*.

This club was her husband's domain, *his* country club, *his* oasis, the one place she only visited at select times. Tonight was only the fifth time in the five years they were married that she had accompanied him.

"Five years," she muttered behind the fake smiles and kisses on dry cheeks. *Five long fucking years of this kind of nonsense*. Parties full of folks with empty faces to match their empty souls, who lacked even an ounce of true concern for her well being. Their faces would be forgotten on the ride home, and the empty promises of keeping in touch would fall the way of most New Year's resolutions.

Worse, whenever she attended *his* country club functions, he would find some excuse to run off with the guys and leave her standing alone, yet again longing for affection. Later, when he was drunk and passed out, she'd have to settle for the mechanical yet reliable tenderness of her Hitachi magic wand.

Often she would find her husband in the company of one of the looser women at the club, just talking he would claim. Yet Maya never heard a single rumor about his improprieties, only that he was one cheap son of a bitch at the bar.

One of the wives had told her to get over the lack of attention and enjoy the perks of marriage to a wealthy man.

"Get some cock on the side," she'd say with a wicked grin. "Preferably a big black stud...a quiet one."

Maya had nodded and changed the subject. Yet the idea would fester at the back of her mind, teetering on the edge of fantasy and action. Still, for some of these folks to suggest a dalliance with a black man amused her.

She laughed outwardly every time one of the partygoers told a black joke about Liza and Rastus fucking in the mud or made a crass comment about black people rioting in the streets. Inwardly she would cringe, of course, but because of her education and social status, she wouldn't complain. They all thought she was more white than black and didn't demean her for being mixed race. She would hear how well spoken she was in contrast to some sales clerk with a foreign accent and unpronounceable name. Sometimes she would excuse herself from those conversations and escape to the powder room where she'd punch at the air and give them the finger from behind the closed door. She was sick of enduring dumb, xenophobic comments:

"They expect entitlements."

"Slavery was so long ago...get over it."

"No black man will ever date my daughter," often

followed by, "Look at the fine ass on *that* black chick."

But regardless what many white men around her said, their lily white wives often had a different opinion of black men:

"I would never marry one, but my God, that one time I was with a black guy..."

Often the stories began right there. *That one time I was with a black guy...*

"It was the best sex *ever*. Jim still thinks he's the only guy to ever make me come. Ha."

"I couldn't take it. Seriously. All he did was slide the head in. I came so hard I screamed. So I just sucked him off and swallowed his cum."

"After he helped me lose ten pounds, Raheem, my personal trainer, slipped what felt like ten pounds of dick inside me. If that black man had as much money as he had cock, I swear I'd marry him."

Maya never admitted to anyone that she'd never had that *one time* with a black man. She was surprised she hadn't even told Rebecca that fact, though Maya trusted her assistant and considered her a BFF, best friend forever.

Bored out of her mind, she watched the crowd. Occasionally folks would come up to her, ask her where her husband was, and shoot the breeze before moving on in search of the next person to impress.

She spotted her husband across the room, conversing with a burly black man sporting an unkempt beard. She smiled in their direction, and the bearded man raised his glass to her. Maya returned the gesture before strolling to the bar.

With a glass of scotch neat in her hand, she found one of her favorite spots in the club, a windowed wall. She stared out at the mountains in the distance, bathed beneath the moon's pale rays. A man coughed behind her. She turned to see the square-jawed beau with the striking blue eyes from the gym. "Oh my." She smiled as that tingle blossomed between her legs. “Are you stalking me, sir?”

“I’m rich. I don’t have to stalk women.”

“Oh, and modest too.”

“You forgot incredibly handsome and truly unforgettable.”

“I’m married, in case you’ve forgotten.”

“I haven’t.” He smiled. “Your husband is a lucky man.”

“You know Albert?”

“He and I have crossed paths, yes.”

“Not friends?”

“Oh, no. Hell no. I’m afraid we will never be friends.”

“Why not?” She took a step toward him and noticed his eyes rest on her cleavage. “Jealousy? Envy?”

“Hardly.” His eyes traveled up her throat to meet her gaze. “I don’t like the way he treats his wife.”

Her legs got a little weak as she felt the heat rise between her thighs. Her heart began to beat faster before the bearded black man from earlier stepped up, clamped him on the shoulder, and turned him away. Maya watched him walk off without another word.

“It was nice talking to you,” she muttered.

She took a sip of her drink then turned back to the view outside the window. Obviously her husband was not the only man who took business over beauty. Her skin was flushed and her chest heaved as she took a trip down short-term memory lane, remembering the handsome man’s steel blue eyes and the intensity they had when they’d met hers. She just needed to get laid. She just needed her husband. She just needed him to hold her close and thoroughly fuck her.

“Penny for your thoughts.” Albert wrapped his arms around her waist and pulled her close.

She shivered, surprised by the sudden public display of affection. He must have taken a happy pill, his nickname for the blue pills, because she felt him press his rigid cock against her rounded backside. "Just admiring the view..." Her voice trailed off as his tongue hit that sweet spot on the left side of her neck. She giggled then turned around to face him.

He kissed her tenderly.

She melted in his arms. "What has gotten into you?"

"My friends and their wives can't stop talking about you and your gown."

She felt a tingle deep in her belly that she hadn't felt in a long, long while. It was the tingle that only her husband could stir, like loosed butterflies that flittered to her head and her toes. Now was no different than the first time.

"Are you ready to go?" He gazed at her lustfully.

"Of course." Visions of riding him beneath the passing streetlights ran though her head. "I've been ready since we got here."

"Your body...in that gown...I'm surprised I haven't ripped it off you already. Let's go somewhere and ravish each other."

"Sounds like a plan to me." His jacket hid her fingers while they performed a delicate dance against the bulge in his crotch. "We simply must put this big guy to work." Her smile shone wide and bright. "But that lump is going to make it a little awkward walking out of here."

"What shall we do? I mean, we could just let my hard-on lead the way."

"No, thanks. I don't want other women to imagine your cock." Maya laughed. "Just hold me at the waist from behind and don't let go."

They danced their way out of the room, the very picture of a loving couple, all would say, finding their passion again after a brief absence.

They got in the limo. Of course, he sat on the right and laughed as he motored up the partition.

"Walking out with you holding me...and you were so

hard against my ass...it was so erotic..." she felt breathless, "I'm soaking wet."

"Let me see."

She gasped as he slid two fingers effortlessly past her cherry colored thong and into her wet folds. She felt her juices run down her inner thighs. She hugged his neck and kissed him on the lips.

"Hmm... You're right, but I'm sure I can get you much, much wetter."

"Make it rain, baby, make it rain." She inhaled and slowly pumped herself against his fingers, which soon numbered four. "Oh god." She moaned. "I want you." She pulled his hand out from between her legs and reached to unbuckle his belt. "I want you inside me."

"Most definitely."

She slid the belt loose while his hands found her breasts. He freed her right tit from her gown and fondled it lovingly. She groaned, yearning to put the nipple between his lips.

Meanwhile, she dug for his cock and smiled once it sprang free from the confines of his boxers. "There's my favorite toy."

His cell phone rang.

They looked at each other, a comical and erotic sight all at once; he with his cock sticking straight out of his unzipped pants, and she with her right breast nestled snuggly in his hand. She was beyond aroused, happy he was showing her some attention. "Please, honey," she begged, hoping the word honey would not let her plea go ignored. "Don't answer it. Not now."

He looked at her...then at the phone.

She stroked his hard cock, hoping to distract him, but he wasn't deterred and grabbed the phone. "Hello."

She pouted momentarily then got an idea. "Okay." She wiggled down his lap and legs to the floor of the limo. "You gonna pick that phone over me..?" She held his cock in both hands now.

"Yes, Jackson," the all-powerful Valdis growled into the phone. "This had better be...ah...important." He looked down at her.

She smiled wickedly. "I warned you not to answer the phone." She stuck out her tongue and licked slowly around the pink rim of his shaft.

"Jackson, your timing sucks," he said, trying not to cry out as her tongue traveled from stem to stern and back again. "Whatever the issue is, I'm sure it can wait until morning. Good night." He hung up and thrust his throbbing erection into her mouth. "Yes." He groaned. "Suck that dick, you bitch."

She gagged and tried to lift her head up, but he forced her mouth down on him, all the way to his zipper.

He liked to call her a bitch when she gave him head, and though his disrespect bothered her, she never complained, just got the discontent out of her system in the gym during her kickboxing class. Besides, the attention was worth the verbal abuse.

He jammed himself deeper into her mouth and down her throat.

Maya couldn't move, so she fought to breathe on every upstroke. She decided to enjoy giving him head, still happy he was paying attention to her. Just happy he was showing her some affection and appreciation.

Her mind wandered as his hips moved at their own pace. He enjoyed the skillful caress of her tongue and the firm stroke of her hand. Maya lost herself completely into what she was doing, though she imagined the long thick cock in her mouth was attached to a more deserving man, a man who truly cared for her, an idea that aroused her more. Soon her mind floated to a place where she made love to this fantasy man's shaft, while in reality, her own hand traveled down between her thighs and played freely within her folds as her honey seeped down her dark thighs.

Too soon, he growled and erupted in her mouth without warning. "Swallow it, bitch."

She slurped and gagged down his cum, knowing she was next to explode, but before she'd sucked him dry, he fell asleep, and within seconds, his once proud erection withered down to its normal flaccid state and hung limply out of his open pants.

She swallowed. "What the fuck?" The car kept moving and Albert snored. "Motherfucker." Aggravated, insulted, and still thoroughly aroused, she slid over to the left, tucked her breast back into her gown, and looked out at the city streets as they rushed by.

Tonight would be another night with her Hitachi. She would have to buy stock in the company and come up with a name for her own, since she used it so damn much. She looked at him, amazed a man in such good condition had the stamina of a narcoleptic cat. She saw the bottle of champagne on the limo bar, shrugged, and poured a glass to wash down the lingering taste of cum in her mouth.

Her mind wandered as the streetlights streaked by, then she texted Alanza, her maid, and asked for a bottle of wine to be left in her room. Alanza texted back, stating a red would be sitting by her bed. *"You are the best,"* Maya texted, jealous that Alanza was with her man.

Probably getting some good dick, unlike my sorry ass.

Alanza was dating a black man. *Lucky girl.*

Maya's mind wandered back to the cock she imagined sucking while going down on her husband. At first, it belonged to the man from the gym and the party. The bulge she'd seen in his slacks was quite nice, and she figured he was blessed. But then the cock in her mind grew greater in length and darker in hue. She licked her lips and had to stop her hand from traveling down her body as the memory turned as vivid as it was while sucking off her husband. It would be in her mind again, later tonight, after a soothing bath in lavender and a nice long drink while staring at the sky. Then it would be time to plug in her Hitachi and think about that cock.

Hmm...If I ever did meet that cock, would the same fate befall it? Would I be so into pleasing that cock I would make it explode before it ever got a chance to enter me?

She giggled, hoping it would go either way.

The guy from the gym and the party was lean muscled with an impressive bulge. And while a black cock was a fantasy, he was a reality. And that made him dangerous.

"For the sake of my marriage, I will live in a fantasy," she whispered.

So when her mind wandered to what else she would do, she made sure it was a big black shaft in her mouth, in her hand, and in her pussy, instead of the white man from the party. Her mind was filled with pleasure as an image of her riding this imaginary black cock filled her inner eye. She looked again at her husband, flaccid and still asleep. "Fucker," she spat, truly angry and hurt. *Thanks for nothin', honey.*

Her mind's eye envisioned riding that ebony dick as her Hitachi wand worked its magic on her clitoris. She licked her lips, her mind in its new happy place.

What a cock. Big. Hard. And black.

Chapter Three

THE NEXT MORNING, ALBERT KNOCKED on the locked bedroom door. "My love, are you awake?"

"What do you want?"

"Unlock the door."

Maya sighed as she sleepily stumbled out of bed. She saw her Hitachi still plugged in, sitting on a towel on her nightstand, and she deftly unplugged it and slipped the toy under her left-hand pillow. Satisfied, she adjusted her nightgown and strode to the door. "Keep your hands off, you hear?"

"I just want to talk."

She swiveled the lock.

He immediately pushed his way inside. "What a way to end the night, huh?" He still wore his tux. "I woke up in the limo."

Maya made a face as she plopped down on the bed. "Epic."

"What's the matter? Weren't you satisfied? I took two pills."

"So what? That didn't stop you from once again diving head first into our little routine."

"What routine?"

"The routine where you call me a bitch, quickly come in my mouth like you have somewhere else to go, and then promptly pass out. That fucking routine."

He sighed heavily and walked to her, his hands jammed into his pockets in his normal apologetic stance. "I'm sorry. I shouldn't have taken a Valium, too. Along with the alcohol and my busy schedule, the combination got the better of me. Why didn't you wake me up when we got home?"

Maya glared at him. "The driver offered to help me get you inside and in bed, but I told him to leave you there. I needed some *alone* time." She glanced at her left-hand pillow. "I tucked your dick back in your pants, of course."

Albert smiled. "And then what did you do?"

Maya fiddled with the edge of her top sheet. "I took a hot bath."

"And..?" He sat on the bed and rubbed her bare leg.

"And...I went back to the car. You were still passed out, but your blue pills kicked in when I rubbed your cock, so I unzipped your pants and rode you like a horse with no name."

"You raped me?" He looked aghast. "I feel so violated." He said it in a girly voice.

She hit his arm. "I hate you. You got me all hot and bothered and left me hanging again."

He laughed. "Hanging?" He pointed to his crotch. "I have your cum on my dick that says otherwise."

Maya blushed. "Okay, I came once, but I was only half satisfied."

"You got off. Isn't that what you really wanted?"

She sat forward and took his hands in hers. "Would you be happy with only a fifty percent profit? I wanted to feel your arms around me and my arms around you, and we could come together, like we used to do when we were madly in love with each other. That's what I wanted last night."

Alanza knocked on the open door, respectfully using the wall to stay out of sight. "Breakfast is ready."

"Thank you."

They both stood in unison. He smiled at her. "Whatever has you in a tizzy, it's over now, and I have the perfect remedy for your woes."

"What would that be, a proper fucking?"

"Yes...while we're on vacation."

"Ha. I've gone on vacation with you. You might be there, but you're not *there*. You're on your phone, business calls, deals that can't be passed by or details that have to be worked out. Like the time you turned our suite in downtown Boston into a makeshift office. Or how about the luxury cabin we had to share with a potential business client you were trying to steal from a rival? Hell, one time when we went to Jamaica, you stood me up for dinner over fucking fantasy football."

"Now, Maya, we have talked about your language. A woman of your stature—"

"A woman of my stature deserves a man who will dote on her. Show her some attention. Some affection. You know a chair is not a chair unless someone is sitting in it."

"What on earth are you babbling about?"

"I'm just saying that a room is not a room—"

"What?"

"And a house is not a home, baby."

He huffed. "I don't get it."

"A wife is not a wife when she's alone. I'm not meant to be alone. Make this house a home and show me some damn affection."

He sat back down, surprised by the palatable anger in her voice. "Very well then..." He looked at the floor. "I'll leave my phone here. How about we vacation on our favorite island? It's exotic, remote, and has very few cell towers."

"If you leave your phone at home you don't need *any* cell towers."

"Now come, come, Maya. We most certainly need a phone in case of an emergency."

"You never mean what you say." She sat on the bed and leaned against the headboard. "You never will leave your cell phone at home for me."

"Okay, I will this time."

The thought of having him all to herself made her nipples swell and strain against the silk of her nightgown.

Staring at her nipples, his erection grew beneath his pleated slacks.

She got up on her knees and dropped the left strap of her negligee. "Then let's practice what we're going to do on vacation."

He stood and walked toward the doorway. "Now come on, Maya. In order for us to frolic, I must do my work. So hold onto whatever tantalizingly erotic thought is racing through that pretty mind of yours...hold it until next week—"

"Why not this week?"

"It takes time to get my business straight enough for me to leave for three days."

"I want you for five days."

"Five?"

She dropped both straps, allowing her full, supple breasts to spring free.

Albert marveled at her body.

"Five long, luxurious days, baby," she cooed. "With me and these puppies." She gave them a jiggle.

"Okay. But no sex until our vacation." He blew her a kiss and walked out the door, closing it gently behind him.

Maya wanted to scream. He had done it again. Got her hot and bothered only to leave her dripping.

With a sigh of exasperation, she peeled off her drenched panties and fished under her left pillow for her toy. "Guess my breakfast is going to get cold."

Sadly, she turned the switch to *high*.

Chapter Four

MAYA FELT HER FEET being dragged across a smooth and cold floor before she heard a door open and felt a burst of fresh air hit her face. She inhaled as the sunshine hit her skin, and the smell of the ocean wafted to her nose.

I'm still on the island.

She was relieved to see the once dark blindfold brighten, and she could see, albeit faintly, through the thin white material.

A blurry black SUV sat in the distance.

She felt the ground change texture, wincing as her feet were dragged on a jagged surface.

"Pick her up, mon," the leader's gravelly voice rang out. "Watch her pretty toes. As little damage as possible Bossman said. She is going to make him a lot of money."

She felt a swift smack on her ass as she was not-so-ceremoniously hoisted into the air and cradled in the arms of a rather large man. His scent was a combination of weed, cologne, and a smidge of body order.

"Lots of fuckin' money."

She heard a car door open, then the chime before another door opened. *Okay, he's the driver.* Why that mattered, she had no idea, but since she was still clueless about what the fuck was going on, knowing the driver was something of a revelation.

The big strong man set her in the car. His rugged hands were surprisingly gentle as he situated her on a leather seat. She heard and then felt him grab the seatbelt and drag it across her body. Unlike the man who did most of the talking, he seemed to purposely avoid touching her anywhere feminine. She heard the belt click.

"Not too tight?" he asked.

She shook her head.

"Man," the same guy said, slamming the door. "She smells like piss."

She heard multiple doors open, and felt the car teeter as the men got inside. She could see the shapes of their bodies: one behind the wheel, one in the passenger seat in front of her, and the third sitting next to her. She smelled the same scent as before and felt a muscular shoulder brush against her arm, momentarily, as he belted himself in.

"Stop squirming, mon," the guy behind the wheel said while starting up the car.

She heard the engine change tone as the transmission slipped into drive and the car started moving. She looked toward the window, but only the sun's unrelenting light filled her vision.

"I hate riding in the back," the big man next to her whined, a tone she found strange for a criminal.

She saw the outline of a big meaty hand hit the fellow in the passenger seat.

"Switch."

"No," the driver shouted. "Bossman waiting. Just fucking deal."

"But she stinks, mon."

He was right. She needed a fucking bath.

Chapter Five

THE COFFEE HOUSE WAS crowded and noisy as Maya Valdis finally approached the counter to place her order. "Good morning. I'll have a chocolate latté. Medium... No. Better make that a large. I deserve it. And three medium caramel swirl cappuccinos."

The dashing man behind the counter smiled genially as she looked over the assortment of goodies. "And a dozen glazed donuts and two blueberry muffins."

The man, whose nametag read *Finn*, smiled brightly. "My pleasure," he replied with a thick British accent then rushed off to fill her order.

She felt good while she waited patiently in her black Minolo boots, black cashmere coat, and black and white dress. The other folks in the line would note her affluent appearance and marvel at the humble tones in which she spoke.

She admired Finn as he performed his job, remembering how she had once juggled a job and college. He turned to his left, grabbed a pair of tongs, and deftly picked up two big blueberry muffins.

Then she had a thought as the man placed the muffins in a bag. "Could you put one more in a separate bag, please?"

He did what was asked of him without complaint then returned to the counter in front of her. "That'll be thirty dollars."

Maya handed him a bank card.

"Credit or debit?"

"Credit, please."

She took the receipt and signed it with the pen Finn held out to her. The fact she'd run a fingertip across his hand in the process didn't go unnoticed.

They then traded: Maya took the bags, Finn took the receipt. Satisfied, she handed him the bag with the lone blueberry muffin. "Have a nice day." She winked at him and turned away in a flourish of beauty and regality.

Before Finn could reply, she was already outside, and as her trendy cashmere coat waved in the breeze, she felt proud of her small act of kindness.

#

A large black man with an unkempt beard watched shapely Maya sashay toward her place of business. A broad smile crossed his hairy face. The man leaned on a silver Mercedes Benz as it idled at the curb, his eyes shielded under a grey baseball cap. He was totally content to stare at Maya. She seemed to glide down the sidewalk. He watched, pleased, as every man who crossed her wake stared at her, and some even turned around to watch her pass. He gave a satisfying grunt before climbing back into the luxury car.

His right-hand man spoke as soon as the car pulled away from the curb. "She legit," he said more than asked.

The bearded black man nodded his equally unkempt head, now free from the confines of the baseball hat. "Mr. Valdis is right. She will make me a rich man, against her will, of course."

Chapter Six

MAYA WALKED INTO THE lobby of her office suite where her assistant and receptionist, Rebecca, greeted her from behind a high tan counter.

"Good Morning, Maya. Your husband called and asked that you call him right away."

"He better not change our vacation plans."

"Vacation?" Rebecca smiled.

Maya held out the blueberry muffin bag. "One for me and one for you." She pointed at the coffee and donuts. "One cup of caramel cappuccino is yours. The others are for my honey bunnies in IT. Oh, and you can have a donut too, along with your blueberry muffin."

"But I don't like blueberries." Rebecca blinked behind a pair of oversized oval glasses. The burgundy colored frames matched her skirt and boots. Very trendy. Today she had her blond locks swept back in a neat ponytail, tied with a single white ribbon. "But I do appreciate the cappuccino. My favorite."

Maya was already heading to her office when she stopped abruptly. "Darn it." She turned back to Rebecca. "I keep forgetting you don't like blueberries, because in my mind, how can anyone not like blueberries? Next time I'll get you a sticky bun. Meanwhile, you can have as many donuts as your blueberry deprived heart desires."

"It's fine, Maya. At least you thought about me. Besides, I already ate breakfast."

"Then let's do lunch. My treat."

"No offense, but you always buy lunch."

"True, true, but today, let's splurge."

"Ma'am..." Rebecca paused, remembering her very cool boss hated being called *ma'am*. "Uh, Maya, you don't have to do that. I'm fine."

"Nope. I'm the boss, and I make the rules, and today's rule is we splurge for lunch in honor of me forgetting my world-class assistant doesn't like blueberries." She grinned. "Besides, that extra muffin provides me with a mid-morning snack."

"Okay." Rebecca hoped the calories from the muffin went straight to Maya's curvy hips. "Thank you." She held up the cappuccino in salute.

"Come with me." Maya strode to the counter and claimed the bag of muffins then walked down a long hallway with Rebecca in tow. Other than the guys in IT, they were the only two occupants of a corner suite on the top floor of a fifty-five-story building that her husband owned. When they arrived at Maya's office, she set the muffin bag on the entry table and shook off her coat, which Rebecca took and neatly placed on a hanger.

"I can hang up my own coat, been doing it since third grade."

"Really..." Rebecca sighed and hung the coat on the ornate cast iron arm of a coat tree by the door. "Must we talk about this every day?"

"You're not my slave." Maya walked up to the floor-to-ceiling windows that accentuated the corner office and took in the magnificent view. At first, the dizzying perspective had scared the beejezus out of her, but after a while, the panoramic view of the city became a source of peace and comfort. "I need you as much as you need me."

"I know that, but your husband pays me to take care of you, and I always do my job." Rebecca found Maya's exotic beauty intoxicating. With the city's skyline in the background, coupled with Maya's allure and bright smile, Rebecca had to admit there was something sensual about her.

Maya turned around to face her. "I think you do what you do, not because it's your job but because we're best friends."

"Thank you." She stared at the top of her boss's dress. It was white and adorned by artistic lace in black, which accentuated her firm breasts while the dress's form-fitting bottom caressed her thighs just right. A vision of Maya naked gave Rebecca a rush of desire. She coughed, hoping that would explain the bloom of color to her cheeks.

"Sit." Maya moved to her desk. "I want to tell you about our vacation plans."

"I'll go get your coffee first," she said softly before rushing out as quickly and calmly as she could.

Maya's desk phone rang, and she shuddered at the caller ID display: her husband. He'd better not be calling about their vacation. She glanced at the digital clock on her desk. It was time to open for business, and for some inane reason, she made sure her hair was just right before she sat down in her comfy leather chair and hit the speaker option. "Yes, Albert."

"Just making sure you made it to work," he said matter-of-factly.

"Where else would I be?" She leaned back. "If I'm not here, I'm at the gym, or at the house, waiting for you to come home."

"I know, I know." He sighed. "So what are you doing today?"

"Uh, working."

"What would you rather be doing?"

Maya grinned. "You really need to ask?"

"Stay focused, Maya."

"Oh trust me." A vision of his cock, erect and proud, appeared in her head. "I'm focused."

"Other than fucking, what would you rather be doing?"

Maya pursed her lips. "Uh, I guess working out at the

gym or reading a book. Maybe some yoga."

"Well, how about all of them?"

"Does that include making love to you?" she asked sweetly.

Valdis laughed. "Uh, of course. Yes, yes you can do all of those things every day."

"You mean..." She dropped her voice to a seductive whisper. "I could make sweet love to you every day?"

"Now, Maya, I can't do it every day."

"Okay, every other day," Maya said playfully.

"Maya, focus. Get sex out of your mind and think about being on vacation every day for the rest of your life."

She sat up straight in her leather-backed chair. "What are you talking about, Albert?"

"I want you to sell your business."

She scoffed. "Who would want to buy my company?"

"Me."

She couldn't find words to respond. Her tongue turned to sandpaper.

"I'll take good care of your business."

"But what would I do?"

"Enjoy your life. Have some fun. Go on vacation for more than five days."

"With you?"

Albert cleared his throat. "Uh, uh, we'll see."

"What fun would it be for me to spend my vacation alone? You should retire too."

"Why? Because I'm over fifty?"

"No, because you've earned it."

"But I have a business to run. Our marriage is nothing without money."

She sighed. "Then I'll keep working until you decide to retire."

"Maya, my dear, be reasonable. You hardly do anything. The IT department runs your business, and your customer service department is located in Pakistan. All you do is get dressed up in designer clothes to sit on your pretty little ass all day and twiddle your thumbs with Rebecca."

"Do you really think my ass is pretty?"

"Of course, but that's not the point."

"Then I'll sell my business when you retire so you can rub my pretty booty as we lounge on the beach under the sun."

"That's not the deal I have in mind."

"Then consider it a counter offer. My company for your, ahem, company."

"So that's a no?"

"Are you going to become my personal masseuse and sex slave?"

"No."

Maya pouted, a little hurt that he wasn't even trying to play along. "Then it's a no from me until you retire."

"Okay...there's one more thing. I noticed on your credit card statement—"

"Why did you look at it? It's my money—"

"Maya, one...don't ever interrupt me, and two...you need to stop treating your secretary to lunch every damn day. It's costing me too much."

"Blah, blah, blah." Maya giggled. "Someone woke up on the grumpy side of the limo. Maybe if you had stayed awake long enough—"

"Maya, just be quiet and listen."

"Are you mad at me?" She leaned closer to the speakerphone. "You want to come by and punish me? Oh, I know...tonight, let's do it again in the limo...before you pass out this time."

"Why do you act as if you're starving for affection?"

"Because I am, baby. I get wet just thinking about you."

He cleared his throat. "I have another call. I'll see you tonight, and in the meanwhile, I want you to think long and hard about my offer." He hung up.

"I love you," she said to a dead line. "I love you too." She mimicked his voice poorly.

Leaning back, she stared out her window. A blue sky hung high above the city, with a few scattered clouds floating by on the breeze. She thought about Albert and what he'd said about selling her business to him. While lounging around all day seemed like fun, she knew it would get old fast.

She heard the phone ring in the lobby. Rebecca answered after the third ring. "Hello and thank you for calling the Serpent and the Fire dot com. How may I help you?" A pause. "I'll transfer you to our technical support department. Please hold, and once again thank you for calling," Rebecca finished with a happy tune in her voice.

If I sold my company, what would happen to Rebecca and the IT boys? I have to stay just to make sure they have jobs. Besides, I'd miss this view from my office windows.

She'd founded her business during her freshmen year of college. She saw a need, so she took advantage of an opportunity. Soon, she was making so much money she had to hire a customer service staff and a computer tech team to keep it all up and running.

Then she met her husband.

It was right after graduation, at a job fair. He was recruiting recent grads, and Maya needed help to run her business. The moment her eyes met his, she fell hard and fast. First, his money was attractive; he was a billionaire. Next, he had the swagger and confidence of an older man in charge. Plus, he was downright sexy from the way he walked to the way he gazed into her eyes. Back then, he actually paid attention to her. The way he listened to her, talked to her and gave her ideas, she knew he believed in her. He didn't even hit on her. She had to ask him out on their first date.

She'd never forget their first kiss, because once he got the hint, he ran with it. And while she had never put out on the first date, by ten that night her future husband had her naked on his penthouse sheets, crying out his name. Then eight months later he'd asked her to marry him.

"Yes," she screamed while his head was between her thighs. "Oh God, yes."

Today, she had to shake her head at her affluence, despite the loss around her. Now, only the tech team remained, but at half the staff she originally had in place. The customers she once communicated with on a daily basis now just clicked on their Internet favorites or tapped an app to get the same high quality products and service.

But without her smile and cordial assistance.

Albert had wanted her to outsource to a warehouse overseas. "Cheap labor," was his logic, but she shook her head, put her foot down, and gave him a magical blowjob. "My warehouse and its staff will remain here," she had said, pausing to slowly stroke his rock hard cock. "Cheap labor or not, charity begins at home, and the US is home to my company."

He said nothing, choosing only to push her mouth back on his throbbing member.

So here she sat, in a big pretty office, along with a capable assistant, and nothing important to do. The damn Internet monitoring service her husband owned basically ran her daily operations. Albert Valdis damn near owned her company already. Nothing left but the paperwork to make it legal, but she'd never agree to sign everything over to him.

She tapped the intercom phone. "Rebecca, I'm going to the gym."

***

Maya was halfway through her workout on an elliptical when he walked by. "Hi," she said, surprised that she'd spoken first.

His crisp blue eyes sparkled as they met hers. "Hi there, again."

This was Maya's favorite time to work out, when the morning crew of muscle heads and other workout enthusiasts were either on their way to their offices or homes. The smaller number of folks exercising meant easier access to the machines and fewer stares at her booty. She loved the attention her exotic looks gained her but not when she was all sweaty.

But here was this sexy rugged guy in front of her, slacks on, jacket and shirt slung over one shoulder, and a duffle bag strapped over the other. He wore a tight t-shirt that showed off his exquisite biceps and abs.

"It was nice to see you at the country club party."

"Yeah, you too. Sorry I had to rush off." He spread his arms. "Like now. I've got to get back to work."

"I think you're a little underdressed for work."

He laughed. "Oh, I'm upstairs. Up on the 50th floor. Besides, I run my own business, so I don't have a dress code."

"Now isn't it a small, small world." Maya smiled. "My office is on the 55th floor." She couldn't help but brag.

"Must be nice."

Her eyes dropped to his groin. The bulge made her imagination run wild and her pussy clench with anticipation.

He grinned. "I must come up to see you sometime."

Maya's mind snapped back to reality. "I'm married, remember?" She thrust out her hand to showcase her ring. The gesture was more for her than him, a weak attempt to hide the fact that, for a moment, her pussy was in control of her emotions.

An obvious side effect of a husband who only bangs me once, maybe twice, a month, if I'm lucky.

The man standing before her oozed sex appeal, but she dared not indulge. Hell, she hated being sexually frustrated.

"I know you're married. You always bring it up." Then he stepped in close. "But are you really happy?"

Maya stared into his hypnotic blue eyes, a clever answer at least a light year away while she fought the burning urge that blossomed within her. She blinked. "Yes, I'm happy." Her lying throat turned dry. "Very, very happy."

"Sure you are," he said with a wink and a half-hearted salute. "Have a great workout."

She instantly regretted not having a witty comeback as the man and his cute backside left the gym. She felt the tingle down below diminish and eagerly went back to her workout.

Maya had to laugh to herself as she got into her rhythm on the elliptical. She looked up at the bay of TVs, choosing to watch ESPN instead of the *Daily Show*.

Her mind drifted again. *Who was that guy*? *And why the fuck am I feeling hotter than July down there*?

She turned up the speed, determined to exercise away her arousal, but he was still on her mind.

And she liked it.

Chapter Seven

AFTER HER WORKOUT, MAYA sat staring aimlessly out her office window, as Albert's offer to buy her business still whirled tumultuously in a mind now full of troubling thoughts. Rebecca sat on the other side of her desk, blissfully eating the lavish takeout lunch she and Maya shared, though hers sat half eaten.

"You know," Rebecca said out of the blue. "I've never worked for a woman married to a billionaire."

"It isn't all it's cracked up to be." Maya sat forward in her chair and wagged her plastic fork. "It's more stressful than any normal marriage."

Rebecca's expression drooped. "What do you mean? To have all that money...if living your life is stressful, count me in."

"Oh yeah, the money is nice, and don't get me wrong, I love it. But...but sometimes..."

"Sometimes..." Rebecca prodded.

Maya sighed, closed the Styrofoam container, and set her fork on top of it. "We've got to work hard to get that money, which makes it hard to find quality time to spend together. It's not easy working hard for the money."

Rebecca snorted. "Oh yeah, I see a ton of sweat on your brow."

Maya shrugged. "Okay, maybe *now* that's an exaggeration, but I used to work hard. I loved it, and while I love the life I'm living, I miss parts of the life I once lived."

"You miss working hard?" Rebecca replied. "You are *so* weird."

Maya laughed. "I mean, I miss certain...things. Things not related to work."

"Like..?"

"Like when I first got married..." Maya's tone lightened and her face shined. "Albert and I would spend the days and nights together. We snuggled up in the morning, woke up late, and just hung out and talked. We'd go to the park, the movies, or maybe just take a long walk and just be together. Hell, we once went skinny dipping." She sighed. "Now I can barely get him to come home to me. And if he's home, he's either working in his study or asleep on the couch."

"I'm sure he's busy," Rebecca said. "Maybe you should retire. Sell this business and enjoy the fruits of your labor."

"Have you been talking to my husband?"

"N-no...of course not."

"He wants me to sell."

"Maybe you guys can have a kid, which would give you the perfect excuse to sleep in."

"Have you been stranded on a desert island all your life? You obviously don't know anything about having kids."

"No...but I bet if you were home more, your hubby would be home more."

"Sitting around all day eating chocolates and chasing a baby around is not for me." Maya shuddered. "Besides, if I sell, you and the IT guys could lose your jobs, and that's not something I want on my conscience."

"Don't worry about me." Rebecca looked Maya straight in her eyes. "If the new owner doesn't want us, I have a man who is more than capable of taking care of me. And with IT in such high demand, the boys would be okay, too."

"But I wouldn't. I know it seems as if I sit on my butt all day, but I do enjoy my job. I like working on new ideas, getting in new products, finding new ways to market my brand. I just miss dealing with people."

"To each his own, but if it were me, I would sell."

"But it isn't up to you." Maya huffed. "And I would appreciate it if you would change the subject."

Silence fell between them. Maya looked out the window, her mind even more troubled than before.

#

Rebecca glared at Maya. *Bitch thinks she's in charge. In charge of what? Not a damn thing or anyone. Her husband runs this show.*

Rebecca had a brief yet intense carnal thought about Mr. Valdis before quickly going back to Maya. She was still staring out at the view. "Have you thought about having a man on the side?"

Maya blushed. "Are you kidding?"

"Your husband has been lacking in his affections, so have you ever thought about having some cock on speed dial."

"No." Maya gasped. "That would be cheating."

"Only if he found out." Rebecca grinned slyly. "Besides, with men of his stature, you can bet he has some pussy on the side. Power and money are intoxicating to *some* women."

"Women like that are whores. Besides, my husband would never cheat on me."

"All men cheat. Or want to, besides, you're avoiding the subject."

"I don't need just any dick to fulfill me. I want my husband's dick to fulfill me."

"Hmm, I know when I want to be fulfilled and my guy isn't around, I grab my buddy out of the drawer, drop the batteries in, and let him tuck me in at night."

"Yeah." Maya sighed. "I've got a Hitachi wand I've recently named *The Rock,* and I've got a subscription to Pornhub so I can watch all the big black cock I want."

Rebecca frowned. "You like black guys?"

Maya laughed. "Girl, I'm half black on my daddy's side. Have you never noticed my year-round tan?"

"I never really thought about it. Just figured you spent a ton on tanning booths." Rebecca laughed. "Damn, no wonder you like black dicks. To be honest, I like all dick, don't care if it's black or white, it just needs to be big, hard, and full of cum. But I will admit I do love a big black cock inside me. I've had five. Shit, I lost count of how many white guys I've been with. How many black guys have you fucked?"

Maya pursed her lips.

Rebecca looked over the frame of her glasses. "No way. No fucking way. A black chick who's never been with a black guy?" She clapped her hands. "Now that is classic."

"I don't know any black guys. My mom is white, and my black dad was gunned down in a drive-by. Wrong place, wrong time. I was barely two and I don't remember him."

Rebecca nodded solemnly.

"My mom moved me out to the country, back with her white family. We lived with an aunt who was nice and smelled of syrup. They taught me how to be a lady, and what I had between my legs, underneath my blouse, and inside my skull were all valuable, and to never let anybody, especially a man, ever take them for granted. So I listened, and because of them I became who I am, a white black girl."

"And beautiful," Rebecca added.

"So I've been told." Maya sighed. "The first black cock I saw was in a porn flick, and to this day, I have yet to see a black man naked, hard, and ready to fuck. Now that I'm married to a white man, that won't ever happen. It'll just have to remain a fantasy of mine."

"If your husband isn't taking care of business, and it ain't like he would know, why not indulge in some strange cock?"

Maya shook her head. "I took a vow. If I get horny, I take matters into my own hands...no pun intended."

"Okay." Rebecca shrugged. "But if you change your mind, I got some BBC I can highly recommend."

"Big Black Cock?" Maya laughed as she stood. "No thanks." Walking to the windows, she felt that tingle again as an image of a hard black shaft slid into her, making her gasp at its girth and length. She shook her head to brush away the erotic image, but there it lingered, as big as day and as hard as steel.

No. No. No.

Chapter Eight

"HEY," MAYA HEARD FAINTLY. "We here now, American Beauty." The SUV stopped. Doors opened. She heard a seatbelt unsnap and slide across her body. The same pair of strong arms scooped her up like a baby to carry her. "You relax right now."

She heard satisfaction in his voice.

"Soon as we clean ya up, you'll be good as new." He then spoke quieter. "Just do as Gilbert say and you be fine. You about to have a good life. Well, a good life for a whore."

Maya's heart lurched. "I'm not a whore."

"Shhhh," the big man hissed. "Gilbert close now, girl. Hush now, or we both gonna get it."

"Tell me your name," she whispered.

"Elgin," he said quickly. "You talk too much. Women to be seen not heard unless told to speak."

The big man started walking, and Maya fell silent, listening to a world she could not see. She could tell they'd gone inside; the air turned colder and his footfalls echoed on a hard floor. Occasionally, she felt him step up a short stair or two, and then the ground would level off. Through open windows, she heard birds and water crashing against the shore outside. She inhaled, smelled something familiar and couldn't help but smile. "Ganja?"

Elgin laughed. "You smell it too, huh? You behave, you get some. You cause a ruckus, you get slapped. Understand now, eh?"

"Okay."

The big man isn't so bad after all.

"Gilbert, she is here."

She heard a door open and a raspy voice. "Take her upstairs." He coughed.

She figured Gilbert had just entered the room.

"First pass the duchie."

Maya tensed. She heard him take a long toke.

"Yeah," Elgin murmured, holding in the smoke. There was silence for a moment, and then Maya felt a cigar full of weed touch her lips.

"Smoke, bitch, now." It was Gilbert's raspy voice close to her ear.

Maya took a toke and coughed hard.

"She be used to that American shit." Gilbert laughed. "This here home grown true, true Jamaican. None better, girl."

"Give her more," Elgin said. "Make her easier to deal with now."

The cigar touched her lips again. She stopped coughing long enough to suck in the smoke.

"She got nice lips, mon," Gilbert said. "Okay, enough." He snatched it away.

Maya coughed once but managed to hold in most of the smoke.

"Yer welcome." Gilbert chuckled. "Take her on up now. Taite and the girls waiting for her."

Exhaling, she heard Elgin take one more hit before he turned left and started up a set of stairs. They seemed to last forever, yet the big man didn't sound out of breath at all. She had a thought and leaned her head against his chest. He said nothing, but she felt his grip tighten around her. She had found an ally, or at the very least a man she could manipulate if needed. And she was going to have to do some serious manipulation to get out of this mess.

But still: *Where is Rebecca? Hell, where is Nick? Most importantly, where the fuck is my husband?*

Her mind was full of questions when a woman spoke. "Oh, so she must be the new girly. Elgin, why you carrying her like a baby?"

"Hush now, sis." Elgin adjusted his big arms before gently setting Maya's feet on the floor. He snatched the blindfold off her face, breaking his streak of gentleness. "Maya, this here be my sista, Taite."

Taite looked her up and down. "She look like shit."

Maya placed her still bound hands over her eyes, as they struggled to adjust to their sudden freedom.

"Gilbert say clean her up so she can meet him."

"Come on now." Taite grabbed the disoriented Maya and took her into an ornate bathroom. She heard the door close behind her and blinked a few times.

"Give it a chance now," Taite said. "All that blinking won't make yer vision clear any faster."

"Oh..." Maya stopped talking in mid breath and looked around. "Who are you people? Who's in charge?"

Taite laughed. "He not here. Besides, Gilbert is not who you need worry about now." She stopped at the tiled edge of an oversized sunken bathtub. "Bath time, girly." Taite untied the ropes binding Maya's wrists. "There now. Strip and clean yerself. You smell like piss."

"I couldn't help it."

"Don't talk *now*, girly. Don't think about runnin'. Don't think about escapin'. Whatever you thought of, Bossman done already figured out." She walked into a closet.

Maya took off her clothes and slid into the tub's warm water. It was perfect. Not too hot or too cold and she sighed, feeling better as the water temporarily soothed her tortured body.

Taite returned. "Bossman like for us to bathe then shower afterwards." She placed a towel and a robe on a bench between the bathtub and shower. "I'll be back in twenty minutes. No shit now or Bossman will hurt you. Hurt you bad if you can't make him money, too." She walked out the door and locked it behind her.

Maya looked around the sunlit room. There were three windows with iron bars to her right and a floor to ceiling mirror to her left. The closet door was still open, and she could see it was long and deep. She saw gowns, lingerie, summer dresses, and other women's clothing mixed in with suits and button-down men's dress shirts.

She scooted to a bathtub pillow on the other side of the large oval tub and rested her head. The weed was strong, like the stuff she had shared with Rebecca and Nick.

Which is probably how I got into this mess in the first place.

Again, as panic filled her heart and mind, she took in a deep breath. She was alive, and right now that was a big reason to celebrate, but she had no idea where she was or why she was here. She just wanted her husband to swoop in and rescue her before she became somebody's sex slave for an hour at a time.

She shivered at the thought and dipped her head under a mini ocean of bubbles. When she came back up, she got out of the tub and shuffled to the shower. She opened a heavy glass door and turned the spout, stepped in and closed the door. Hot water rained down on her. She selected a washrag from a neat pile on a high shelf. There were several bottles of shower gel on a low shelf to her right. She chose a lavender blend and took in its scent as she luxuriated under the cascading water. She knew, in order to live, she would have to impress this Bossman character.

And in order to escape, she was going to play the fool.

And play him good.

She stepped out of the shower and basked in the softness of the towel she'd wrapped around her body. She jumped a little as the door to the bathroom slowly opened.

Taite came in and closed the door behind her. "Ahh. Feel better now don't cha, girly?"

Maya nodded as she looked at the woman. Taite's

close-cropped afro accentuated her high cheek bones. Her dark skin was radiant in the sunlit bathroom.

"Gilbert had to scare you a bit. Just do what yer told, and he can be sweet as pie."

Maya hugged herself. "Where am I?"

"Not far from the city. Near the port."

"I was at a resort on the other end of the island."

"Hmm, hmm. So was I when they got me."

Maya slipped into the robe. "How long have you been here?"

Taite shrugged. "Two years or so. My brother, that fat fool who carried you in, owed some money to some local businessmen, and when he couldn't pay up, they snatched me. He went to Bossman, who got me free, but now I gotta pay for my freedom from him. So my brother is here, looking out for me until our debt is paid."

She looked at Maya. "Now, before you go making some plan for some great escape, let me tell you how it is. You thinkin' you can seduce your way out of here. Whip some of that pampered American pussy on them eh? No. These boys treat pussy like a cigar of weed. Not something you fall in love with, just smoke it 'til it's all used up. So your pussy, no matter how good ya think it is, won't set you free." She stepped into the closet. "You might also be thinking you can escape in the night. Nope. I tried. Most cops bought here by Bossman. They found me, brought me back, and I got beat. Then I got to spend a week in the hole." She stepped from the closet and held out a blue summer dress. "Here, put this on. Bossman likes us in dresses." She ducked back into the closet.

"The hole?" Maya shed the robe and slid into the dress.

"Yeah, girly, a pit they toss you in. Guards use it to piss in, so you can imagine it's not high on my list of places you should go. That is the first punishment for trying to run away."

"What's after that?"

"Trust me..." Taite came out with a pair of slippers in hand, each with a massive fuzz ball on top. "...if you get the hole, you won't ever break a rule again." She held up the slippers. "Wear these. Bossman been talking about you. Excited for you to get here." She paused for a breath. "You might want to practice kissing ass, literally, because that's what you gonna have to do to stay on his good side."

Maya looked at Taite, who appraised her as she stood fully clothed. "No underwear?"

Taite shook her head. "No need." She walked toward the door. "Follow me now, girly, and act cool. This ain't America. This is a man's world, and you must jump when told, or get used to hitting the floor after you get slapped."

They walked down a hallway to the left of the staircase Elgin had carried her up. The weed made her walk slowly, and she noticed Taite did the same. Now that she thought about it, everybody around here moved slowly.

Except Gilbert when he slapped the shit out of her, she was pretty sure he didn't move slow. As a matter of fact, that slap was the first time a man ever put hands on her.

The strong weed took her mind from Gilbert, and a goofy smile crept across her face as she walked on a cream colored marble floor. She admired the seemingly artistic cracks running among the tiles. The walls were a chocolate brown with white molding, which sectioned off the wall; each showcased either a painting of flowers or some ornate vase. This kidnapping pimp named Bossman had good taste in décor and women.

Taite looked at her. "That weed don hit cha, huh, girly." She laughed, and Maya laughed with her, watching her round ass jiggle underneath her white linen dress, which somehow made Maya think of her husband.

She smiled at the thought of him. He could be a neglectful asshole at times, but she knew, right this very moment, he was on the phone, calling Federal agency after agency, using favor after favor to find his missing wife.

Yeah he is an asshole, but he's my asshole.

"We here," Taite said.

Maya took in her surroundings. There was a myriad of folks of all shapes and sizes surrounding a large round pool. Maya noticed the men wore anything from a casual shirt and slacks to Speedos, while many of the women who weren't clad in skimpy swimsuits opted to walk about naked. Maya felt out of place in her blue dress, despite how short it was, but preferred the garment to walking around butt naked. Whatever this place was, it was as if a party was going nonstop. The folks around the pool were laughing and dancing. For a second, the revelry distracted her from the fact she was a prisoner.

Taite looked surprised. "Wasn't prepared to see her here. Look at her. She go to America and come back thinking she some kind of fashion model."

Maya caught sight of Rebecca in a string bikini. She smiled wickedly and tossed her head full of blond hair. Maya's jaw dropped. "What the fuck is Rebecca doing here? Is she a prisoner too?"

Taite nodded. "She was Bossman's favorite."

Holy shit. Maya's mind reeled. *Rebecca is a fucking whore working for Bossman. How the hell did she end up working for me?*

The gentle ring of a small bell jarred Maya back to reality. Taite touched Maya's shoulder. "Here the ass kissing starts. Be quiet and cool now, girly."

Maya saw Rebecca look across the mammoth pool and followed her eyes. For the second time thirty seconds, her mouth fell open in complete amazement.

The large black man with the unkempt beard walked in, smiling, dressed in a white polo shirt, black and white checkered pants, and white loafers. A cigar hung precariously from the corner of his mouth. His eyes scanned the area and fell on Maya. "My dear sweet Maya. Your beauty is a godsend." He walked to her. "I want to thank you, thank you so much for joining me in my humble abode."

"I've seen you at my husband's country club."

"Yes." His voice sounded as deep as the pool. "When I am stateside I am a proud member of a country club. But here, here I am a king. And your beautiful ass will make me a much richer king. My dear, I believe once you get used to our way of life behind these walls, you will be a very happy woman."

"Fuck you," Maya spat. "When my husband finds out I'm here, he'll rescue me." She saw Rebecca step up behind the big man and snicker. "Rebecca? What's so funny?"

Bossman didn't let her answer. "Well, my pretty. Your husband already knows you are here, but as for a rescue by him. Not likely."

"What the fuck is going on?"

"We will get into all that later, but now, it is time for your first class. I'll be the teacher and you the student."

One second she was standing upright, the next she was falling in the pool, her left cheek and ear stinging and ringing from a swift backhand blow, even as the water swallowed her up.

"Rule one. From this day forward you are to speak only when told to speak. Your opinion means jack shit to me."

He reached down with one hand and pulled her from the pool by her neck. He held her there, her toes barely touching the water as she clung to his massive forearms in hopes of supporting her weight so her neck wouldn't break.

"I hate this lesson, I truly do, but you need to be put in your place. You must accept your fate, my dear. Your husband is a memory. The life you once led is a thing of the past. Your future belongs to me. So save the questions. Enjoy the ganja and the ocean. Luxuriate in the fact that men will pay thousands to fuck your pussy, and I expect you to be on your best behavior. If you fail me, fail to pleasure a client, then..." He flipped her upside down and jammed her face under water and held her there until she thought her lungs would burst.

Finally he pulled her head out of the water. "Then I feed you to the sharks, but only after some locals fuck you for five days straight."

Maya fought to breathe.

"You understand?" He dunked her again.

Maya heard nothing but the splashing water from her feeble efforts to escape.

Bossman smiled. "I like this one." He looked around at his women, his eyes resting on Rebecca then Taite. "She's got spirit. Will take a strong hand to break her."

Maya's efforts to surface grew weaker.

"My, my, I will so enjoy breaking this one." He held her head under for a few more moments. Her struggling slowed almost to a stop. "Now perhaps she is ready to learn." He hoisted her up and dropped her onto the cement deck.

Maya coughed and took in deep breaths as the big man stood over her.

"Maya, you were a queen in your world, but know this is my world, and you are now my bitch."

Maya sucked in air then spat water as she strained to look up at him. "Fu-fuck you."

"Oh, I like her." Bossman kicked her in the face.

She saw the white loafer as it came to her eye, a blinding white light encompassed her vision, and a sharp pain radiated from her nose down to her feet.

"Learn your place, bitch."

Where is my husband?

She fell into the black pit of unconsciousness.

Chapter Nine

MAYA WALKED INTO THE coffee shop.

Finn smiled at her brightly. "Good morning, Maya."

"I'll have a—"

"Chocolate latte," he finished. "It's the size I don't remember."

"I'd like a large one, please." She noticed how his cheeks flushed at her comment before he turned to make her drink.

A young blonde walked over to him, her face a mask of bewilderment. "Boss, I can't get the dishwasher to work."

Finn sighed. "It's jammed again. I'll be back there in a minute."

The girl hurried off as Finn brought Maya her drink. "Anything else for you?"

"Is this your business?"

"Took my inheritance and bought it from a lovely couple seeking to retire in Florida."

"The Bensons, yes...I've been coming here for years. So, they're retired? Good for them. From one business owner to another, congrats." She handed him a twenty-dollar bill.

"I figured you were a self-made woman. You carry yourself with such regality." There was admiration in his eyes as he took the money.

She looked away, her cheeks flushed. He gave her the change, and she put a five in the tip jar.

"See you tomorrow?" he asked.

She shook her head. "I'm going on vacation to

Jamaica with my husband."

"Lucky man. Perhaps you'll let me buy you a coffee when you come back."

Maya felt a tingle in her pussy. His smile was infectious and his eyes held hers under their mesmerizing stare. At times like these she cursed Albert for not taking care of his husbandly duties. Her mind raced for something clever to say but settled for: "That would be very nice. I'll be back in five days."

"Have a great time. I look forward to seeing you again."

She waved and walked away with a smile.

***

Rebecca quietly knocked on Maya's office doorframe and noticed her boss's chair faced away from the door. Her cell phone lay on her desk. She waited patiently for Maya's hand to appear from behind the chair and wave her in.

"What is it?" She sounded terse.

Rebecca cleared her throat. "Maya...I hate to tell you this, but your husband just called. Says he can't go on that vacation."

"He called you?" Maya swiveled her chair around. "I've been calling him and texting him all damn day...and he called you? Chickenshit bastard hasn't got the balls to tell me himself. And he waits to cancel until the day before..."

"A huge deal has fallen through in Dubai and he has to fly out there. He's headed for the plane right now, told me to tell you he's sorry."

"Sorry? I wish he felt the same level of commitment to me as he does to making money."

Rebecca shrugged. "I don't know what to say."

Maya grunted in disgust. "He never comes through on his promises."

"He did, however, send two tickets for a trip to your favorite island." Rebecca laid the tickets on the desk. "Round trip. Five full days, including a suite in the finest resort."

Maya groaned. "Keep 'em. Take a paid vacation on me. I'll even give you the company credit card."

"Maya, I simply couldn't..." Rebecca had to think fast. "You should go."

"Then come with me. Let's spend my husband's money together."

"But...what about your business? I should stay—"

"Hell, we hardly do anything..." Maya picked up her desk phone and pushed the button for IT. "Hey, John. I'm going away for a little while. Yes, my husband knows." She rolled her eyes. "Yes, I'll be careful. No, I won't travel alone. I'm going with Rebecca. Yes, she knows to be careful too. Stop trying to be my mother. I want you to run things while I'm gone. For the next five days... No, you can't have my car...not the company credit card either. Would you stop?" Maya shook her head. "No, John, you can't put a strip club tab on your expense account."

She hung up and smiled at Rebecca. "I told you the IT boys would do anything for me. So it's settled. You, me, and a tropical isle for five days."

"Okay. You twisted my arm."

They laughed like a couple of school girls.

"Now..." Rebecca said coyly. "What happens there stays there. I won't tell a soul if you happen to live out your fantasy with a nice big black dick."

"You just want to live vicariously through me."

"I've already lived it but wouldn't mind living it again."

Maya frowned. "If you're going to get your freak on, maybe we should get separate rooms."

"No." Rebecca grinned. "If I get lucky, we'll go to his room."

"Then I'll have time alone with my Hitachi."

"Really?" Rebecca frowned. "You're not seriously taking a sex toy to an island resort. You may as well bring sand for the beach."

"What would you have me do, fuck some stranger?"

Rebecca nodded vigorously. "Hell, yes." She leaned over the desk. "Who would know?"

"You."

Rebecca shook her head. "Come on, Maya. We both know I wouldn't say shit for two very good reasons. One, you're my boss, and this is the coolest job I've ever had, so selling you out and fucking up a good thing...I'd never do that. And two, I plan on being too busy doing my own fucking to even care what you're doing."

"That's not the point—"

"The point should be you getting your groove on and not relying on your sex toy. Think about it. Why would Mr. Valdis allow you to go away for five days on a tropical island and not go with you?" She smiled. "Come on. He can't expect you to behave."

Maya thought about that. Had he given her a free pass? He obviously didn't think she was important enough to come along. *So why not*? *Why not get some strange black dick*? She thought about her fantasy in the limo. While her husband's cock filled her mouth, a long rod had filled her imagination. She remembered how hot she got just thinking of that cock as she sucked the head until it exploded...but not as swiftly as her husband's dick came in her mouth. Then she imagined a phantom black cock staying rigid as she climbed aboard and slid the long dick deep into her pussy.

Fantasies can come true...

She shuddered. "No, no. I'll have my fun, but play with my toy. That's the right thing to do."

"Okay, fine. That means more dick for me."

"Get ready to go shopping." Maya walked toward the

restroom with that big, stiff, and long black shaft still on her mind. She shivered with wild delight at the thought of actually fucking one of those wonderful cocks.

How would Albert know? Would he even care?

A vision of her on her back, watching that fantasy cock slide inside her pussy almost made her swoon.

Chapter Ten

BOSSMAN SIGHED. “American women are always so damn stubborn.” He snapped his fingers. Elgin and Gilbert rushed over. “Taite, watch her now,” he bellowed. “You got nursing, right?”

“No, Bossman,” Gilbert answered for her. “That be Rebecca.” He pointed at the nearly naked young woman Maya knew.

“I should have known my former crown jewel had multiple talents.” The big man gestured to Rebecca, who obediently strutted up to him. “You look out for her. She struck her noggin against my shoe, right sharp. You watch her now.”

Rebecca nodded and started to walk away, but he grabbed her by the crook of her arm. “Now, that don’t mean you take a break.”

“I have to change clothes.”

“We both know what her husband wants me to do with her, but his needs are not mine, and should an accident befall her while under your care, my dear, I promise one will befall on you, as well.”

Rebecca pulled against his grip. “Nothing will happen to her, Bossman. You can trust me.”

“That’s why you’re my number one.” He kissed her lightly on the cheek then smacked her shapely ass. “Now go on and change. Taite, stand over the American ‘til Rebecca gets back. Then I got some fuckin’ for all of you to do.”

Chapter Eleven

REBECCA SAID A SILENT PRAYER as her fingers dug into the armrest of her seat in the cool, clean van while it rounded a nasty curve. For a moment she paused in awe, staring out at the familiar yet always breathtaking view of the ocean crashing against the shore. But as the driver took another sharp bend just a tad too fast, her gaze turned to one of anger and shot daggers at his sweaty back. Once the road straightened, she took a deep breath.

"Remember..." Rebecca said to Maya. "Whatever happens here stays here." She looked down the road as the resort drew into sight. "Oh my." She feigned surprise. "It's so beautiful."

"It is," Maya said with a smile. "And there won't be anything happening here that needs to stay here."

"Keep telling yourself that."

The pristine shuttle slowly ascended the final hill before the resort. This was Maya's fifth time coming to the magical island, and the third time her husband failed to come along. She hated that, she truly missed him, in so many ways, but she pushed her blues to the back of her mind and smiled at Rebecca who was raving about the ton of men Maya was going to meet. She then turned away and enjoyed the view, even as her hands held each armrest in a death clutch. There was only one part of her many trips here that she hated, and that was this road to the resort. Officially, it was a one-way road, and often, vehicles were coming down and going up at the same time.

Rebecca chattered on. "I saw how you and that guy in coach checked each other out. I think you got that itch."

"No, no," Maya said as the shuttle, at least in her anxious mind, teetered on the edge of a curve that, if handled improperly, would send them hurtling to the rough ocean waves below. Rebecca's inane talking actually helped keep Maya's mind off the fact the road was a friggin' death trap. "All he did was check me out, and I being a lady, just smiled to be polite."

"Hmm, hmm..." Rebecca plastered an annoying smug look across her face. "You know the worst person you can ever lie to is yourself."

Maya groaned as she looked around the shuttle and noticed two college-age guys eyeing her and Rebecca. Her gaze fell on the baby blues of a lovely blonde boy whose smile was almost as bright as the sun glaring in Maya's eyes as the shuttle rounded the last curve. She appraised his chiseled physique beneath a blue t-shirt and white linen shorts.

He shot her a wink, and Maya rolled her eyes.

"His body is fine," she whispered to Rebecca. "But he's not that cute."

"But would you fuck him?" Rebecca asked.

"Could you repeat that a little louder? I don't think the village five miles away heard you."

"We heard you," one of the college boys said.

Rebecca turned and looked at them. "Good, now hear this. Children are to be seen and not heard."

The kid who'd spoken laughed. He had a dark chocolate-brown complexion. His impeccable haircut fit his clean-cut face and light brown eyes. While quite toned, he was far too thin to suit Maya's taste in men. *Track or tennis. Maybe if he had twenty more pounds of muscle on him...*

"Oh, no, ma'am," the black kid replied to Rebecca. "We intend to be seen and heard...quite uproariously."

"Wow," Rebecca said to the black kid. "What a pithy comeback. You get that from a movie?" She blatantly looked him up and down. "Hmm, dressed by J. Crew, Lacoste travel gear, well manicured hands, and good grammar, you must be an Ivy Leaguer." She looked at Maya. "And you know what they say about Ivy League boys, don't cha?"

The blonde boy of the duo sat forward. He was a little more heavily muscled, but his blue eyes made Maya feel mildly on edge. "What *do* they say about us Ivy League boys?"

Rebecca leaned forward, her tantalizing cleavage begging for release from the tight confines of her black blouse. "Long money and long—"

"Okay," Maya interjected. The rest of the shuttle passengers, including the driver, laughed.

Rebecca smiled at the blonde jock, who gave her a wink. She then whipped her head around to Maya. "You know, you still didn't answer my question."

"Yes I did, you just didn't like it."

"I didn't hear it," the blonde jock put in.

"Nor I," the black boy said. His curly dark-brown locks frizzed about his head like a wilted afro. "And inquiring minds want to know."

"No, I wouldn't fuck him," Maya said, trying not to smile. "Not even when I was younger."

"How old are you?" the black kid asked.

"What do you think?" Rebecca challenged him.

The kid pursed his lips and appraised Maya. His eyes traveled up her curvy calves, tantalizing thighs, and tempting tits. "Twenty five."

She laughed. "Yes," the thirty-one-year-old replied. "Very good, young man."

"Ladies and gentlemen, we are here." The shuttle driver stopped the van.

Conversation silenced, passengers disembarked the shuttle and stepped onto a bricked driveway. Valets rushed to the small group, and the women smiled as handsome young men with golden brown skin and bright winning smiles took their luggage and piled the assortment on a brass cart.

Rebecca ogled one man's backside and nudged Maya. "Prime beef."

The handsome bellboy turned to her. "Pardon, ma'am?"

Maya giggled.

"I-I was wondering if you guys have some good beef here," Rebecca stammered.

Maya turned her head away to hide her smile.

"Of course, ma'am. Best beef on the island." He turned and pushed the cart toward the resort's main entrance.

"I bet they do."

The cute but cocky blonde jock laughed. "We brought our own prime beef." He pointed at his crotch.

Rebecca giggled at that.

They stepped toward a pair of glass doors, which slid open as they drew near. As they stepped beneath an ornate glass dome, Rebecca gasped. A wide walkway took them over a stream teaming with colorful fish that swam freely beneath a crystal-clear floor. The walkway emptied out onto a marble floor and down an aisle bordered by carved wooden columns that led to the elaborately designed mahogany front desk.

A chocolate-skinned beauty behind the counter smiled at the ladies and welcomed them to the resort. Maya smiled back and gave them their names and waited patiently for their room assignment.

Rebecca whispered in Maya's ear. "Even the friggin women here are hot."

The same bellboy then led them to a trio of elevators. He pushed the *up* button and smiled at the women. "First time on our island, folks?"

"Yes," Rebecca replied.

"No," Maya said.

The college boys said, "No," simultaneously, as they stepped up with their own bellhop in tow.

Maya quickly punched the black kid's arm. "Pididle."

"Ouch," he whined childishly as the elevator doors opened.

The boys' bellhop chortled. "You Americans are funny."

They arrived on the third floor. The college boys and their bellhop went one way; Maya and Rebecca went the other, along with their bellboy. The blonde jock winked at the ladies. Maya turned away, her cheeks coloring, while Rebecca smiled back and blew him a kiss. The kid tried to remain cool, but stumbled as he turned a corner.

The hallway opened up into a tropical-themed foyer, complete with tall leafy trees, mist, and the sound of the ocean bouncing against the shore. The foyer emptied out onto a deck above a waterfall that dropped about ten feet into the salty waters below. Maya wished she could share this view with her husband.

The butt face is probably playing golf in Dubai. She felt more than mildly disappointed.

"Welcome, ladies. It is a pleasure to meet you." A lone man with a deep voice stood behind the desk against the center wall of the foyer. He was about five-ten with a barrel chest and a proud stance. His close-cropped hair was thinning at the top, accentuated by wisps of gray hair that streaked his side locks. "My name is George and it is my duty and my distinction to serve you the entire duration of your time at our resort. My job is to fulfill your every need."

Rebecca said, "Well, since you're taking care of needs, my friend here needs—"

"A restroom," Maya interrupted and turned away from the spectacular view. "Preferably the one in my room."

"Let me lead you to your suite then." He bowed.

The bellboy followed George, who led them a short way to the right this time. “The key, please.”

Maya handed him the card key.

George slid the card in place and opened the door.

Together, the quartet walked into the luxurious confines of the suite. The floors were covered with plush light-brown carpeting that enveloped Maya’s feet when she took off her shoes by the door.

George and the bellboy unloaded the bags from the cart and placed them near the king sized bed set in a cubby across from the living room.

Rebecca smiled wickedly. “Only one bed?”

Maya ignored her as she examined the room. That bed was meant for her and Albert, and now it was virtually useless. She stepped down two steps into the sunken living room, complete with a fireplace, which one could watch from a long couch or a walk-around love seat across the room. Behind the fireplace was a sliding door to the patio, and to the right, a kitchenette and breakfast nook, complete with a small round table already decorated with silverware cutely wrapped in linen napkins. Square gold plates sat empty on the table and adorned an ice bucket that chilled a bottle of champagne.

“Oh, my God,” Rebecca said. “My favorite champagne.”

“Courtesy of your husband, Mrs. Valdis,” George chimed in.

Maya made a face. “He knows I don’t like the bubbly stuff.”

Rebecca held up the dripping bottle. “Guess I’ll just have to drink it by myself.”

The bellboy strolled up and gently took the bottle from her hands. “Allow me to open it.”

Maya walked around a coffee table and headed for the open patio door. She strode outdoors, spied a hot-tub to her right, ornate metal patio furniture, and then she noticed the spectacular view of the island shore and the ocean waves. To her left, the resort sprawled below a cliff, and she smiled at its grandeur. "Amazing," she whispered. "God I wish you were here, Albert. I miss you." She went back inside.

"Is there anything you ladies need?" George looked expectantly at Maya. "There is an online guide to our resort on the laptop in the kitchenette. It can tell you about the restaurants and nightclubs we have here. You can also use it to order room service."

"Can I get some weed around here?" Rebecca asked way too loudly.

"No," George said. "But I can."

Maya's head snapped around. "Really?"

"Yes, ma'am."

"I haven't smoked since college." Maya walked toward him skeptically. "You sure it's all right?"

"Yes, ma'am. Unlike your country, ganja is legal here. Just don't buy it in town or at the airport. You can't trust what you are given."

Maya put her hands on her hips. "Why should we trust you?"

George grinned. "Because we want you to come back more than once so we can get more of your money. So I will get you the good stuff. How much do you ladies need?"

"Fifty bucks worth?"

"Have you smoked our weed before?"

"No."

"Then I would recommend a smaller amount." George kissed his index fingertip. "Our ganja, pardon me for saying so, is not that weak shit you Americans get."

Maya dug a $100 bill from her purse. "Fifty, and papers, and split the change between you two." She nodded to the wide-eyed bellboy.

George grinned. "Okay, ma'am. But do not get mad at

me if you spend your vacation in the bed, sleeping the day away courtesy of our finest island fire." He gently took the bill from her pinched fingers and walked out. The bellboy followed him.

"Oh my, look at you," Rebecca said. "So commanding. So in charge."

Maya laughed. "Funny thing, you would think he'd try to get us to buy more, not less."

"Maybe their shit is some good fire." Rebecca poured champagne into two flutes on the table. "That yummy bellboy did a fine job flirtatiously opening the bottle for us."

"How do you flirtatiously open a bottle of champagne?"

Rebecca handed her a glass. "I thought he was flirting with me, and as for what it looked like, use your imagination." She tapped her glass lightly against Maya's. "Here's to an unforgettable time we can never take pictures of or tell anyone else about. Cheers."

Maya sipped the champagne. The bubbles tickled her nose.

There was a knock on the door. Rebecca answered it. George walked in, hands behind his back. She closed the door and rejoined Maya by the table.

"As you requested, ladies." Grinning, he held out a plain brown bag.

"That was quick." Maya walked to him, opened the bag, and sniffed its contents. "Whew." She reared back and smiled. "That's some powerful weed."

George bowed. "My pleasure." He handed her three cigars he'd taken from his jacket pocket. "I have already prepared these for your enjoyment."

"Thanks."

George took his leave.

Maya rushed up and closed the door then turned to Rebecca who was looking at her expectantly. "I hope we don't get in trouble for this."

Rebecca pointed at the cigars stuffed full of ganja. "Girl, you ready to get fucked up?"

Maya giggled. "Yup." She handed Rebecca a cigar. "Light this one for our IT boys."

Rebecca laughed. "Shoot..." She placed the cigar tip in her mouth. "This shit might be too much for us to handle. Remember what George said. You ain't done this in a long, long time, so take it easy."

"Like you're some expert," Maya scoffed. "And who gives a damn if it's strong. Isn't that what we want? Some King Kong, Mike Tyson, knock you on your ass type weed?"

"How about some king sized dong." Rebecca giggled.

Maya fished the lighter from her purse and handed it to Rebecca. "Just light that motherfucker, please."

Chapter Twelve

ALBERT VALDIS TURNED on the TV and smiled as the newscast began.

"...the disappearance of Maya Valdis, wife of investor and entrepreneur Albert Valdis, from a resort in the Caribbean."

"Oh how sad," Valdis muttered, closed his eyes, and groaned while the newscast continued:

"Local police, headed up by Chief Clive Battersby, are baffled and have only stated that the disappearance is a top priority. They are investigating it as we speak. We also have yet to hear from Mr. Valdis directly, but a spokesperson says he was deeply, deeply saddened by the news and worried sick."

He looked at the blonde kneeling between his legs, his shaft halfway inside her succulent mouth. "Nikki, did you really say that I was worried sick?"

She let him free long enough to speak. "I sure did." She returned to sucking his head like a beloved cherry flavored lollypop.

"Girl..." He grunted in ecstasy. "You're sucking me like you're trying to impress me. You already got me, just as soon as they find her body."

Nikki smiled with her eyes and sucked him in deeper without saying a word.

His cell phone rang. "Shh, don't slurp so loud," he said, "but don't stop. It's Rebecca."

Nikki giggled with her mouth full.

He answered the call. "What's the word?"

"I'm going to be her nurse."

He could hear the mirth in Rebecca's voice.

"She got knocked out after talking shit to Bossman."

"So he bitch-slapped that bitch, huh?" He laughed then spluttered and rolled his eyes as Nikki's skillful tongue hit a sweet spot.

"What are you doing? Are you with someone?"

"Only you in my mind." He struggled to contain himself as Nikki hungrily engulfed him.

"You better not be fuckin' around on me, baby." Her voice softened. "Lord knows I'm in need of some dick since you put me on lockdown with your wife. You need to be on your way here, anyway. Bossman is expecting his money for my freedom, hand-delivered by you."

"But he still won't, I mean, he's still not willing to wipe the slate clean, is he?"

"He's not going to kill her, if that's what you mean." Rebecca huffed. "Trading her ass for mine is one thing, but killing her is against his business savvy."

"Then what about you?"

"I couldn't sleep with that on my conscience."

Valdis smiled. "You like her?"

Rebecca said nothing.

"She has a way about her, doesn't she? Reels you in with those pretty brown eyes, silky smooth tan skin, that truly succulent body, along with a smile that could launch a thousand ships and break a million hearts. You fell for her like I did. So let me tell you what I learned. She's a selfish needy bitch."

He looked into Nikki's eyes as she took him out of her mouth and kissed the head then slid her lips back down his shaft while flicking her tongue along each bulging vein as she went.

"You would be better off without her, Rebecca. As for your conscience, I'm sure you'll sleep quite peacefully in her bed after fucking her husband."

"You promised me—"

"If Bossman won't do it, then only you can make it happen."

"But Bossman told me to watch her, and if anything happens to her, it would be my ass swimmin' with the sharks. So as long as I'm watching her, she's as safe as a babe in the manger."

Valdis shook his head, and to keep from losing his temper, he put the phone on mute. "Let me see those tits, Nikki."

The blonde took his dick out of her mouth and obediently freed her bountiful chest from the confines of her designer bra. The soft valley between her breasts enveloped his throbbing shaft in its warm embrace and stroked him up and down. He knew she felt every vein as his stiffness throbbed within the gap of her cleavage.

"I love your cock," she whispered as her tongue danced around his tip.

"And my cock loves you. Now put it back in your mouth." He took the phone off mute. "Rebecca, my dear, your loyalty is impressive but useless at times. This is one of those times, my dear. You can't be loyal to us both."

"What do you mean?"

His hips bucked for a second and he stifled a moan. "What is more important, being loyal to me or to my wife?" He arched his back under the intense barrage from Nikki's skillful mouth. "You know what I can give you." He gasped. "So you might want to rethink your position. Let me know what you decide." He hung up and imagined Rebecca yelling *prick* into the dead phone.

Valdis closed his eyes as Nikki's lips brought him to a frenzied finish. His searing cum spewed all over her luscious chest while she continued to glide her fist up and down his throbbing shaft. When the pulsing waned, he smiled at her. "Well done. Now get the fuck out."

Nikki tucked her drenched breasts neatly back within her bra and blouse then stood without a word and walked out of the room.

Valdis took a towel from his bottom drawer and wiped Nikki's spit off his wilting dick then leaned back in his chair. He held up the remote and switched over to watch ESPN. "Life is good."

Now if only I can get Rebecca to kill my fucking wife.

Chapter Thirteen

MAYA AWOKE WITH A START. Her vision was blurry, thanks to Bossman's boot that had knocked her out cold, but at least her eyes weren't blindfolded. She tried to rub her face but couldn't move her hands; they were tied to a bed. "What the fuck?"

The room was bathed in white, down to the sheets beneath her. She spied her reflection in a wall mirror across from the bed. The sight wasn't pretty. She had a black eye the size of Texas.

The sound of footsteps drew close. When she saw who approached, a blonde in a white smock and nurse's hat, her eyes snapped open wide. "You fucking bitch," she screamed at Rebecca. "Let me loose. I'll scratch your fucking eyes out."

"Take it easy, Maya," Rebecca said to her former boss. "Calm down so we can talk."

"Talk?" Maya gnashed her teeth. "Oh yeah, we can talk, bitch. Come closer. Let me whisper in your ear. I'll bite the fucker off."

"Okay, have it your way." Rebecca picked up a cattle prod from the floor and jammed it into Maya's side.

The jolt locked up every muscle in her body. Her face contorted into a gruesome mask of pain as she was frozen in place until Rebecca pulled the rod away. Maya arched her back and pressed her head into her pillow. "Oh, my God, bitch..." She panted. "That fucking hurt."

"Call me a bitch again..." Rebecca snapped the rod, which made a bolt of electricity jump from prong to prong. "You'll get more. Now, you be nice."

"Be nice?" She gasped. "Be nice to the woman who smiled in my face while she stabbed me in the back? What the fuck is this shit I'm in? What the fuck am I supposed to do, become a whore for that prick, Bossman?"

"Yes," Rebecca replied. "You're taking my place."

"You're Bossman's whore?"

"Not anymore. I'm free. A client, a frequent client, has bought my freedom, but since Bossman needs a top tier girl, here you are."

"I'm not a whore."

"You fucked the shit out of Nick and me. I mean, you were something else. Eager to please, and oh so into being pleased. Multi orgasmic." Rebecca laughed. "See, guys want a woman who is into it. You know, a chick who likes to fuck, and you, Maya Valdis, love to fuck and suck. You can never get enough. So why not get paid for doing what you love? Besides, girl, you say you're not a whore, but I say all of us are whores in one way or another."

"Speak for yourself, whore." Maya spat at her.

"Come on, admit it. You're a whore for your Hitachi, right?"

"Fuck you. My husband will come to get me—"

"You heard Bossman. There's no rescue coming."

"I don't believe that. Albert will come, and he'll bring hell with him, bitch."

"What did I tell you about calling me a bitch?" Rebecca jabbed the prod into Maya's side again.

Every muscle screamed to get out of her body. She couldn't think, she couldn't breathe, she just wanted to die...until Rebecca retracted the prod, leaving Maya mad enough to kill.

"I wonder how this will feel on the bottom of your pretty little feet."

"No, no." Maya tried to protect her feet, but they were tied down and vulnerable.

Rebecca giggled. "My how the tables have turned.

See, back in the states, you were the boss. It was your company, your office, and I was your bitch. Now I'm in charge, and now you're my bitch."

"I treated you good," Maya said slowly. "I never fucked you over in any way. I took you to lunch, shopping, a vacation to the island. I would never poke you with a fucking cattle prod."

"True..." Rebecca turned off the device. "You were a good boss. In fact you were a great boss, a smart boss, but a blind boss." A wave of sadness flowed over her face, but too quickly it was gone. "Once your husband introduced us, I knew I had you. So eager to help out a struggling woman because I reminded you of who you used to be, right? Girls looking out for girls, but did you even do a background check? Hell, my interview was over lunch, and then we finished up at the bar. And you only asked me one question about my office skills. *Can you type?* Damn, you were too fucking easy."

"So let me get this straight," Maya said, still tugging futilely on the ropes around her wrists. "You're complaining that I gave you a job with virtually no questions asked?"

"And look where it got you."

"So the fact you and your crew kidnapped me, knocked me out, and now you're gonna try to turn me into a whore...that's all my fault?" Maya shook her head. "You have to be out your damn mind."

"Look where you are, and look where I am. And you still don't see how being nice got you here. Not only are you too fucking nice, but you only see what you want to see."

"What the fuck are you talking about, you crazy bi—" Maya's mouth abruptly shut mid-word.

"Watch it." Rebecca brandished the cattle prod.

She glared at Rebecca. "Fuck you."

"You can be mad all you want, but maybe if you saw

me and your husband as we really are, and not as you want us to be, you might have caught the hints he was dropping and divorced him."

Maya felt all her bravado leak from her soul. "What does my husband have to do with all this?" She looked into Rebecca's eyes, seeing the truth before she even spoke. "No, please no. Please, please, please don't tell me you've been fucking my husband."

Rebecca sighed. "Just so you know, it started before you and I met. He hired me to work for you, said, if I did my job perfectly, my life would change, and I could leave this whore house behind. I have a chance to live like you do, only without having to get up and go to work. Forget that. And I damn sure won't complain if he only fucks me twice a month, 'cause with his money, I can rent a dick whenever I please. And Albert said he'd watch, and I said I would watch him fuck any chick he wanted. And even now, you scoff at the idea of your husband's cock in some other pussy. I see your face. That is some shit you would never fathom doing with him, but you sure did share with me and Nick. Maya, Maya, Maya. Now do you understand why you are the old and I am the new?"

Maya just stared at her, unable to speak under the roar of her beating heart.

"This is not personal for me. I really like you, but in order for me to get away from here, I needed to find someone to replace me, and well...you're it."

"Rebecca, please. I—"

Unceremoniously, Rebecca turned on the cattle prod and jabbed Maya again.

Her body squirmed as the voltage ravaged her body and her will to live.

"No, Maya." Rebecca pulled the prod away. "No begging. You are taking my place and that is that. You can resist your new life or fucking deal with it."

"I'll resist," she hissed through clenched teeth as tears

welled in her eyes.

"I thought you might take that road." She reached in the pocket of her white smock and pulled out a hypodermic needle.

Panic tore through Maya's chest. "What the fuck is that?"

"Something that will ease your transition from wife to whore. I think this will change your mind about fighting your fate." She grabbed Maya's arm.

"No." Maya struggled, even as the needle pierced her skin. "No..." Her voice faded as a wave of warmth encased her in a soft caress. She smiled as her body got lighter and her eyes got heavier.

"Now then..." Rebecca leaned in close as darkness filled Maya's vision. "Just so you know, after Bossman and his boys took you away, I fucked Nick...or rather he fucked me. And that big black dick was good, too...really, really good. Now, what did you say...something about resisting?"

Chapter Fourteen

THE ELEVATOR DOORS SLID OPEN, which immediately solicited a robust laugh from Rebecca and Maya, before the latter put her fingers to her lips. “Shh,” she ordered. “We’re too loud.”

Maya almost dropped her purse.

Showered, fed, and incredibly high, Maya and Rebecca stumbled out of the elevator and stagger-stepped toward the resort’s swimming pool. Towels draped their waists while flattering bikini tops, red for Rebecca and turquoise for Maya, accentuated their bouncing breasts.

“You sure we can smoke by the pool?” Maya asked as they got closer to the sliding glass doors that led outside.

“Girl, relax, it’s cool.” Rebecca put on her sunglasses as they reached the doors. She took in a deep breath. “Damn. Now that’s a pool.”

An expansive pool with a sky blue bottom filled the entire central area between the resort’s three buildings. Guests sat on lounge chairs, drinking and laughing while others swam and played in the pool’s crystal clear water. Sunken bars were located at the north and south ends of the pool, complete with stools and tables for folks to enjoy their drinks and meals without leaving the water. Behind the south bar was a spectacular view of the ocean, serenely lapping at the nearby shore.

“I could get used to this kind of life,” Rebecca said with a bright smile. She looked at Maya. “Guess this is nothing new to you.”

“No, but every time I come here, I fall in love with it all over again. Now let’s go find a spot in the shade.”

"Not too much shade," Rebecca chided. "I'm working on my tan."

The setting sun provided a breathtaking backdrop to what was a beautiful day. They found a pair of empty lounge chairs. Maya spread out her towel and sat down. "Perfect view. We can see the pool, the bar—"

"The men," Rebecca added. "In fact two are walking this way right now."

Maya and Rebecca watched the two guys approach carrying tall glasses topped with umbrellas. Each wore island swim trunks, flapping sandals, and big wide grins. "Ladies," a now familiar voice said. "Fate has been kind to us." It was the blonde jock with his black buddy.

"Not you two again?" Rebecca sneered.

"Now what is wrong with us?" his dark-skinned friend asked. His lean body looked a lot sexier with only the swim trunks on. "You don't even know us." He put out his hand, damp from the condensation around his drink. "I'm Trevor and this is Larry."

Rebecca looked at him from behind her oversized red sunglasses. "I'm Rebecca and this is Maya."

"May we join you?" Larry looked at a pair of chairs to Maya's right. "These taken?"

Maya huffed. "Knock your socks off."

Just then, all heads turned to face a diminutive raven-haired beauty in a black string bikini. Her large breasts and thick thighs fit her toned, petite frame. Her smile was bright and her light colored eyes contrasted perfectly with her dark lashes. She sashayed toward them with a muscular man clad in a pair of Bermuda shorts and an open Hawaiian shirt over broad shoulders. He stared out from under a mop of curly blond hair. "These are ours." He gestured to the chairs. "I'm Cole and this lovely woman is my beautiful bride Portia."

"We just got married." Portia adjusted a pair of black shades.

"Holy shit," Rebecca said with a giggle, her eyes keyed on Cole "You guys look like the boy and girl next door...but on steroids."

Maya smiled as she admired the diminutive black-haired woman standing statuesque before her. "I'm Maya, and smarty pants here is Rebecca."

"A pleasure," Cole said.

Portia hugged him close. "We've been dating a year, and a month ago Cole asked me to marry him. My parents wanted a big wedding."

"Yeah," Cole griped. "They wanted a fucking horse-drawn carriage, doves, and other expensive shit. My baby here was stressed out from planning the affair, so I said fuck it. We eloped and hopped a plane over here."

Portia giggled. "Our parents are pissed as hell."

"How romantic." Maya noticed Portia kept looking her way. "These two bozos are Trevor and Larry. Come join us." She opened her purse and produced a cigar.

Cole dropped his glasses, revealing his red eyes. "Already had some, thanks."

"I'm sure we can have more." Portia hastily sat by Maya.

Trevor and Larry sat next to Rebecca.

Maya fished out a lighter and lit the cigar.

"I love this view," Portia said.

"Well..." Maya took in a deep long drag. "It's about to get a hell of a lot better."

Cole looked at Trevor and Larry. "Where you guys from?"

"University of Pennsylvania," Trevor said.

"We're Philly boys," Larry bragged.

"Yeah, we wanted to celebrate graduating early. So we came here 'cause we wanted weed, wine, and hot women."

Maya inhaled smoke. "I hope you find what you're looking for."

The college boys glanced at each other. Larry shrugged. "I think we already have."

Maya exhaled, cleared her throat, and handed the cigar to Rebecca. "Now, don't fuck up the rotation. Everybody just pass to the left."

Portia's delicate hand touched Maya's shoulder. "Why to the left?"

Maya felt a tingle where she didn't expect to feel one.

Cole laughed. "The song, girl. You know the one...about passing the dutchie on the left hand side..."

Portia looked at him blankly.

"*I said...*" Larry sang.

Cole sang along with Larry and Trevor. *"Pass the dutchie on the left hand side..."*

Portia looked confused. "Is that what that song is about?"

All the guys laughed.

"Shh." Rebecca handed the cigar to Larry, being sure to trail the tips of her fingers on the back of his hand. "Not so loud, college boys."

"Party pooper." Larry took a hit. For a moment, he was fine, then his face turned crimson, and his eyes bulged.

"Don't fucking cough," Rebecca demanded.

He handed the cigar to Trevor, and as he struggled not to hack up a lung, he calmly stood, set his drink down on a table between Maya and Rebecca, and then jumped into the pool, coughing as he surfaced. "Wow."

"My man." Trevor took a hit while the others laughed. "Damn." He grunted. "What the fuck is this shit?"

Rebecca smiled. "Only the best ganja around." She looked at Maya. "And George thought *we* couldn't handle this shit."

"Oh, I can hang." Trevor cleared his throat twice before taking a short toke on the fat, well-rolled cigar. "Damn," he said, his eyes already glazing over. "That's nothing like we get at home."

Cole took the cigar from Trevor's outstretched hand. "Give me this, weaklings." He took a long deep toke.

Rebecca watched as he kept sucking on the cigar and inhaling the smoke. "Damn." She looked at Portia. "Does he suck everything with such gusto?"

Portia rubbed the V of her thong. "You bet."

"There," he said, handing the cigar to Portia.

The women stared at him. Any second he'd keel over.

"What?" A puff of smoke came out.

Rebecca licked her lips as her eyes drifted down to his crotch. "Guess you *can* hold your own."

Cole smiled, exhaling. "Yeah." He turned to Portia. "Baby..."

"Yes," she said sweetly.

"That is some strong ass shit." His body teetered to the left then the right, until finally he fell back in his chair.

"Ha," Rebecca laughed. "You ain't no *smoka*," she teased.

"That ain't no ordinary ganja," Trevor replied.

Portia looked nervously at the cigar. "Do I dare?"

"Hit that shit." Maya gave her a sly smirk. "I got your back."

Portia took a short toke, her eyes never leaving Maya's. "Oh my." She fanned herself. A short cough escaped her lungs and she handed the cigar back to Maya. "Damn."

"Told you," Cole said, lying on his back, his fingers laced across his chest. "Some strong shit..." his voice faded and he closed his eyes, totally blitzed.

Maya giggled. "Is that normal?"

Portia stared at her husband's crotch. "My man can chill. We don't smoke very much." She draped a towel over his midsection, being sure to bunch it up around his cock. "He gets hard when he sleeps."

"Why hide it?" Rebecca asked.

Portia was about to reply when a deep voice came

from behind her. "Good afternoon."

Tremors of delight skittered down Maya's spine. He stood at least six-four, dressed in a pair of khaki slacks, black sneaks, and a black polo shirt with the company's security emblem on the left side of his chest. His dark beard was well trimmed, and hard large muscles rippled under almond colored skin. He looked at Maya, his eyes bright and cheerful. Her mouth dropped open, the lit cigar inches from her lips. At that very moment, she felt her pussy twitch.

"Is that ganja, miss?"

Maya tried to speak. "I-I-I..." but his deep sexy voice was echoing in her head, and her heart slammed against her chest as her pussy throbbed with wild abandon.

He held out his hand. "Allow me." He took the cigar from her fingers, gently. She actually swooned slightly before she braced herself against the armrest of her chair.

He sniffed the stogie and took a short toke. "Okay, now." He handed it back to her. "You got the good stuff, but do be careful in the pool." He softly laughed before giving them a nod as his eyes locked on Maya's. "Enjoy."

The women watched him walk away, enjoying the bounce of his step and the shape of his ass as he walked back inside the resort.

"Well, you sure are one smooth operator." Rebecca snatched the cigar from Maya, who just stared at the space where he once stood.

"Been a long time since a man took my breath away," Maya breathed.

"It's this good-ass weed." Rebecca took a hit. "Too strong for you all." She put it out. "Come on and get into the pool with me."

Maya shook her head, still reeling from the security guard. "I-I need a minute, to uh...gather myself."

Rebecca smiled. "Hmm, hmm... Come on, Trevor."

He looked up at her. "Okay. If I drown, it's your

fault."

She stood, dropping her towel, and his eyes traveled up and down her curvy figure. "You'll be all right." She grabbed his hand and led him to the pool. "I know mouth-to-mouth." They jumped in.

Portia watched as Maya settled back in her chair. "You okay?"

"Wasn't expecting this weed to be a religious experience. All I did was take two maybe three hits, and now I'm stratospheric."

"Well, just enjoy the sunset with me." Portia took Maya's hand into her own.

Rebecca watched as the two women talked in their chairs. With her head just above the water, her eyes traveled around the building, then settled on the sexy security guard staring at Maya from a darkened balcony. His eyes met Rebecca's.

A hand crept up her bikini top, and she felt Larry's hard cock against her backside. "Marco," he said.

Rebecca nodded in the security guard's direction before playfully slapping Larry's hand away. "Polo." She grabbed his cock beneath the water. "Game on."

Chapter Fifteen

A FEW HOURS LATER, Maya and Rebecca headed back to their room. Portia, Cole, Larry, and Trevor tagged along. "I know one thing..." Maya unlocked the door. "I got the munchies. Are we eating in or out?"

"How about both?" Larry dropped to the sofa, propped his legs on the coffee table, and stared at Rebecca walking toward him with a towel and a sly grin.

"Think you could handle that?" Rebecca bent over. Her full breasts filled his vision as she applied the towel to his damp hair. She dragged her hand behind his ear and down his neck to his chest where her hand rested momentarily so her fingers could deftly tease his right nipple. "Hmm, hmm. Just as I thought. Still wet behind the ears."

Portia giggled as she and Cole settled on the love seat. "We're hungry too."

"Room service?" Trevor stated. "Or we could just go to one of the restaurants."

"Trevor..." Maya said. "I'm high. Very, very high. I just want to chill in my room, stuff my face, and get high some more."

Trevor shrugged. "Fine by me."

"So it's settled." Maya clapped her hands. "Is there a menu around here somewhere?"

"I have no idea what I want?" Rebecca said.

"Me either," Portia replied. "Seafood, steak and potatoes. All I know is, I just need to put something in my mouth."

Trevor, Larry, and Cole shared a wicked look and

then laughed.

Portia jokingly punched Cole on his arm while Rebecca shook her head before sitting between Trevor and Larry. “Boys will be boys, won’t they?”

“Still in a frat boy state of mind, I see,” Portia said to her husband before kissing the tip of his nose.

“What do you expect from us?” Cole grumped. “We’re high, horny, and you all look great in your bikinis.”

“You talkin’ bout an orgy?” Rebecca rested her hands on Trevor and Larry’s thighs.

“Uh-uh...” Cole looked at Portia.

Rebecca laughed. “Don’t go lookin’ at your woman to get permission.”

“Well, to be honest...” Portia shot Maya a come-hither look. “We have discussed threesomes and foursomes. I suppose it would be okay to have one here. You know what they say, what happens here stays here.”

“That’s Vegas, baby,” Rebecca retorted. “You in Jamaica, girly.”

The two guys on either side of her laughed.

“Besides, what’s with the fake British accent, anyway?”

“It’s not fake,” Cole snapped.

Rebecca made a cat noise. “Calm down, Hercules, but I must admit, it’s kinda nice to see a man so protective of his honey.”

“Yes,” Maya said. “It is.”

“My accent isn’t fake,” Portia replied. “I lived in London for fifteen years. My father’s company moved us there. I loved it, but I love home too.”

“Where’s home?” Maya asked. “Wait before you answer that, I need a menu.”

“And I need some more weed.”

“I gotcha.” Cole kissed Portia. “Be back, dear. Gonna get our stash and see a man about a horse.”

“Just make sure you put the seat back down,” Portia

said.

"Hey, man." Trevor stood up. "I'll go with you." He looked down at Larry. "You coming, dude?"

Rebecca smiled while she walked her fingers up and down Larry's leg. "You coming, Larry?" she teased.

He stood up, an erection poking out, which made the women gasp then laugh. "Not yet." He proudly walked to the door.

Cole pointed at Larry's tent. "Aim that somewhere else, bro."

Trevor opened the door. "Larry has no dick control."

"My, my." Portia looked at Rebecca. "You had quite an effect on him."

"Oh that? It was nothing. College boys are easy. Larry is young, dumb, and full of cum. Just another dick to conquer."

"What is he, a challenge like Mount Everest?" Portia joked.

"You did see that monster lump, right?"

Portia shrugged. "Cole is enough for me."

Maya grinned knowingly. "He's the only guy you've ever had, isn't he?"

Portia blushed. "I've been with other guys. Two before Cole. He was the first guy to make me come, and my God, he made me come good. I was screaming and pounding the headboard. My flat mates teased me for weeks."

"You inspired him," Maya said. "Must've been that video vixen body you have."

"I used to do gymnastics in college."

"What do you do now?"

"I'm a coach at a local gym and I give private lessons to girls who compete." Her eyelashes fluttered at Maya. "I must say, a complement like that coming from you is very flattering."

"You two want to be alone?" Rebecca chimed in. "I

can go with the guys, you know."

"How about getting me a blunt first?"

Rebecca huffed. "You're not my boss."

"Please?"

Rebecca rolled her eyes and stood up. "Where is it?"

"On the patio table...I think."

"Don't bother looking," Portia said, "Cole is bringing some."

Rebecca clapped her hands. "See? Cole is bringing some."

The door chime sounded.

"There, Portia, I bet that's your sexy husband now." Rebecca strolled toward the door. Her bikini top had slipped down enough to reveal a nipple.

"Yes, he's *my* sexy husband," Portia responded. "Emphasis on he's *mine*. So tuck that boob back in where it belongs. I don't want you giving him any ideas."

"Bet you're no fun in a threesome." She opened the door.

***

The room service order was placed and more cigars were rolled around well designed lines of weed. They decided to smoke while they waited for the food, which they were assured would arrive in under twenty minutes.

"By the way," Portia said slowly through a haze of smoke. "I was also a cheerleader in high school and college."

"And she still has the body for it." Cole kissed her cheek.

"Not without effort," Portia chimed in. "I go to the gym daily."

"Me too." Maya inhaled smoke. "Gotta stay in shape...with all those younger girls wanting to steal my husband."

Rebecca giggled. "It's not what you got, girlies, it's how you use it."

Maya and Portia continued their conversation about physical fitness while Cole admired his wife and Rebecca stared at his crotch, which, the longer he stared at Portia, the fuller his shorts got. Their eyes met briefly. Rebecca returned her wanton gaze to the center of his pants, making Cole blush. He quickly tightened his hug around Portia.

Rebecca suppressed a giggle. "With Trevor and Larry gone, I feel like a third wheel."

"Where did they go?" Maya asked.

"To get some more smoke." Cole struggled to avert his eyes from Maya's chest.

A knock at the door ended their conversation. Rebecca got up, not without brushing her freshly manicured nails against Cole's right arm as it rested on the sofa. Portia missed the gesture, while Cole resisted the urge to admire Rebecca's ass as she opened the door. The server carried a tray down the short staircase and placed it delicately atop a matching gold cart. Both gleamed in the room's light, as did the server's smile. He bowed and left the foggy room.

"Good grief, let's eat." Cole rubbed his hands together.

The quartet dug into their meals, and the conversation started up again.

"So..." Rebecca looked at the newlyweds. "What fantasies are you two going to live out while you're here?"

Portia looked surprised. "Uh, uh..." She looked at Cole who reveled in the attention he was getting from Rebecca.

"I guess whatever happens, happens. As long as it happens to us *together*, right, Cole?"

"Yup, together." He nodded, being sure not to stare too long at the curvy blonde Rebecca or at Maya's rich brown skin.

Rebecca grinned. "Really, Cole, what fantasies do you want to explore?"

He looked at her, and then Portia. "I guess a threesome with my wife and one other woman," he replied with reluctance in his voice.

"And with someone we both like." Portia said that while gazing at Maya.

Rebecca grinned and licked her lips. "Me or Maya?"

Portia giggled. "Either or both."

"Definitely not Larry and Trevor," Cole responded.

"Why, Cole, you wouldn't want to watch those two guys fuck your wife?" Rebecca leaned forward. "How about while I orally ravage your cock?"

"Uh, gonna plead the fifth on that one." He was visibly aroused while at the same time incredibly uncomfortable. "I'm high but not high enough to admit to that." He looked over at Maya, who looked fantastic in her bikini. Cole loved how the lighter colored outfit accentuated her soft brown skin. "What about you, Maya?" He hoped to steer his way out of Rebecca's seductive web. "You have any fantasies?"

"Nah." Maya shrugged. She ignored thoughts of her absent husband coupled with the fact she didn't pack her magic wand. "Just here to get high and have fun."

"That's a lie." Rebecca pointed at Maya who was sitting on the bed, eating from a plate of shrimp and mangos. "She wants to fuck a black guy for the first time ever."

The silence in the room was tangible as the young couple stared at Maya in sheer astonishment. She coughed as Cole looked at her incredulously.

Maya drank some water in an effort to quell her cough then shot a nasty look at Rebecca. "I never said I would live out a fantasy. I'm married. Happily married, well, somewhat. And just because I'm half black doesn't mean I've been with a black man."

Rebecca snorted. "Not like your husband would know. Incidentally, where is he again?"

Maya frowned in annoyance at Rebecca's cryptic tone. The stares coming from Cole and Portia unsettled her, as well, but she had to stick to her vow: no big black dick. "Albert's not here. That's all that matters."

"Why?" Portia sighed. "I couldn't imagine coming to such a beautiful and romantic place without my Cuddle Buddy, Cole."

He blushed. "I asked you not to call me that in front of folks." He threw a sideways glance at Rebecca who grinned at him.

"Oh, it's okay, Cuddle Buddy," Maya said, happy to get the spotlight off her problem.

"Maya's husband paid for all this, so he's here in spirit." Rebecca picked up a new cigar. "Round two, folks?"

"We're only on round two?" Portia asked quietly.

Cole grunted. "There's no way I'd let my lady come down here alone. Three words. *Dexter St. Jock*."

"Who the fuck is Dexter St. Jock?" Rebecca asked.

Cole looked at her, surprised. "Famous Eddie Murphy skit about women going on a trip to an island paradise, like this one with girlfriends, like you two, and getting fucked by some guy with a big black cock."

"Mmm," Rebecca purred. "Sign me up for that exotic vacation." She took a wooden match and carefully lit the cigar, making sure all sides were burning evenly. "How about you, Maya?"

"I got a big dick..." she snapped. "At home."

"But it's not here," Cole said.

"And it damn sure ain't big and black."

"How would you know?" Maya scoffed. "You haven't seen my husband's cock."

Rebecca slowly twisted the cigar between her full lips while giving Cole a sensual sideways glace as she licked the bottom of the tip. "I can imagine—"

"Don't even go there," Maya muttered with a frown.

Rebecca busted out laughing, and Maya couldn't help but join in.

Albert and Rebecca fucking...how absurd.

"Temptation has a way of rearing its ugly head." Cole shot a glare of envy at the cigar between Rebecca's lips.

"I wouldn't cheat on you, baby." Portia draped her leg over his, and then rubbed his left thigh.

"You say that now..." Rebecca took two puffs and breathed in deep before passing the weed to Cole. "But you are not like my friend over there." She exhaled smoke. "Her husband constantly lets her down, leaves her hot and horny." She dragged her finger against Cole's as the cigar passed between them. "She deserves a thorough fucking on vacation."

"Enough about me." Maya gave Rebecca a shut-the-fuck-up look. "You're fucking up my high." *And overstepping your bounds*, but she dared not say it. She still had to share a room with her.

Cole coughed.

"I'm just saying, Maya," Rebecca continued over Cole's coughing. "He should appreciate you more."

"He does...in his own way."

"Not material things, either," Portia said. "He has to spend quality time with you." Gingerly, she reached for the cigar in Cole's hand, but he coughed and jerked it away from her. "Hold still." Then she laughed at his calamity and grabbed his hand to take the cigar while his body jolted with each cough. She examined the cigar. "I like my blunts like my cocks, fat and long." She gave the ladies a sly wink while her husband got up to find a bottle of water. "Just like my man's dick." She slid the cigar between her rounded lips and took a quick toke.

Rebecca frowned while checking out Cole's ass as he walked away. "Well, I hope you can handle his dick better than you handle that cigar."

In mid toke, Portia busted out laughing, and when she gasped another breath, the smoke filled her lungs even faster. Her eyes bugged out, and she handed the cigar to Maya who was trying not to laugh. Portia patted her chest as a cough erupted from her throat. "That's some wicked shit."

Cole returned holding out a full and opened bottle of water for his bride before sitting down and drinking one for himself.

Maya grinned. "You two lightweights can't hang." Then as she took a toke, she looked over at Rebecca and noticed how she was staring at Cole's lap. Again she wondered if Rebecca and Albert had fucked. *Nah.*

She breathed in the smoke, and closing her eyes, mild euphoria caressed her inner being. She thought about her husband and Rebecca naked in bed, and then pictured the young couple on the love seat naked and fucking. Her pussy clenched. She breathed out then brought the cigar up to her lips again, while her eyes remained closed.

You should be here, Albert. You promised you would be here. Maya shook her head. *Not the first time you said one thing and did something else*.

Inwardly she frowned, now angry at him. She wondered what he was doing right now. She pictured him at a strip club with some silicone doll's tit in his mouth and ass cheek in his hand. *Dubai my ass.* Maya inhaled another long drag and pictured that wonderful black cock. *Big, long, veins popping, throbbing inside me or gushing in my mouth. How would Albert ever know*? *Rebecca wouldn't tell him. How would he know I got some dick? How would he know I got some nice big black cock while on vacation*? *Hell, would he care*? Maya smiled. *Maybe I will indulge myself. Maybe I will just get me some—*

"Puff, puff pass, mofo." Portia giggled.

Maya's eyes snapped open. "Sorry...my mind

wandered." She handed the cigar to Rebecca who was looking at Maya's chest. "We can tell. Look at your nipples."

Oh dear. They'd swollen enough to make an impression in her bikini cups.

"You were thinking about that big black dick, weren't you?"

"I-I..."

Cole saluted. "Here's to hard wood and hard nips."

Maya frowned. "Whatever." She got off the bed and walked over to a chaise chair across from the couple. Rebecca sat on an oversized ottoman. She held out the cigar to Cole. "Your turn to suck on the smoking dick."

The other ladies laughed with her.

"Could we not call it that?" Cole asked. "It'll fuck up this whole smoking experience for me."

***

Maya awoke in her bed, still clad in her turquoise bikini, with Rebecca at her side, snoring loudly. An oversized white t-shirt covered her curvy frame. Maya looked around the dimly lit room. Cole and Portia were nowhere around. She liked the pair more and more as the night progressed and figured after three room service calls and smoking on the same cigar all night, they'd all passed out, but sometime before dawn the newlyweds must've made it back to their own room.

Probably to fuck, which is what I would be doing if my husband had come along.

She lay back on the bed and stared up at the ceiling. She loved Albert, fiercely, but at times, he was such a jerk. He had a way about him; his talk, walk, style. She knew he loved her, in his own way, of course. Their sex was great despite its sporadic nature.

And that was what baffled her. He didn't fuck her

more than twice a month. *What kind of husband is that?*

And Rebecca...

Maya looked at her friend who was still sleeping and snoring. *What the fuck has gotten into her? She is so damn quiet at the office, but here...* Maya shook her head. *Maybe it's the weed. Maybe that's what has her secure enough to come out of her shell and encourage everyone to fuck everyone else.*

"I know she needs to stop snoring," Maya said out loud about a foot from Rebecca's ear.

She snorted and twisted onto her side before snoring again.

Maya smiled.

Something about white girls with big tits...

She thought back to her two college roommates who used to drive her crazy at night: they were also well endowed. Maya was blessed, as well, but a nice C cup always took second to a D in some men's eyes. She got out of the bed and thought about closing Rebecca's mouth. Or, better yet, she thought to look for something she could use to tickle Rebecca's nose.

But instead of fucking with her friend, Maya decided to pee. Or rather her bladder decided for her, and as she sat her delicate derriere upon the porcelain throne, her thoughts again traveled to the big black cock in her dreams, that ebony phallus that could drive her over the edge of pleasure like no other dick before it.

Maya waved off the thought of finding a real one.

Dick was dick was dick.

It was the man who made sex special. She started the shower and dropped her swim wear on the floor outside the stall.

More importantly it's how I feel about the man, and how he feels about me that makes the sex good.

She thought about her husband and how his lovemaking was more than excellent, although it would be nice if he'd give it to her more often.

But then, a fantasy kicked in, remnants most likely of the high still titillating her body. She was in a room similar to her suite, only it was all white. The pillows, walls, ceiling, all white. Only the window was colorful, a spectacular view of the sun and the moon, one rising, one setting against a mountain sky with an ocean surging beneath.

She lay on a king-sized bed, atop white sheets, bouncing up and down as she felt the dick from her dreams slide in and out of her sweet sex. She couldn't open her eyes as strong hands glided up and down her body and drowned her in bliss. The shaft was so smooth, so thick, so good. She tried to open her eyes, but she felt an explosion brewing.

Her head tilted back, the shower water hit her now heated body as she polished her skin with a soft wash cloth and fragrant soap.

Now she was on her knees, backside sticking straight up as that dick slid inside her from behind. Strong hands gripped her hips, and the thrusts, at first, were slow and deliberate, each long stroke driving a pleasure-filled moan from her lips. Soon his hips picked up their pace, and before she knew it, he was slamming that big black cock in and out of her so fast that the sound of skin smacking skin mimicked the applause of a thousand people. Her heat grew ever closer and closer to coming...

"No," she shouted to her subconscious mind and eager libido.

The water rained down on her, and the fantasy refused to let go. She had that black cock in her hands, so big, so hard, but when she looked up at his face, it was hidden behind a blurred veil.

All she could see was his mammoth cock.

It was all she wanted... *No. No big black dick. No fucking without my husband.*

She turned off the shower and stood to let the water drip off her body. Her knees trembled and her pussy ached. She needed her husband, or at least the damn wand.

Why the hell didn't I pack the damn wand?

Then she remembered. Rebecca had talked her out of taking it, in favor of a new one still in the package. So Maya had left her faithful Hitachi at home. Then Rebecca failed to bring the new one. She'd planned it that way, for sure, leaving Maya with no alternative but to seek relief elsewhere. She felt a dark cloud over her head. Her mind raced back to Cole's words about temptation, now sounding truer than ever.

Just one fuck, just one black man, Maya insisted and her pussy clenched in anticipation. *And that's all it would be, a meaningless yet thorough fucking.*

She took a deep breath and stepped out of the shower and began to towel off. *No fucking*. She looked at the bathtub. The faucet came out just far enough. She could prop her legs just right and have a good old fashioned come that way.

No dick.

No white dick, no black dick, just her husband's dick when she got home. And, oh boy, was he gonna get it the next time she saw him.

Then a flash filled her mind's eye.

The big back cock throbbed in her hand and erupted in a river of cum that shot all over her body as she convulsed from her own overpowering orgasm.

Must be the weed playing with my mind.

"No strange dick," she muttered, but when she looked into the mirror and met her own gaze, even her reflection doubted her conviction.

Chapter Sixteen

SOON AFTER DRINKING a cup of green tea while watching the sun rise, Maya brushed her teeth then put on a sports bra and shorts to go to the gym. And after lacing up her running shoes, she got one of the card keys off the dresser and softly closed the door behind her.

She went back the way the cute bellhop led her when they arrived. Maya had been here alone before but still got lost every time she tried to find the gym. Her husband usually led her around the place. She remembered the one time she was here with her husband that he had actually spent time with her, which culminated in them fucking every night.

Ahh, the sweet memories.

But those memories, while pleasant and erotic, did not shed any light on where the gym was located. So she took out her phone to call the front desk but didn't have the number in memory, so she decided to go downstairs and ask somebody in person.

The elevator doors slid closed and she rode it to the lobby. As the bell tolled and a mechanical voice softly announced the lobby, the elevator jerked to a stop. She dropped her phone and looked down as it hit the elevator floor. "Damn." She knelt to pick it up just as the doors opened.

"Good morning, ma'am," a deep baritone voice rang out.

Maya's gaze snapped up from her phone, and right away her heart began to flutter, and her mouth fell open as her eyes locked on a massive bulge in a man's pressed slacks.

She forced her eyes to look up and appraise the dark brown security guard who stood before her. The Adonis she'd first seen at the pool wore a tight black polo stretched over his muscular frame. He stood straight and proud, with a well maintained haircut and clean fingernails.

"Please allow me." He kneeled down beside her and picked up the phone then stood straight again, all in one fluid motion. "Here you are." He held out a big wide hand. "May I?"

God, is he as big everywhere..?

"Yes," she croaked as she attempted to clear her throat in as classy a manner as possible. "Thank you." After accepting his offered hand, she rose effortlessly as he helped her stand. She admired his round shoulders so as not to allow her gaze to traverse back down to his crotch.

He stepped aside, holding out his free hand. "After you, ma'am."

She blushed like a school girl. "You're so kind." Demurely, she stepped off the elevator, and she read his nametag as she passed by.

Nicholas.

On second thought, she turned around as he got on the elevator. "Excuse me, Nicholas."

He looked at her, appraising her toned legs and healthy hips. He had checked out her shapely ass while she sauntered off the elevator. Yeah, she was the same woman at the pool. He also did not fail to notice the large handfuls beneath her sports bra. He imagined with some pleasure fucking her...if everything went as planned. "Yes, ma'am."

"Maya..."

An old couple got on the elevator.

"My name is Maya. I'm in the executive suite."

The old woman groaned. "Listen to her brag."

Maya ignored her. "Can you tell me where I can find the gym?"

"Ask the front desk," the woman snapped, jabbing a finger at the elevator console.

Just before the doors slid shut, Nicholas smiled at Maya. "Take a left and follow the signs."

"Thanks again." She bit her lip as the door shut. "Damn." His bright grin flashed through her mind.

Maya strolled toward the gym. A smile warmed her entire being. Nicolas was so fucking cute. Big smile, nice even teeth. She wondered if fate was tempting her.

Colorful signs led her to a pair of heavily tinted glass doors. She pushed her key card into a slot in the wall, and the doors slid open to reveal a gym double the size of the gym in her office building. She was impressed for the second time today.

The first time was Nicholas.

She stretched before hitting the machines. No hurry. She was on vacation. Yoga next. Thoughts of Nicholas danced through her head as she breathed deep and meditated. *He was big, but was he big everywhere*? She headed to the cardio equipment, glad the place was nearly empty, just a few folks scattered about. After ten minutes on the treadmill, she moved to an elliptical for another ten, and then finished up her workout with the weights. Nicholas popped into her head again. He was gorgeous. A fantasy come to life. Big strong arms and chiseled chest. His legs looked full and robust beneath his slacks. And in her mind's eye, she could see him, and feel him inside her, making her drown his hardness in a gush of her nectar.

She set the bench press machine back in place and closed her eyes, trying to get the sexy security guard out of her mind.

"Ahem," a male voice said from out of nowhere.

Maya's eyes flew open and her head jerked around to her left to reveal Cole with Portia and Rebecca. "Are you three a team now?"

"I told you she would be here." Rebecca laughed. "It's

what sexually frustrated women do."

"No it's not," Portia said. "I work out all the time, and I'm far from sexually frustrated."

Cole shrugged. "What can I say?"

Maya asked, "What are you doing here?"

Cole struck a Superman pose. "We gotta work out, too."

Portia's eyes met Maya's. "You look great."

Rebecca frowned. "But she's all sweaty."

"Accentuate the positive." Maya laughed. "I'm almost done."

"Hey, it's cool." Cole stuck out his chest. "I'm going to hit the weights." He gave Portia a kiss and then nodded to Rebecca and Maya.

As he walked away, Rebecca whistled low. "Portia, my dear, he is undercover cute."

"And all mine," the raven-haired beauty replied.

"Aww," Rebecca cooed. "You're protective. But come on, Portia. I thought you guys said you were gonna live it up while you're here. Can't I have a little bit of Cole-cock? Just a taste of what you are going to have the rest of your lucky ass life?"

"Mmm, I don't know," Portia purred. "If I let you borrow him, you simply must promise to give him back. And I'll need some more of that absolutely magical ganja. It made me, so, so..."

"Hungry?" Maya finished.

"Horny?" Rebecca offered.

"Is it supposed to do that?"

"It's a nice side effect." Rebecca looked at Maya sadly. "Hungry? Really? Girl, you need some dick."

Before Maya could reply, the glass doors slid open, and Nicholas strolled in.

"Oh, my God," Rebecca said and right away looked at Maya. "That's all yours, girl, oh yes, that's for you. I bet your name is tattooed on his cock. Oh shit, he's coming this way." She turned to walk away and pulled Portia with her.

Maya just sat there. Rebecca's voice faded underneath the pounding of her heart.

Nicholas stopped about five feet from her and smiled that dazzling smile. "I see you found your way."

She felt her lower lips moisten. "Thanks to you." She'd said it far more huskily than she'd intended.

Oh, my God. I'm so wet.

He spread his massive arms. "I am sorry about that old woman in the elevator. She is a regular and she is a bit possessive."

"Possessive maybe, I'm not sure of what, but she's a bitch most definitely."

"Yes, she can be a bitch, especially when it comes to her only living nephew."

"Oh my God." Maya's mouth fell open. "I'm so sorry I called your aunt a bitch."

He laughed. "It's okay. My mother has used much harsher language when referring to her oldest sister."

Maya felt seduced under his appraising eyes.

"I hope she will not distort your perception of our resort."

"No, no way, not at all." Maya's gaze landed on his midsection then basked over the bulge of his crotch. "I love this place. Every inch of it."

"Is there something..." he stepped closer, "...I can do for you?"

She stood, holding onto the handles of the bench press machine as her legs grew weak in his presence. A thousand erotic thoughts ran through her mind, all of which centered on a big black dick. "I'm fine for now, but..." A sudden jolt of confidence let her next words loose. "...could you check on me every now and again? My husband isn't here, and I..." She imagined kissing his full lips and him kissing hers down below. "I might need—"

"Might need me to check the locks," Nicholas

suggested.

She noticed his growing bulge. “Yes, Nicholas.” She showed him a conspiratorial grin. “Most definitely the locks. Thoroughly.”

He smiled as he licked those beautiful lips. “Fair enough. By the way, my friends call me Nick. My shift ends in two hours. Perhaps I can check on you then.”

“That would be perfect.” The distance between them was getting smaller by the second. “I’ll feel so much safer knowing you are around.”

Nick held out his hand. “It will be my pleasure.”

“Mine too.” She shook his hand, again marveling how one so strong had hands so soft. She watched him stroll out the door as she bit her bottom lip.

The split second Nicholas was out the door and out of sight, Rebecca rushed up to her. “Girl, what was that?”

Maya laughed. “Just having some fun.” She jostled her wedding ring. “No hubby.”

Portia scowled at her. “Perhaps your husband will show up.”

Maya saw disappointment in Portia’s expression. “Maybe—”

“That’s wishful thinking,” Rebecca said. “That black man and Maya were doing more than flirting. I could feel the heat, girl, from a thousand yards.”

“Whatever,” Maya replied coyly.

“But you do realize that guy has the dick of your dreams.”

“How would I know that? I haven’t seen it. Besides, he might be gay.”

“No way he’s gay. He was looking at you as if you were his salvation.” Rebecca grinned. “Just say the word and I’ll leave the room tonight so you guys can be alone.”

“I might but just so I can have an intimate moment with the tub’s faucet.”

“Girl, stop playing. You want to fuck, he wants to

fuck, and your husband is not here."

"But he's here in spirit," Portia chimed in.

Rebecca rolled her eyes. "Okay, the newly married smurf thinks all men are created equal and act like Cole."

"But Maya has a good man," Portia insisted. "I can tell."

"He always finds something better to do than be with his wife," Rebecca shot back. "Please join us in the real world where there are good men, bad men, and dick men. You have a good man, Maya is married to a bad man, and that black man has the dick she's always wanted." She looked back at Maya who was throwing darts with her eyes. "Doesn't he, Maya?"

"Jury's still out," Maya snapped, yet she pictured his bulge and thought Rebecca might be right, though Maya would never admit it.

"It's not too late to have that moment of bliss with him," Rebecca said.

"First, I hope it would last longer than a moment, and it's too late because I'm married."

"Yeah." Portia cheered.

"Stop it," Rebecca said. "Stop playing and go get you some. You know, treat yourself."

"It's not too late to resist temptation," Portia said. "But once you spread your legs, there's no going back."

"Girl," Rebecca growled. "Temptation has already moved in, and he's six-foot something with a body like The Hulk and he's ready to fuck. And Portia, my dear, as much as you want this to have a fairytale ending, I do believe Maya is going to ride that black cock to heaven, and her husband can go to hell."

Portia said nothing while Rebecca walked toward the stationary bikes, then: "Some friend she is, Maya, egging you on to shag another man. But I have faith in you."

Maya smiled wanly, fearful that Rebecca was right and Portia was dead wrong.

Chapter Seventeen

NICHOLAS SAT IN a dark corner of a crowded bar, staring dolefully at the fat envelope on the table in front of him.

"It's all dare, mon, take it." Gilbert smoked a joint that barely contained the copious amount of ganja within. "That cash will go a long way."

"How is she?" Nick was still looking at the envelope.

Gilbert smiled. "More than fine. We takin' good care of her and that world-class pussy she got between them fine legs."

Nick's hand shot out to wrench Gilbert's skinny neck. "I never liked you," he said through clenched teeth. "So watch what you say about her."

Gilbert smiled as he calmly brought his left hand into view and stuck a silver barreled .38 in Nick's face. He cocked the hammer back as the joint dangled precariously from the corner of his lips. "Careful now."

Reluctantly, Nick released the weasel.

"I could pull this trigger and take the money and no one here would even blink." He sighed. "Pussy is pussy, a commodity like oil, gas, water even, none of it worth dying for. So take what you earned from fucking the American bitch and live your life. You got it good, mon, at that resort. Steady job, good pay, and endless access to top-shelf pussy. Why fuck it up over one American bitch?" He slid the hammer back in place. "Take the money, mon. Forget the bitch." He stood and walked out.

Nick's hand fell on the envelope as he watched Gilbert leave. He was right; no one was looking at them.

He examined the thick envelope. A good deal of money for a job well done.

So why did he feel like shit as he pocketed the envelope and walked out into the sunshine?

Maybe because I sold out the best woman I ever met.

Chapter Eighteen

MAYA STOOD ALONE ON a pier, drinking a glass of red wine. A light blue dress loosely entwined her body and flowed with the ocean breeze. With her eyes closed, she listened to the waves and the sounds of nature all around her.

Why aren't you here, Albert?

Sadly, she opened her eyes and watched the sun as it slowly faded beneath the weight of the night sky. Cole, Portia, and Rebecca were in the restaurant behind her, eating with the college boys: Larry and Trevor. She welcomed having the two twenty-something boys around; they stopped Rebecca from endlessly nagging her about fucking Nick.

Granted, she thought about Nick a lot. She had to take a longer bath than normal to quell the tingle between her thighs, but while she was happy about finding the handheld hose, the pleasure it brought her was not satisfying enough. It would be just about to send her over the edge when she'd take it away, the thought of a fat cock filling her mind instead.

She credited horniness and endorphins instead of the weed. Hell, she still might have been high. Whatever it was, she wasn't going to allow lust to step between her and her husband no matter how much he neglected her. Besides, the disappointed look Portia had given her earlier still haunted her, which made her admit that Portia's disapproval exacerbated her own guilt for even thinking about doing the deed with Nick.

But why should I feel guilty? Albert's not here. He's

somewhere else doing God knows what while I'm here alone.

She sipped her wine, hoping to quell her illicit thoughts.

"Maya," a soft voice said.

She turned to find Portia striding toward her. "We're all going back to the suite. Rebecca invited those two boys. I mean, they're cool and all, but all they talk about is weed, football, and sex."

"They're college guys, Portia." Maya glanced into her wine glass. "Weed, football, and sex are all they know."

"I've no experience with college boys. I didn't live on campus."

"Neither did I." Maya swallowed a gulp of wine. "I graduated with as little extracurricular fucking as possible. In fact, I didn't have sex until my twenty-first birthday."

Portia blushed. "I was twenty. And well, you were right. Cole was my first. I mean I gave guys head and all, but he was the first to fuck me." She smiled. "He was the first to earn it, you know what I mean? But still..." She swallowed. "I like women, too."

"Really?"

"Why else would I agree to a threesome with Cole and you?"

Maya nodded. "Or Rebecca."

"I worry about the way she ogles Cole. I'm not as in to her as I'm into you. I think she wants Cole and me to fulfill our fantasies with you so her freaky butt can watch."

She wants to join in, Maya thought to say but instead: "Okay, girl. I'll join you in a little while to put a leash on Rebecca. Meanwhile, I want to finish this wine and enjoy the sunset. Just make sure you count me in the rotation when you puff-puff-pass."

"Good, the party will be even, three girls and three boys." Portia gave her a light kiss on the cheek before she moved away, almost skipping back into the restaurant.

"Now that is one hell of a woman in one hell of a body." The thought of touching it made Maya's pussy thrum.

"Is everything all right?" a deep voice said from behind her.

She jumped and dropped her wine glass into the ocean below her. "Oh shit." She watched the glass sink, then she turned to Nick, and the thrum increased to a downright throb.

"My apologies for startling you," he said in his sexy tone. "I was trying not to scare you...guess I failed miserably."

Maya laughed. "How about an A for effort?" She appraised him in his impeccably pressed uniform. *How about an A for everything, period, you sexy motherfu—*

"Maya?"

She heard Nick call her name and snapped back to reality. "I'm sorry. You were saying?"

"I asked if you would like another glass of wine."

"Yes...of course, please."

Nick gestured to a waitress standing in the doorway of the restaurant. The woman rushed up right away, and Maya assessed the very short and very curvy woman with lots of caramel skin showing.

"Yes, Nicholas," the girl said in her delightful Caribbean accent.

Maya enjoyed the sound of his name, and she grinned as she noticed how much the waitress seemed to like saying it.

"Will you bring our guest another..." Nick looked at Maya.

"Cabernet Sauvignon," she finished for him.

The girl's devilish eyes shifted from Maya and back to Nick. "Of course." She shot Maya a nasty look before walking away.

Maya touched Nick's arm. "That girl likes you."

"No kidding. She was in my room one night, drunk and naked."

"And..?"

"I called some of my security guys to haul her out. Cost me a few bucks, but I got rid of her."

"Why?"

Nick looked long and deep into her eyes. "She's not my type."

Maya looked toward the sunset, already feeling that ache again...but: *He deserves to know the truth about me.* "I'm married."

"Happily?"

Maya was about to say *not entirely* when the waitress came back. She handed her the glass and a napkin. "Enjoy," she said with a fake smile then hustled off.

Maya swirled the wine around.

Nick pointed at her glass. "I see people do that a lot with wine. Why?"

"So it can breathe, baby." She held the glass deftly as she swished its contents. "By agitating the wine, it allows oxygen to get in, and that allows the wine to open as it softens and reveal its aromas." Maya looked at him with a sweet smile as she put the glass to her lips. Their eyes never wavered as she took a measured sip.

Nick grinned. "The first part of what you said went right over my head...about aromas and agitation, but I must admit I liked the way you explained it." He watched her beautiful throat swallow. "I'm no wine drinker. I like beer."

"I used to drink beer, but my husband is into wines, which pretty much means I'm into wines, too."

"You must enjoy it."

"Very much." She looked him up and down, a habit she was beginning to enjoy. "You're still in uniform. Am I to take it that I won't be your lone security issue tonight?"

"Alas, no."

"Alas?" Maya repeated. "My, for a security guard,

you are well read. I'm surprised you don't know about wine."

"Of course I know about wines. I just wanted to make conversation. And I am well read. Far too many folks died for me to be able to read."

"I see."

He shrugged. "It's just that, at times, I get tired of folks thinking I am not educated because I'm black and work security at a resort. It's a cool job and I'm proud it puts food on the table and a reasonable roof over my head."

"A reasonable roof?"

"One with just a single leak will do."

She laughed.

"I am working a few extra hours tonight, but that will not restrict me from checking in on you."

"Good. And to be honest, I'm not entirely happy with my marriage. Sometimes I can't go to sleep without a glass of wine."

"What about after a good fuck? Do you still need the wine?"

Maya looked at him over the rim of her glass, her pussy throbbing madly under his gaze. The sensation began to override her thoughts, guiding her mind and body to a place she didn't dare go. "I don't know." She swallowed another sip of wine. "My husband is not here to fuck me."

He smiled before he gestured in the direction Portia skipped off to. "Why are you not with your friends?"

"Later." Maya looked him up and down, her panties in desperate need of a change. "Right now, I'm enjoying the view."

When Nick turned to look at her, she was staring at him. "Ahh... Unfortunately, my break isn't much longer."

"How long?"

"Not long enough to do what your eyes tell me you want."

For a moment, the heat passing between them was

almost palatable, amplified by the silence they shared. Finally Maya spoke, her eyes never leaving his, even as pier torches automatically lit and blazed around them. "There is something in this tropical breeze that brings out romance...and desire."

"I suppose that is why so many writers come here." Nick drew closer to her. "To add depth to their works."

"Writers? I thought you would have said lovers."

"Them too, but isn't that obvious?"

"I suppose so. Are you from here?"

"I live here, work here, but I'm from Davenport, Iowa. My father is from here, and when my time in the service was done, I came here. I wanted a job without all the hustle and bustle of life in America."

"There are a lot of perks to this job," Maya noted. "The view, the ocean, the ganja."

Nick grinned. "And you."

"Oh, yeah, I almost forgot about all the women, both the islanders and visitors."

Nick looked at her. "I must admit, Maya, that you have ruined that aspect of my job forever."

She looked at him skeptically. "Now just how did I do that?"

He gazed out at the ocean. "Hmm..." He turned back to look her in the eyes. "To start with your natural beauty, and your aura, your songbird voice, hell, I even love the way you walk. When you leave, it's gonna be hard to forget you, Maya."

"You're too kind." Maya blushed. *This guy knows exactly what women want to hear.*

His expression turned serious. "You mentioned a husband more than once. Why is he not here?"

"Business. On purpose, I believe. Bailed on me the last minute."

"How unfortunate for him. He should be here to make sure you do not dine alone."

She didn't take her eyes off Nick. His musky scent was overpowering, and she worried her anticipation would seep out and drip down her leg. "Perhaps you could, you know, temporarily take his place as my dinner partner."

"I'm off tomorrow night." He pressed his bulge against her hip. "How about dinner first, and then some dancing?"

"That's funny. Most men just want to fuck me, not romance me."

He gazed at her beauty, illuminated by the torchlight. From her pretty feet nestled inside a designer pair of flip flops, up her sculpted legs to her shapely breasts, her cleavage beckoning him, he was enamored. "You are beautiful enough to deserve both."

Maya smiled. "Are you the man to give me both?"

Before he could reply, his handheld radio squawked. He sighed while snatching it off his belt. "This is forty-three."

Maya saw the phallic shape bulging in his trousers.

"I understand."

She watched his cock-bump diminish as he listened to the dispatcher.

He looked at Maya. "I have to go."

"Duty calls." She turned back to the ocean with a smile. "Find me when you can."

"I will find you." He turned away.

"You better," she whispered.

But your husband, Maya...what about your vows, the look Portia gave you?

Maya sighed then looked up at the starry sky. "What should I do?"

A bright streak blazed against the glittery background and burned out before it touched the water.

"It's just one time," Maya said to the remnants of the shooting star. "What can it hurt?" She slapped the railing. "One fucking time is all."

Tears blurred her vision of the heavens.

God damn you, Albert Valdis.

She dumped the dregs of her wine into the water below.

Chapter Nineteen

MAYA FELT HANDS touching her body, rubbing her sensually, which solicited a soft moan of pleasure from her full lips. Her mind swam in a drifting fog above a huge bed surrounded by the surreal eyes of blurry faces. A pair of hands rubbed her feet, made her giggle and squirm. A moan of pleasure escaped her throat as a new pair of hands slid between her soft thighs and touched her wet flesh, making her shiver and gasp with delight.

She looked up to find Nick smiling down at her, his hard naked body at arm's length, allowing her eager hands to blaze a trail across his chiseled chest and taught abs.

"Nick, what's happening to me?" Her voice reverberated down a long dark tunnel.

His cock began to rise, the ebony shaft like a lusty monolith begging for her touch.

"Taste me," he said, standing over her.

She said nothing as he moved closer. Her mouth willingly opened, engulfed the proffered head, and her lips slid down the thick shaft. A slow carnal groan escaped his throat. Pleasure captured her mind as she licked up and down the hard cock in her mouth.

"Maya," Nick cried as her tongue waggled around the rim of his head. He tasted sweet as mangos. She savored every inch of him, taking her time as she sucked and licked. His hips found a blissful rhythm with her mouth, but soon he was forced to pull away from her lips to stave off his pending explosion.

She looked down to see another man between her legs, forcing her to cry out as his tongue found her sweet spot. With a moan she tried to move away, but Nick and the man held her in place. She took Nick's erection into her hands and massaged him from top to bottom. He cried out and stood on his toes as she worked him up and down and rubbed her lips around his tip once more. His eyes closed as she slid her tongue in a slow sensual circle around the pink skin of his head then she guided him into her mouth only to cry out as the man's hedonic labors gently prodded her clitoris to a euphoric climax. Gasping and shuddering, she smiled down at the man between her legs. He looked up, revealing her husband's face, wet with her juices.

"Albert, what are you doing to me?" Her voice again a faraway echo.

"Suck that black dick, bitch," he demanded.

She turned back to Nick and softly glided him deeper into her warm, inviting mouth and ravenously slid her tongue against every vein and every curve.

Nick's ethereal form fell into a trance as if hypnotized by her skillful mouth, and his hips began to move on their own volition. His eyes slid shut, and she knew all he could feel was her amazing mouth, satin soft lips, and amorous tongue guiding him to a climax. He moaned in blissful agony as his cream flowed heavily into her hot, fervid mouth.

She sucked him eagerly, refusing to let go until his legs trembled and he had to snatch himself out of her mouth. Then with pleasure, he watched her husband fill his mouth with her wet folds. She groaned as her husband delighted her body. This was what she wanted. This was what she always wanted from him: to love her, take the time to be with her, make her feel like a woman again.

His eyes met hers as his tongue ravished her clit. The orgasm she'd coaxed from Nick had brought her closer to her own. She moaned and closed her eyes. Her hips flowed up and down like waves, some crashing into Albert's mouth, beseeching him to eat her more forcefully. She pressed her head back onto the pillow and grabbed Nick's cock to hold his still erect masterpiece like a handrail to heaven, squeezing it with every lick of her husband's tongue.

She stiffened her leg muscles as she felt her climax building, starting down in her toes and traveling like a hot wind up her body.

Her husband must have sensed her heat too, as the movements from his mouth became more deliberate, licking harder and probing deeper.

She felt him slide his tongue up and down her folds, forcing her hips to mimic his frantic pace. She faintly heard voices talking softly in the background, but the tongue's dreamlike pace found her pearl. His lips latched on and his tongue lapped it without mercy. Her hips bucked, completely at the will of her husband's mouth, and her groans grew louder.

Nick's hand caressed her right breast as she clung to his cock. The tongue slid tantalizingly up and down her folds from her pearl to her wet opening, then her back arched and she cried out as her climax reached its peak. Her husband's mouth left her pulsating flower, and a moment later, he slid his meaty cock into her vagina. She maneuvered her legs to rest on his strong shoulders, and she took Nick's head back into her mouth as her husband thrust his dick in and out of her.

The men lifted her off the bed. Nick pulled out of her mouth and scooted his body under hers while Albert set his girth on her lips. As she propped herself up on her arms, Nick slid into her pussy from behind. She cried out then her husband shoved his cock into her open mouth. She groaned around the thick shaft as Nick, driven by lust, began to piston in and out of her, bouncing her firm backside against his abs.

Her body began to shake as both men fondled her breasts while her husband's hand slid downward to softly stroke her clit. He fell out of her mouth as she moaned in ecstasy.

Nick kept slamming into her from behind, growing more rigid with each stroke, and she took her husband into her right hand and began to stroke him up and down.

"Come, woman," she heard someone say from far away.

"Wha—" Her mouth slammed shut and her eyes rolled back as she felt her juices rain down Nick's shaft. *"Oh my God,"* she cried as a second climax hit her. Her hips bucked wildly on Nick, who growled as he pulled out and spewed his cum for a second time.

Her husband watched her lustful delirium and reached his own explosion, pumping hot lava onto her face and chest.

She heard a hearty laugh. "She is a suitable replacement." It was Bossman's cruel voice.

Maya opened her eyes in time to see two naked men walk away from the bed, which was small with cum-stained sheets. "Nick?"

No response.

"Albert?"

No response.

"What have you people done to me?"

Then she remembered:

"...something about resisting..."

Realization punched Maya in the gut. What happened was real, but the men were strangers. The drug had fucked with her mind. Her libido couldn't take her whorish behavior and inserted men she cared for in place of the men she didn't know.

"What the fuck?"

Rebecca suddenly appeared, dressed in a white smock and holding a syringe in her hand. "Very impressive performance, Maya."

She felt a prick on her naked thigh and clenched her

fist as her vision grew hazy and her head felt heavy. “Noooooo...”

***

Bossman looked at Rebecca as they walked down a long hallway. The big man smiled at the woman, his eyes lingering on her full chest as it set snuggly in the confines of her tight white smock. “You will be missed, my dear.” His baritone voice rumbled from deep inside his throat. “I should have asked your new benefactor for double the money to take you away. However, the surrogate you found, she will do well, of that I am certain. Her body is exquisite and she is very, very impressive in bed.”

“Just make sure she’s high,” Rebecca replied. “She gets it done.”

“I am satisfied. Now all we have to do is wait for your rich man to bring me my money and pick you up.”

Rebecca looked at him in bewilderment. “The money isn’t already here?”

Bossman shrugged as he turned toward the stairway. “Haven’t heard from him in hours.”

“But he was supposed to be here by now.” Rebecca’s mind raced. *Where is the motherfucker?*

#

Bossman had reached the top of the stairs when Gilbert ran up. “Problem at the resort, sir.”

“What kind of problem?”

“Talkers. Chief and the police woman are asking guests about your new lady.”

Bossman scowled. “Be sure to remind everyone on this island why some things are better left unsaid.”

“But...even the Chief of Police?”

Bossman sighed. “Of course not Clive, or Adrian for that matter. Just anybody who decides to speak about that which is not to be spoken.”

"You know George known to sing for dollars."

"Well," Bossman pondered as he started to walk down the hall. "Should the birdie sing, clip his wings."

Chapter Twenty

MAYA ARRIVED AT THE door of her suite around ten in the evening, her mind filled with the desire to feel the island's sweet, sweet ganja tickle her throat. She had waited for Nick to end his shift by killing time at the bar and talking to other tourists. However, the longer she waited for Nick, the more disappointment set in. Finally the bartender told her Nick was busy because the resort was short of staff. So alone and somewhat drunk, she'd bid the bartender goodnight and left, frustrated and in need of some island comfort.

She hesitated outside her door with the card key poised at the slot and listened intently yet heard nothing inside. She couldn't imagine them going to bed this early.

"Maybe they're not here," she muttered before sliding the card into place and gently opening the door. She closed it quietly and took off her shoes. The suite lights were out; only the glow from lamps outside shown through the windows. She took the steps down into the living room but stopped when she heard a sigh in the semi darkness.

As her eyes adjusted, she saw Portia lying on her back on the couch, her bare cherry tipped breasts jutting proudly on her chest, and her dreamy eyes gazing lustfully at something just outside of Maya's line of sight. Cole's head was nestled between his wife's thighs, his tongue lapping her tantalizing fruit.

Maya dropped to the floor and scooted behind the walk-around love seat. She peeked around it and watched as Portia licked her lips and moved her hips, her eyes never wavering from whatever she saw. Maya couldn't see what it was, but she heard groans, and soon she heard skin meeting skin in that oh so familiar fucking fashion.

Who's fucking on the bed?

With her lust at a boiling point, she ventured to see what Portia was watching, and at the same time, keep her own presence hidden. Her desire for her absent husband, coupled with her longing for Nick, already had her thoroughly aroused, but this voyeurism made her pussy wet with desire. Her mind reeled at the thought of a threesome if she had come back with them. Maybe she'd be sucking on Cole right now or *maybe Portia would be licking my pussy...* Those thoughts ended abruptly once she saw the action on the bed.

Rebecca was sitting backward on top of Larry's cock and facing Portia on the couch. Larry's head was on the pillow, his face a mask of contentment as her meaty pussy bounced up and down his thick shaft, leaving an ever growing pool of her juices on his balls. And then there was Trevor struggling to maintain his footing on the bed while Rebecca hungrily sucked his black cock. He fell out of her mouth and she looked back at Larry, whose eyes were closed and mouth agape.

The action between her legs must have been intense. When Rebecca grabbed Trevor's rod and shoved it back in her mouth, her hips pumped with wild abandon and her body trembled in bliss.

Trevor's face contorted as he tried to pull his cock out of her mouth, but Rebecca grunted in protest, clamped him tighter in her jaws, and continued her assault on his friend.

Maya turned to see Portia running her fingers through her husband's hair while he slid his tongue up and down her folds, taking his time, feasting on her nectar as her hips moved in scintillating union with his tongue. Maya's pussy dripped just watching him enjoy the flavor. She shifted her gaze back to the bed just in time to see Trevor's hips gyrate wildly as his cock unleashed a torrent inside Rebecca's eager mouth. As she grinned around his girth, cum leaked past her teeth to drip down her chin, and despite his pleas, she wouldn't let him go. His blond-haired pal watched him jerk and shudder, probably thinking about football to stave off his own growing climax.

Wide-eyed, Maya suddenly wished she had left the restaurant with them. What she wouldn't give to taste that cum and play with those bodies...

Rebecca finally released her mouth from around the college kid's long thin rod. He fell back on the bed, panting. "White bitch is for real." He held his hard-on like he was glad to get it back.

Rebecca turned to look down at his blonde buddy. "Your turn to come, baby," she said with a snap of her hips. She bucked her pussy back and forth and ravaged the rigid cock that battered her sensitive walls. The boy's face contorted as she sent him to the edge.

"I'm going to come," he roared and pushed Rebecca off him to grasp his swollen shaft.

With a mischievous laugh, Rebecca took his hand away and set her dripping pussy over his open mouth. Ravenously, he began to lap her juices, making her moan as she and Portia stared at the throbbing cock that stood proudly on its own. Rebecca's eyes met Portia's, the thick, pulsating rod like a tower between them, which made the newlywed buck her hips, forcing her husband to suck her sweet spot.

Maya couldn't help but cup her right breast and tickle the tip of her nipple as Larry's rigid cock throbbed twice before a trickle ran down the shaft. Each woman groaned softly as they watched thick streams of his cream suddenly surge into the air and land in milky puddles on his muscular thighs and abs.

Rebecca giggled and stroked him, which made him buck his hips more violently. He tried to squirm from the relentless grip on his now oversensitive shaft, but Rebecca smothered his face with her dripping flower and hungrily dropped her mouth over his throbbing cock.

Maya twisted back to see Portia grab her breasts and jut her hips out as Cole's lust-filled kisses brought her to an intense climax.

"Cole," she breathed. Her body trembled as he got up on his knees and slid his enormous erection inside her. He leaned down to kiss her while her explosion subsided, then slowly, methodically began his own journey to heaven. Their passionate kisses increased the tempo of his thrusts, and soon the trio on the bed was eagerly watching the couple on the couch moan inside each other's mouths as their bodies convulsed in blissful harmony.

Licking her lips, Rebecca crawled off the bed and slinked over to the couple, who were kissing as Cole's cum dripped onto the cushions below them. At first, Rebecca rubbed Cole's back, and then his ass, then her hand traveled down to his hanging cock.

He stopped kissing Portia.

Rebecca smiled and leaned into them, choosing to sensually kiss Portia first. Cole could only stare, his mouth open and his rod throbbing as he watched the two women kiss passionately.

When Rebecca pulled back, Portia looked up at Cole. He nodded. Rebecca gestured to the two college boys with a come-hither motion of her index finger.

Maya watched, her panties pulled to the side and her fingers digging in as the duo walked to the couch, their hard dicks wagging in front of them.

Rebecca went back to kissing Portia as Cole leaned back and stroked his own cock. Rebecca's hand slid between Portia's thighs. She trembled under the touch of the woman's expert fingers.

Then Rebecca leaned back to allow Larry to kneel between Portia's open legs. He took the head of his cock and rubbed it up and down the folds of Portia's still dripping box, then slowly pushed his way inside.

Maya was sure Portia felt every thick inch of his shaft stretch her wet opening to its limits.

As Portia gasped, Trevor stepped up and slipped his dick into her mouth. She groaned as both dicks filled her. She looked over at Cole, whose eyes met hers as Rebecca, now kneeling between his spread knees, took his cock into her hands.

At first Portia frowned, jealousy painting a mask of reluctance all over her face, but she didn't stop sucking Trevor's engorged cock.

Rebecca looked at her as she held Cole's fat mushroomed head only an inch from her full pouty lips. "Just roll with it, girl." With her eyes staring deeply into Portia's, Rebecca slowly slid her lips down Cole's shaft, which made him groan and close his eyes.

The look of pleasure on his face made Portia moan as well. Her hand grasped Trevor's sack; she groped it slowly while moving her tongue up and down his length in unison with the long deep thrusts of Larry's cock in her pussy. She never once took her eyes off her husband.

Cole's heavy eyes opened, weighed down by lust and weed. He focused on the two college guys pleasuring his wife, which made his cock throb in Rebecca's oral embrace. When he saw Portia close her eyes to fully enjoy the barrage of carnal lust, he whispered to Rebecca, "Fuck me."

Her mouth released him. She crawled up on his lap and dropped her succulent pussy on his saliva-soaked cock. He rubbed her silky smooth back as her heart-shaped booty bounced up and down on his rock hard plow. He looked at Portia who was suckling Trevor's dick. Her knees were spread wide to allow Larry maximum access as his muscular backside pumped wildly between her creamy thighs. Cole settled back to enjoy his own carnal ride.

Maya's fingers played freely between her legs, her

panties now sitting on the floor beside her. She wanted to join in, knowing she would be more than welcome...by Portia especially, so she concentrated on watching for the bride's pussy each time Larry momentarily pulled out of her dripping valley, then teasingly slid his slippery shaft back inside. In that short bit of time, Maya caught glimpses of Portia's meaty folds. Her lips were full and luscious and glimmered with sweet juices in the dim light. Maya knew that woman's shaved rosy flesh was hers for the taking...the tasting. All she had to do was strip to the buff and reveal herself to the participants, but this orgy was not what she really wanted.

She wanted to fuck, but more importantly, she wanted to be the star of the show, not just one of the extras. The sex had to mean something to her personally. She wanted to make love and be made love to...very, very badly. She really wanted her husband, but more than anything, as she watched Trevor's skinny black shaft slide between Portia's ruby red lips, she wanted a black dick, a big black dick. And damn it, she could have one. All she had to do was let Nick take her, forget about Albert, forget about her vows, and let her fantasies come true.

"Fuck it," she whispered. Her probing fingers were just moments away from taking her over the edge. *I'm going to find Nick before I explode.*

Carefully, she crept back to the door.

Well, maybe one more look before I go.

Maya glanced in the mirror and saw Rebecca's head fall back as she bounced on Cole. *God, that looks like fun.* Trevor pulled back, grabbed his cock and let it spew thin streams of cum on Portia's perky tits, suddenly mixing with Larry's cream as he pulled out and shot his wad on her chest. Her vacated well of lust pulsed and dripped in an orgasm of its own.

Maya's tongue flicked between her teeth and licked her lips. How could she walk away from such temptation?

The college boys were spent, and Cole wouldn't be worth much when Rebecca got through with him. Nick was Maya's only hope to find her own release, her own fantasies fulfilled. *I have to find Nick.* She grabbed her purse and picked up her shoes, quietly opened the door, stepped out, and then quietly closed it again.

In the hallway, she bent over to put on her shoes. Just as she began to stand straight, she felt a man come up behind her. A thick cock pressed against her ass, and a pair of strong arms wrapped her in their masculine embrace.

Fear began to rise in her chest, until she took a deep breath and smelled him. A smile spread across her face. "It's about time you found me." She leaned her body back into him and rubbed her hand down the left side of his leg. "I thought you forgot about me."

"Did you miss me?" Nick asked softly in her ear.

"You have no idea what I've been through." She breathed and turned in his arms to face him. "You have no idea how much I want you."

Nick cupped her ass as she pressed her soft body against his hard frame. "Shall we go inside and see what pops up?"

"Uh..." She looked at the door. A vision of Portia's pussy flashed in her mind. Portia would be a distraction from what she really wanted, and she didn't want to share Nick with her or Rebecca, not now...not tonight. "Let's go to your place. Everyone is naked in there."

"Oh really? Maybe we should join them."

"No," she said breathlessly. "That's not what I want."

He stared at her, his light brown eyes searching hers. "What is it you want, Maya?"

She felt him pressing against her, hard and thick. He could have her right now, and that thought alone made her speak the truth. "I..." Her mouth lightly touched his lips as she spoke. "I want you..." she breathed, "...to make love to me."

Their lips met in earnest. Maya groaned with pleasure, and as their tongues entwined, her legs wrapped around him, and she hoped he'd take her to the floor and ravish her right now. Her need to feel him inside her overshadowed any modesty or fear of being seen.

He twisted her about until he had her cradled in his strong arms. "I have the perfect place for us."

Her head fell on his chest while Nick carried her down the hall, and a few moments later he stopped and set her down before a pair of large chocolate-colored doors. "This is the Presidential Suite."

He slid his card key in, and the door opened to reveal a room bathed in white with dashes of gold on the pillows, vases, and tables. Candles lined the room, accentuating its natural ambience. Maya enjoyed the feel of a black and gold drape covering the sofa; its designs resembled a caramel swirl in a chocolate latte. The soft white sofa cushions wrapped her in luxury as she sat down. She smelled jasmine in the room. "Jasmine. My favorite."

"I know. I had a bouquet brought to this room."

"And just how did you know that I'd come here with you?" She smiled at him.

Waves crashed against the shore below the open windows.

"A little birdie told me." Nick retrieved a thick cigar full of weed from his pocket. He lit it and handed it to her.

"My. You thought of everything."

"No. I only thought of you."

She was about to speak but found herself blushing. Demurely, she glanced away and inhaled a deep drag, held it a moment, then exhaled. "It's so nice to be thought of."

"You are the only thing on my mind tonight." He held out his hand.

She took it, and standing up, she handed him the cigar as he led her toward the bed. As rose petals across the comforter came into view, she gasped. "You romantic devil, you."

He smiled. "I'm off duty, and I figured I could find out the answer to my question from earlier." He handed her back the cigar, exhaling.

Maya took a toke, her eyes locked on his as she wondered what question she'd left unanswered. She closed her eyes, inhaled even deeper, and felt the smoke permeate her lungs as both her heart and pussy throbbed with anticipation.

I'm really about to do this. I'm really about to get my first big black dick. Oh my God, what about my husband? What if he finds out? What if I took this risk and the sex isn't any good? Fuck!

She inhaled another toke to calm her frenzied mind, and she held in the smoke as her eyes remained closed. *What do you want?* She heard him ask within her head. And she had told him. And the answer was still the same. She exhaled the smoke through her nose, dragon-style, then took another hit. *Happily married?* She'd answered that question too. Baffled, she exhaled. "And what question might that be?"

"Whether you need a glass of wine after a thorough fucking."

"Oh, that question." Her mind flashed back to the orgy she viewed in her suite that had brought her precariously close to the edge of a thunderous orgasm, and her body's reaction to those vivid memories assured her that the need to have a screamer of her own was still boiling within her. "Well, before that query is answered, another has to be answered." She slipped off her shoes.

"And that question is?"

She took a single step in his direction. "Are you going to fuck me thoroughly?"

"I thought I might try."

She breathed out while handing him the cigar. "Oh really?" She already felt the weed's effects. "Now..." She stepped closer to him. "...will you make me squirm and scream?"

"I have no desire to make you scream. My desire is to be with you, all of you, mind, body, and soul. Pleasure is all I want you to have."

"Doesn't sound like fucking. Sounds more like making love, don't you think?"

"Maya..." Nick closed the space between them. "Why in the world would there be anything else between us?"

Maya was speechless as, without warning, his arms wrapped around her and pulled her close. She felt his length and girth grind against her as their hips met. Maya groaned against his mouth, opening hers fully, her head falling back slightly as her legs weakened. As she fell toward the bed, his strong arms gently slowed her fall and delicately laid her on the bed of rose petals.

She stared up at him from her pillow, craving to see what her mind had only imagined, his big black dick.

"You are so beautiful." Nick kicked off his shoes, climbed onto the bed, and levered his body over hers as their lips passionately bonded again.

Her eager fingers worked to undo his pants. She had the belt unbuckled when he got up on his knees and began to undress. His uniform shirt came off first, revealing an ebony chest of rippling muscles, washboard abs, and biceps of steel. Maya drooled in eager anticipation of what she would see next. As his pants fell around his thighs, his cock proudly stretched the cotton of his underwear. In the material, she made out the impression of his head, its broad rim, and the edges of a still swelling shaft. She said nothing as she hungrily stared at the Adonis before her.

He slowly pulled down his undershorts, and her eyes grew wider as each inch of him was slowly revealed until the swollen head finally popped free.

"Oh my," she breathed. *What a beautiful cock.*

He laughed softly, shucked off his pants, and reached

for her. They stared into each other's eyes as he explored beneath her dress. Surprise flashed across his face as his hands touched the bare skin of her pussy.

"It got really hot in my suite." She cringed at the thought of Rebecca finding those soaked panties behind the love seat.

He chuckled and again melded his lips with hers. He felt her hands on him, feeling him as if he were a prized possession. She squeezed his mushroomed head and stroked the shaft from tip to base and back again. Her hand barely encompassed half his girth. Their lips pressed together as his arms wrapped around her. Somehow her breasts came free of the confines of her dress, and an erect nipple found its way into his eager mouth.

Maya groaned as he started to slowly and sweetly kiss his way down her body until his face hovered over her mound. "No, not now. I want you inside me."

Supporting his weight on his strong arms, he mounted her, his penis poised at the edge of her valley, his head gently pressing against the wet folds of her lips. She felt the lust take over completely and pushed her pussy against the head, unable to wait any longer. She felt him slide in just an inch and stop, teasing her for a moment, and she embraced that moment by gyrating her hips ever so slightly, teasing him in return. Her actions removed any doubt he might have had about what she desired, and finally, he slid his beautiful cock inside her. As she felt his girth stretch her opening like it had never been stretched before, she cried out in pleasure.

He didn't start pumping her like she was some kind of whore, but paused and stared into her eyes. She swallowed, hoping her lust wouldn't reach a screaming crescendo too quickly. She pushed her pussy against him, causing Nick to push back against her, and she had to resist the urge to start pumping his shaft like mad.

Slowly, he pressed deeper inside.

"Oh, my God." Her head fell back. "Oh, oh, Nick." Her eyes closed tightly.

"But it's only halfway in." Nick kissed the side of her neck.

Goose bumps skittered across her luxurious skin.

He whispered in her ear. "Are we making love yet?"

She inhaled. "To hell with making love, just fuck me, Nick, fuck me like I've never been fucked before."

Their bodies began to move in amorous unison.

She felt herself drift on a wave of salacious joy beneath his strong, hard body. Music played in her mind as her fantasies merged with reality. She had imagined this moment a thousand times.

Once you go black, you never go back.

She wondered if that was true. If so, Albert was doomed to jack off for the rest of his life.

Briefly, she thought of how her husband had made love to her, an unintended comparison, but when Nick began to swivel his hips, her memories of Albert faded as Nick's movements caused her to cry out. A sudden flood of ecstasy flowed freely through her body. She raked her nails across his broad back and shuddered beneath him.

He just made me come.

Maya looked at him, her mouth agape as he moved his big dick in and out of her body.

I've never come that quickly...or is there more coming to come?

Nick leaned in to her face. "Are you okay?"

Maya stared into his eyes. "Just shut up and fuck me."

Their pace quickened, both overcome with desire. They kissed again, deeper this time and more frantic, tongues and teeth and lips colliding.

She felt him harden with each plunge, as if his cock was getting ready to explode, filling her more completely than ever. She spread her legs wider and threaded them through his arms until her ankles found their way onto his shoulders. Now every plunge to the bottom stretched her insides to the breaking point.

She trembled as he quickened his pace.

"Holy shit," Maya whispered into his kissing mouth. "Oh, my God." She groaned, swimming in sheer bliss, each desperate breath a reprieve from drowning in a sea of lust. And her heat was getting hotter. "You're doing it again..."

"Doing what?" he asked, breathlessly, still leaning on his arms above her, his back straight, his hips surging like the most magnificent fucking machine ever made.

Before she could say *you're going to make me come again*, her eyes rolled up into her head, and her back arched. Her mouth fell open in a silent scream, and on top of that, Nick sucked her right breast into his mouth.

"Ahh," Maya yelped as she tightened her walls around his shaft, and the nipple in his mouth grew even harder. She shivered from head to toe as every muscle in her body rejoiced in orgasmic ecstasy.

"Oh, yeah, yeah, yeah..." Nick snatched his cock out of her as it erupted, and he let loose ropes of creamy white cum on her belly, hoping no one down the hall had heard his own loud cries of pleasure.

Maya, feeling her explosion subside, took him in her hand and stroked him as his body convulsed above her. Finally, when the gusher ended, Nick leaned down to kiss her tenderly, while her fingers lightly massaged him and she felt his full and bulging veins.

"Wow," was all he could say as he rolled over on his back.

"Damn, baby..." Maya breathed. "Damn, hmm, shit."

He gasped. "I can't breathe."

Maya laughed. "Damn, I was that good, huh?"

"I run three miles a day, and ten minutes with you took my breath away."

"Twice, baby," Maya said, her cheek against his chest, her right hand basking in pleasure while stroking his still rigid shaft. "You made me come twice in ten minutes. That, baby, is a record." She rubbed her thigh against his thigh. Her body still wanted more from him.

He laced his fingers behind his head. "So shall I call room service and get you a glass of wine?"

"I've got what I want." She held his cock and stared at it as it throbbed in her silky smooth grasp.

A sudden vision of her husband, waving at her and smiling, popped into her mind. *"I love you,"* he said in her vision, followed by the last time he'd left her hanging, which ended any notion she was happily married. She shook Albert out of her mind then relished Nick's giant shaft in her hand.

I don't want to think about anything else tonight, just this big black dick.

She slid down his abs, put her tongue on his ebony tip, licked off the last drip, then slipped her open mouth over the head and sucked it like there was no tomorrow.

Chapter Twenty-One

NICK HAD HIS ERECTION well in hand while thoughts of making love to Maya played in his head. After a long guilt-ridden shower, he lay on the bed naked, his muscular frame still damp. The envelope and its contents rested on a nightstand next to a smoldering cigar. The sweet smell of weed drifted in the air.

He couldn't get her off his mind. The three times they were together were incredible. She had looked at him with such lust...and love. She was so soft and so sweet, and Nick wondered what kind of man would ever let her go on vacation alone. What kind of man would ever let her go, period?

Then he remembered...he was just that kind of man. He had let her go.

His mind's eye showed her in the shower, in her blue dress, and it showed her on top of his cock, her face a mask of pleasure as she leaned down to kiss him. As memories of Maya tormented him, he stroked his long and rigid shaft. How could he forget holding her soft breasts in his hands from behind as she slammed her backside into him, driving him into her deeper and harder? The way her smile arched at the corners of her mouth, and the way her loving eyes would look into his. The way she said his name. She was a damn walking wet dream come true.

And he'd sold her out for a year's pay in a raggedy ass envelope.

Stroking himself harder, angrier, he groaned in pain and pleasure as the memory of her orgasms filled his mind. The vivid marijuana-induced visions of Maya flooded his very soul, and he felt himself plunge over the edge. He couldn't help but call out her name as his mind painted a portrait of her beautiful smiling face. His back arched and he wrapped both hands around his erupting cock to finish.

He tried to excuse his cowardice by telling himself he was in it for the money. And the money was good. Real good.

"Damn." He grunted as he looked at his cum-covered hands. "What the hell is wrong with me? I can't fucking believe I miss her like this."

Nick's mind took him back to the biggest regret he'd ever had:

There she was, wrapped in a white sheet and draped over some big man's shoulder. And there he was, more than capable of taking all three of the intruders out, lying naked on the bed and held back by his word and the speaking end of a handgun. But what did he do? What did he do after making love to such an intelligent, sensual, and wonderful woman?

Nothing. Not one damn thing.

And he hated himself for betraying her.

And no amount of money would satiate his remorse. Again his mind reminded him that Maya was everything he ever wanted in a woman: smart, loving, gracious, beautiful, and damn amazing in the sack.

He toweled himself off and chose to stay naked on the bed. After lighting the cigar, he breathed in the ganja. Once again his mind drifted to the beautiful American, and his cock rose to the occasion once more. His right hand stroked it up and down as he recalled how good she felt in his arms when they drifted off to sleep. And just before her eyes succumbed to the efforts of the sandman, she'd smiled and said his name softly. He marveled at how nice it sounded coming from her loving lips.

He closed his eyes while his hand glided up and down his hardness. The weed just made it easier for him to think of her and their passionate lovemaking. He saw her orgasm in his mind over and over and over again, felt her body shudder with pleasure beneath him, heard her cry out his name.

“Maya,” he whispered as he came a second time. Cum dripped onto his inner left thigh. Once again, it was her beautiful smiling face that brought him to bliss. Those eyes and those lips. “She is so fucking beautiful,” he said to his empty room...his empty life.

He shook his head in disgust. Not for the ejaculate mess he’d made again, but for karma. He knew he would pay for what he had done. Life had a way of getting people back when they did dirt. “Maya,” he cried as he held his dying dick in his hand. “Oh, baby, forgive me for what I have done. Please, baby.”

The big black man cried himself to sleep.

Chapter Twenty-Two

TWICE THEY HAD SEX before passing out on the comfy king-sized bed in the Presidential Suite. Maya found herself swimming in guilt-free dreams of her and Nick walking along the beach, holding hands and talking the talk of a love that was new. At one point, her husband slipped into her dream, his own cock, rigid and strong in her hands, and then he and Nick ravaged her body.

But that didn't last very long. Even in her dream, Albert had somewhere else to be.

So that left her and Nick alone in her subconscious mind. Then the dream got hot, too hot to remain a dream and she woke up. Her eyes opened, and she reached down to find Nick hard and ready. She smiled and climbed on.

Nick awoke to Maya riding him, her eyes closed as she swiveled her hips on top of him, living the dream. He fucked her thoroughly one more time.

Two hours later, Maya's body jarred her awake with a desperate need to pee and take a shower. She slowly and gently got out of the bed so as not to wake Nick, and slinked into the bathroom. She loved the resort's shower and was languishing beneath its warm waters when she heard the door open and felt Nick come up behind her.

"May I have the soap?" he asked, sliding it from her hands.

Maya said nothing as she leaned back against him, feeling him hang long against her butt cheek. *Guess I wore him out*. She smiled. Then he throbbed, and she felt his dick stiffen. *Then again...* Maya reached back to take it, but Nick had the audacity to turn away.

"I just want to get cleaned up real quick."

She twisted him around. "So while you do that, I'll do this." She knelt down and, after taking him into her mouth, all his protests ceased. Shower water cascaded down his abs. His cock swelled in her mouth, getting bigger and bigger, and the soft head banged against the back of her throat. His eyes were closed. She felt his legs quiver with pleasure...

There was a knock on the door.

"It's five o'clock in the morning," Nick grumped. "I better get that."

She made a popping sound as she released him with a final suck. "Whoever it is, kill him and get back in here."

"Hold that thought." He walked naked to the door. "Who is it?"

"Rebecca. Is Maya with you?"

Maya froze. She was busted. She'd never hear the end of it. Fighting panic, she shut off the shower, and wrapped only in a towel, sat on the bed and snatched the weed cigar from the nightstand.

"What do I tell her?" Nick whispered.

"Just let her in."

Nick opened the door and stood behind it.

Rebecca walked in talking. "Girl, where were you? You missed it. We had one very hot impromptu group fuck. Oh and your girl Portia is a closet freak..." Her voice trailed off as she saw Maya's exquisite body wrapped in the beige towel, and she was lighting a fat blunt. Rebecca grinned mischievously. "Girl...have you been fucking?"

The door closed behind her.

She turned around to see Nick naked and at half mast. Her mouth dropped open then she swallowed dryly. "I'll take that as a yes." Her eyes never left Nick's gorgeous cock, still semi erect as he swaggered into the bathroom.

"You okay, Rebecca?" Maya laughed. "Shit, I thought you were no stranger to big black cocks."

"I've seen black dicks before. It's you that's got me shocked."

Maya dragged on the cigar. "Whatever."

Rebecca took off her shoes, walked to the bed, and sat close to Maya. "After all that shit you talked about not fucking a big black dick, and here you are, fucking a big black dick."

"Guess I owe you a thank you." Maya giggled as she handed her the cigar.

Rebecca took it between her teeth. "I had my own fun earlier tonight."

"I bet." Maya pretended she didn't know, but the memory of what she saw in the suite made her pussy clench.

Rebecca held her smoke in...then exhaled as she spoke. "Fucked the college boys." She coughed a little. "Both at the same time...twice."

"Damn, Miss Freak A Leek. What about Portia and Cole?"

Rebecca's smile grew in lustful wickedness. "Oh, I fucked them too."

"Get the fuck out of here." Maya snatched back the cigar.

"No, girl, for real. Of course, Portia was disappointed that you weren't there. I think she likes you...and she was reluctant to fuck anyone but Cole, but once we got her cute little ass high and me and those boys started our show, Cole went down on her, and she got with the program." Rebecca laughed. "She came watching us then she came I don't know how many times as the college boys took turns fucking her."

"I take it you entertained Cole."

Rebecca nodded. "You should have heard him scream the Lord's name."

"How did Portia handle that?"

"Honestly, I don't know. I do believe she had a dick

in her mouth and another one in her pussy." Rebecca shrugged. "After I fucked Cole blind, I took a shower and went looking for you."

Maya looked at her through the haze of smoke. "How did you know to find me here? Shit, I could have been anywhere let alone fucking in the Presidential Suite."

Rebecca looked at her stone-faced, and Maya saw a flash of panic in her eyes, but it disappeared quickly. "Really? You look like you've had the fuck of a lifetime, and you're worried about how I found you? How was the dick? Details, details, details."

Maya grinned, high and not caring about her question anymore. "The dick, the dick is good." She nodded. "Very, very good."

"How many times did you fuck him?"

"Twice." She giggled. "Maybe three times. I lost count. All I know is we fucked and it was good, girl. Damn good."

They shared a high-five then Rebecca leaned in close, allowing her perfume to drift pleasantly to Maya's nose. "So, uh, you gonna share that dingaling, or what?"

Maya frowned. "You wish."

The door opened and Nick came out, his cock hard and sticking up like the masthead of a mighty ship.

Rebecca's hand brushed against Maya's pussy, and she trembled.

"Whoa..."

"Come on." Rebecca kissed Maya's full lips. "What do you say, girl?" She kissed her again, this time a little longer. "Let me get a taste of that cock."

Maya took one last drag of weed, and then gave a long look at Nick's hard-on. *He's not my man. My man is at home, far away from Rebecca's freaky ass.* Maya smiled then shrugged as Nick's footfalls ended at the side of the bed closest to her. "Okay. You want to play?" This time she kissed Rebecca. The blonde groaned as Maya leaned back and let the towel fall from around her. "But just a taste."

Rebecca grinned and turned to Nick. "Oh, I'm going to enjoy this." She seductively crawled to Nick's waiting cock.

He looked at Maya who was watching her girlfriend with some amusement, the cigar once again pressed between her pouty lips. Their eyes met, and she nodded, then reached out and rubbed Rebecca's back as she took Nick's hard-on into her hands.

Maya was surprised how much she enjoyed watching Nick grow even larger as Rebecca stroked him. She was even more enamored with the fact he sought permission from her first.

Rebecca smiled at the thickness she lovingly cradled. "Oh, my," was all she said before engulfing half his length into her mouth.

Nick's head fell back as she began to work him, grunting each time she licked the sweet spot under his head.

Maya put out the cigar, its effects soothing her body as she slid Rebecca's dress off and dropped it on the floor. Then Maya made her own way to Nick, got up on her knees so she could kiss his lips.

Their passion caused him to throb in Rebecca's mouth, soliciting her own groan of approval.

Maya leaned down and kissed Rebecca's cheek as she sucked Nick's cock.

Nick could only watch in awe as the two women then locked lips for a short time before their gazes shifted to him. Without a word, they each took one side of his shaft, their tender lips making him groan, spellbound as they slid their mouths up and down and over him, taking turns sucking on his head and stroking his shaft. Gently, he moved to lie on the bed, where the women continued their oral assault on him, making him rigid beyond description.

Maya sat on him first, her back facing him, as she slid down slowly, and then cried out as he effortlessly flowed into her.

Rebecca kissed Maya's lips before taking a sensual journey down her tender neck, kissing soft skin all the way to her overly sensitive breasts, then choosing to take her right nipple into her mouth.

Full of lust and abandon, Maya placed a soft hand between Rebecca's drenched thighs, which made her groan around the brown breast in her mouth as her tongue danced around the nipple.

Nick closed his eyes and basked in the pleasures of their affections.

Maya's hand was busy on the Rebecca's clitoris, which soon trembled with delight. She cried out in passion as she exploded all over Maya's hand. Her body stiffened, her legs shuddered, and her teeth clamped down on Maya's wanton nipple.

"God that feels good," she breathed.

Rebecca relaxed, leaned back to catch her breath, and watched Nick and Maya continued their lovemaking. Maya moaned with his every thrust. She began to bounce up and down on him, matching his rhythm with her own.

Nick's strong hands found her breasts and clutched them as he played with the nipples, which made Maya's body respond with lustful vigor.

Rebecca watched Nick look down to see his dick going in and out of her pussy, each time seeing more and more of her syrupy essence leave a trail of her desire on the entire length of his shaft.

"Oh yes," was all Maya said as she slammed back on him while her body shivered with pleasure. Her head fell forward, and she giggled yet never slowed her frantic fucking pace.

Rebecca's hand wandered back to Maya's body, found her pearl, and as she played with the engorged nub, she felt her own burgeoning climax begin a slow boil in her loins.

Morning sunshine filled the room.

Maya didn't care about the after effects of this lesbian play on her relationship with Rebecca, let alone her absentee husband. All she cared about was the pleasure coursing through her body.

She felt Rebecca's fingers against her clit, and she savored Nick's deep thrusts inside her. "Nicholas," she moaned as she felt her explosion reach a roaring crescendo.

Rebecca's lips were all over Maya's right breast while she trembled and shook as ecstasy overwhelmed her body. Her head fell back, and her eyes rolled up, and sheer joy spread through her tummy. She bit her lower lip as the explosion rippled through her, an ebb and sway of pleasure like waves against the shore, repeatedly, relentlessly, and absolutely unbelievable.

Nick sensed her orgasmic bliss and increased his pumping, his hands now around her waist, guiding her up and down his stone-hard shaft. Her rapture caused him to sit up and bury his face into her neck just as his cream burst free inside her. His body stiffened and trembled, and he kissed her neck, sending further shockwaves through her body. Once his tremors settled, he fell back to the sheets and licked his lips. "Now that..." he mumbled, "...was a hell of a way to start the day."

Maya giggled as she rose up on her feet and felt him slide out of her.

Rebecca was quick to run her fingers through Maya's folds then lick off the sweet juices. Maya's pussy responded with a flourish of spasms. She sat on the bed by Nick's knees and watched Rebecca lick his semi-rigid cock and squeeze out every last drop of his cum. Then she leaned back against the headboard. "That was fucking great." Her breasts heaved with each breath.

Maya snuggled under Nick's left arm. "Just know you

won't always be a third party, girl."

"Don't be so stingy." Rebecca crawled under Nick's right arm.

"No need to fight over me, ladies," he said, his breathing still heavy.

"Good." Maya sighed. "Cause that would really fuck up this vacation for me."

They fell silent, staying as they were for some time, choosing to remain in each other's arms.

"I wish..." Maya began.

"You wish what?" Rebecca and Nicholas said in unison.

"Oh, it's nothing. It can't come true anyway. I have my life, and Nick, you have yours."

"Please don't tell me you still want to pretend you are happily married," Nick said with some exasperation. "We have something, and we should see where it goes."

"Now, baby, you know we can't—"

"Maya, please. If you were happily married, you wouldn't have fucked me...especially like you did."

Rebecca got up, feeling the mood in the room change instantly. "Where's my dress?"

Maya twisted out from under Nick's arm. "This sex wasn't a sign of my unhappiness."

"It wasn't?" Nick scoffed. "Then what was it?"

"It was lust. Pure and simple. I wanted to fuck a black dick, and you wanted to fuck me. So we fucked. That's all."

"A fuck?" He grabbed his limp cock and waggled it at her. "I was just a fuck?" He sat up. "Okay. If that was all we did, then why were you just wishing that we could be more than a couple of fuckers?"

"It was just a whim. We both know it can't be."

"No. It can be. You just choose for it not to be."

"I can't."

"Why? Because you are married...or because you are

in love? You can't be in love with him if you fucked me."

Maya slapped the sheets. "What kind of stupid ass rule did you just make up?"

"I've been fucked before. I know what a fuck is, and what we did was not just a fuck. It was love. You know it, and I know it."

"And just because we know it..." Maya jumped off the bed. "...doesn't mean we have to live it. We can't live it. And you're right, I won't live it."

"Because you won't leave your husband?"

"I don't even know you, not really."

Nicholas scowled at her, his anger and pain evident on his face. "Then you ain't nothing but another rich-bitch whore like all the rest."

"Why..?" Maya stormed around the room naked. "Why...after a great night of sex, do you choose to be an ass?" She found the towel on the floor and draped it across her shoulders.

Rebecca shrugged into her dress. "I'm sure he didn't mean it." She shot Nick a pleading look.

"Maya." He watched her angrily gather her dress and her shoes. "Come on, I'm sorry." He'd said it halfheartedly.

"That was some weak apology." Maya forced him to stare at her face, despite the radiance of her naked body. "You truly fucked up a great vacation."

Then there was a knock at the door.

Rebecca was the first to reach the door, opening it as Maya walked up the short staircase. Nick closed his eyes when he saw three men burst in...as planned. They grabbed Maya and forced her to the floor. The first man moved swiftly, jabbing a needle into her neck, and the second man pulled a sheet off the bed while the third man held a nickel-plated gun on Nick. Rebecca helped the first man put the dress on Maya, maneuvering her body as if she were a limp rag doll. In under a minute, she was hoisted on the shoulders of the second man, her body wrapped in the cum-stained white sheet. Together, they backed out of the room. The gun aimed at Nick never wavered during their retreat.

The door closed behind them, and just like the solider he once was, Nick did as ordered and waited five minutes before he called the front desk.

You truly fucked up a great vacation...

He didn't even say goodbye, let alone do the right thing and save her. And all he had left were her last words to him, which cut him deep in so many ways.

You truly fucked up...

Rebecca sauntered to Nick's waiting cock. "You'll be paid well for what you did, Nick, but this fucking is for free."

Chapter Twenty-Three

CLIVE BATTERSBY LOVED watching his wife's delicious brown backside slam against his hips as she matched her movements with his every thrust. His hands caressed her silky soft skin, heightening his own pleasure while sprouting chill bumps all over her body, which made her shiver with delight.

Despite ten years of marriage, Clive still marveled at her beauty, intellect, and sexual vigor, not to mention her dedication to cooking and her wonderful parenting skills. She was, after all, the wife of the Chief of Police. It was fitting she was extraordinary, because after all, so was he.

The sun shined through the sheer curtains of their bedroom, allowing him to see her in all her beauty. Through the open doors to the balcony, he heard a car pull up in the drive. He knew it was police business. It had a way of interrupting him at the most inopportune moments possible. Like right now. He was just about to come.

What kind of shit is sitting on my doorstep this time?

"Baby," she groaned, bringing his mind back to their mutual bliss. The youngest Chief of Police in the island's history let out a low growl as his wife bent lower on the bed, arching her spine, which allowed him greater access to her admirable bubble-shaped butt. He slowed his pace, and she cried out as he looked down to watch the fruits of his labor glaze his shaft as her ass trembled in orgasm. He watched a drop of her cum start a slow slide down her inner thigh, ending in a small milky pool on the blue sheets.

"Oh baby, you got me good," she moaned, still under the mercy of her extreme orgasm.

The house phone rang.

And then his cell phone rang.

And then her damn cell rang too.

"Fuck." He pulled out. "I gotta get that."

"No, no, no." Annora looked back at him. "Don't stop fucking me. You haven't come yet."

Clive was sure anyone within earshot just heard her amorous plea. She might have some explaining to do with the kids, but her big brown eyes didn't seem to care about anything but continuing her euphoria. "Clive, baby, put it back in."

The phones continued to ring in unison as he stared at her.

"Please, baby." She twisted around to kiss him. "Please make me come again," she breathed, her voice overflowing with lust as she ground her ass cheek against his rock hard dick.

He leaned over and kissed her neck then placed his tip against her opening.

Annora groaned.

He deliberately slipped in an inch at a time. His rod throbbed as he slowly filled her pussy then slid all the way back out, and then shoved it back in.

She moaned with pleasure as a sudden flood of her cream bathed his shaft. "That's it, baby. That's the spot."

The phones fell silent, leaving them to slam against one another in peace and with as much vigor as if it were their first time. "Oh yes," she cried. "Oh yes, oh..." Her mouth fell open as she felt her body clench then relax. Limbs trembling, she closed her eyes as he kept up his pace, and soon his ramming cock was too much for her. She let out a small giggle and arched her back.

Clive reached around her and took her chocolate tipped breasts into his hands and rubbed them gently as she slammed her full backside against him. She felt the impending explosion, just at the edge of oblivion, beckon her to fall. "Clive," she whispered as he thrust his cock in her two more times, hard enough that she shook in his arms. She reached between her spread legs and grabbed a handful of his balls as her cum drowned his shaft.

He felt his own climax strengthen...*almost there—*

But a hard knock on their bedroom door threatened to destroy the mood. "Go away," Clive shouted.

"It can't wait, Chief."

More knocking.

"Oh, for God's sake." Annora pulled her pussy off his cock in mid stroke and snatched her robe off a nearby chair on her way to the door.

His cock stuck straight out like a cannon on a row boat, locked and loaded but nowhere to shoot. "Fuck."

"Get yer clothes on, Chief." She tied her robe closed while he escaped to the walk-in closet.

Hurriedly, he pulled his underwear over his gradually shrinking erection and climbed into his slacks. Zipped and belted, he said, "Go ahead, Annora. Let him in."

Annora opened the door. "Morning, patrolman."

Patrolman Leon Graham gave his boss's wife a salute while staring at her abundant cleavage nestled in the fluffy white robe. "A woman has been kidnapped from the resort."

"A tourist?" Annora was aware of his prying eyes and didn't bother to hide her bosom.

"Yes, ma'am. She is the pretty wife of an American billionaire, here on vacation. Alone."

Clive shrugged into his uniform shirt. "Come again?"

Annora looked at him, a smile suddenly lighting her face. "My love, you don't have time to come again."

"Gotta come once to come again," he mumbled.

"Seems you've got a pretty wife to find."

"I already found her." He returned her smile.

"Oh, baby," she purred, walking toward him with arms outstretched. "That was so sweet." She gathered him into an amorous embrace. "But I meant the vacationing wife."

Graham watched their banter, rolled his eyes, but enthusiastically, yet subtly, enjoyed the view of her robe-covered backside.

***

Clive walked down the lavish, yet familiar, hallways of the resort toward Maya Valdis' suite. For some reason, whenever he came here, he felt a need to dress exceptionally, and as he straightened his purple paisley tie and smoothed out his black jacket, he still felt uncomfortable in such a ritzy environment.

He rounded a corner and saw George, the concierge, who immediately looked away when he met the Chief's eyes. Clive smiled, knowing George like he did. "Morning." He walked over to the smaller man. "How are you, Georgie. Did you see anything last night?"

George looked down at Clive's fingers as they drummed atop a fifty-dollar bill on the counter. "I would love to tell you, Chief..." He began dragging the money toward him, slyly, while looking away. "But I am on duty."

Clive smiled, playing the game. "We'll talk later, eh?"

George's fearful eyes darted around the lobby as he pocketed the bill.

Is he afraid of me or someone else?

The door to the suite was open, and Clive saw a young couple on the love seat and two young males sitting on the couch. A lone maid stood by the patio doors, wringing her hands. Her nervousness was just as evident as George's.

Lt. Adrian O'Hare sashayed up to him. The only white woman on his team was professionally dressed as always. Today she wore a tan blazer over a pale yellow blouse and black slacks. She always wore slacks, mainly black or grey. Regardless, the pants did nothing to hide her tight and well-rounded derriere. The strawberry-blond officer was confident and capable, and she had been a sexual fantasy of his for some time. Today was no different. She had her cell phone in hand. "Good day, Chief. Care to read my notes?"

Clive glanced around to make sure no one was watching then pulled his reading glasses from his top pocket.

Adrian softly giggled as he took her phone. "I still think the bifocals make you look distinguished," she said with a whimsical smile.

He pretended to read her notes. "The maid's name..."

"Jackie. The college boys are Larry and Trevor, and the two on the love seat are newlyweds, Cole and Portia." Adrian stepped closer to him, giving him a whiff of her enchanting perfume.

He twitched below the belt and quickly thought about his wife. She should have finished him off before answering the door. Now he had blue balls the size of a prized bull's gonads.

"One of these folks was the last person to see the victim, a Mrs. Maya Valdis." Adrian was going through her own issues with titillation due to her proximity to her boss. "I called the husband but got his assistant. She claims the husband is overwrought with grief."

"Impressive." Clive looked at her, immediately suspicious of the husband. "Is he on his way here to help in the search?"

"He's too upset to travel."

"Then I would think he'd use his money to post a reward or hire a private eye." Clive imagined Adrian and Annora naked on their knees before him. "Did he call the consulate? Did we get a call from the US State Department?"

Adrian shrugged. "I can call the office to find out."

"If Annora went missing I would be here." Clive

blinked. "To be quite honest, there is no way I would allow her to go on a vacation without me. But if I did, and she went missing, I'd do everything in my power to find her. Who is this rich guy?"

"Albert Valdis." Adrian gently took the phone from him and scrolled through her notes. "According to Google, he made his money on Wall Street and is worth..." she paused to check the numbers, "...billions, more than my feeble mind can fathom."

"We got a picture of her?"

Adrian pursed her lips as she punched in Maya's name. "Here she is...oh my." She handed the phone to Clive.

He shook his head. "What man in his right mind would let a woman this beautiful come to a tropical paradise alone? What the fuck is wrong with him?"

"Maybe he had more important things to do." She shrugged.

"Or maybe he found some new pussy to fuck. And maybe, just maybe, he knew what was going to happen to his wife. Did you check the security cameras?"

"I've requested the tapes."

"See? There is nothing feeble about your mind."

"Why, Clive, I always thought you liked me for my ass."

"See if we can learn Valdis' whereabouts since his wife got here, and find out who owns any side pussy he might be donkin'. And of course I like you for your ass." Clive walked down the short steps to the living room while smiling at the cluster of folks and the maid. He put away his reading glasses. "Good day, ladies and gentlemen. I am Chief of Police Clive Battersby..." As he walked around the love seat, he spotted discarded panties on the floor. "What's this?" He took a pen from his pocket and lifted them for all to see. "Anyone recognize these?" He was looking at the elfin bride with the raven-black hair.

Her new husband spoke up. “They’re Maya’s—”

His bride punched his arm. “You looked?”

“You saw the short dress she was wearing.”

“Doesn’t mean you have to look.”

“I couldn’t help it.”

She folded her arms and scowled at him.

Clive chuckled. The new husband wouldn’t make that mistake again. *If you look, keep your mouth shut.* He handed the pen and panties to Adrian. “Bag ‘em.” Then he turned back to the group. “I know this is not what you expected on your trip to our island paradise, but we need your help to find Maya as quickly as possible. So we just want to ask you each a few questions about last night. So ladies first? How about you, Jackie?”

The maid looked surprised.

“This way, please.” Clive led Jackie to the patio.

He pulled out a chair for her then glanced at the sky. A storm brewed several miles away from the island. Lightning bolts flashed. “What a view, what a view.” Clive breathed in admiration of nature’s skill as it painted a violent yet captivating mural against the horizon. “This is absolute paradise. No other way to say it. A paradise you and I must keep safe, Jackie.” He sat across the small table from her.

“M-me?” Jackie stuttered.

Adrian sat next to her.

“Yes, Jackie darling. You, me, my partner. All of us. We have a responsibility to make sure this paradise stays that way, and that tourists who come here are happy. And we want them to feel safe. Safe enough to have fun. Safe enough to spend their money. And most especially safe enough to come back and spend even more money. You following me, Jackie dear?”

The nervous maid nodded.

“Good, then you won’t have any problem at all telling me what you saw or heard and know?”

"The-the...lady..."

Clive leaned forward. "Why are you so nervous?"

"I-I..."

"She's got good reason to be nervous, Chief," the resort's general manager, Steven Dillard, said as he stepped through the patio doorway. The pompous bastard wore an immaculate grey suit and a red tie over a crisply pressed white shirt. "Company policy demands employees to protect our guests' confidentiality."

"We're having a private conversation here, my friend." Clive stood with his hand outstretched and a fake smile painted on his face.

"I hope interrogating our staff and guests is not a priority, Chief." Dillard's tone was authoritative and he ignored the offered handshake. "Our guests come here to relax, and our staff needs to make sure those guests are taken care of properly in the midst of this annoying crisis. So any questions you have for her you can ask me."

Clive remained standing, face to face with Dillard. "So you were here last night?"

Dillard frowned. "Of course not."

"Then..." The Chief leaned to the manager's left ear. "...shut the fuck up, and let me find this young woman. The longer she's missing, the more likely some tragedy befalls her, and your lovely resort and your arrogant ass are held accountable for whatever happened. Allow me to do my job so we can both look good and you can avoid a severe beating." He stood straight again. "Do we have an understanding?"

Dillard's face turned bright red as he geared up to comment, but Jackie spoke first. "I saw her around ten or so last night. She was coming out of her room."

"Was anyone with her?" Clive ignored Dillard's cold stare.

"Y-yes."

"Who?"

The maid didn't answer. Her hands trembled as she looked at Dillard.

"Well?"

"I saw her with Nicholas."

Dillard stared at her. "Are you sure?"

She nodded.

"Who's Nicholas?" Clive asked.

"Our head of security." Dillard's eyes never left Jackie, who now stared at the floor.

Clive noticed the exchange and glanced at Adrian, who was sliding her thumbs around on her phone, taking notes.

"Jackie, did you see where they went?"

"The Presidential Suite. Nick uses that room a lot."

"For what?"

She still held her head down, but even her tone was blushing. "Well, see, it's rarely rented out, and Nick has a master card key, and he would use the suite to...to, uh, entertain his lady friends."

Adrian grinned, jotted down more notes, while Clive got the picture.

Dillard stared a hole through Jackie, who wisely kept her head down.

"So...then what?"

"That be it. I saw them go into the room. He was carrying her like they just got married or something."

"Some honeymoon." Adrian whistled. "Maybe the wife had second thoughts and Nicholas got rid of her."

"Or maybe her husband knew about their affair and had his own solution."

"Well, Chief, there it is," Dillard crowed. "You have your man, you have motive. Case closed. Now you may leave my staff and guests alone."

"How is it you're so sure about that, Dillard?"

"Mr. Dillard," he snapped.

Clive sighed, already tired of the man's self-righteous

act. “Let’s have a clear understanding...this case is closed when I say it is.”

“Have you forgotten your place?” Dillard asked indignantly.

“Mr. Dillard,” Adrian jumped in. “I must advise you that if you continue to be a nuisance, I’ll have to take you in.”

“For what?”

“Obstruction of justice and interfering in a police investigation.”

Dillard snapped his head around and looked down his nose at Clive. “You should train your girl to know when men are speaking she is to keep her mouth closed.”

Adrian instinctively reached for her gun, pausing inches from the holster before she caught herself. “Man, you just don’t know, do you?”

“Dillard,” Clive said. “If I were you I would leave.”

He opened his mouth to protest, but Clive got in his face, nose to nose, his size and bulk enough to intimidate the smaller, slighter man. “Adrian, be a good *girl* and escort Mr. Dillard out before a painful accident befalls him.”

Adrian bounced up. “My pleasure.”

Dillard took one look at her then backed away. “I will be sure to take this matter up with your superior.”

“My superior is God, and if you can talk to him, pray for your own ass if anything happens to this missing woman. Oh, and Jackie better keep her job for a long time to come.”

Dillard backed off the patio and into the suite.

Adrian watched him, amused. She smiled at the Chief. “I should have shot him, Chief.”

He gestured a goodbye wave to Jackie. “Go now.”

She flew out of the chair like a frightened dove.

“And send out the newlywed bride...uh—?”

“Portia St. Clair,” Adrian read from her phone.

"Thanks...oh, tell resort security checking the tapes to pay close attention to—"

"The third floor and Presidential Suite."

Clive grinned. "You were born to investigate."

"Maybe." Adrian's grin gained a mischievous gleam. "But that is most certainly not what I do best." She sashayed away.

Clive enjoyed the view of her departure and when she stepped into the suite, his eyes locked on Portia's green-eyed gaze. She turned around to her husband and said something then gave him a quick kiss before getting up. The husband looked at Clive then nodded, a gesture Clive returned as the dainty beauty walked out to the patio.

The petite woman sat in Jackie's chair, her pretty feet sheathed in a pair of tan and turquoise sandals. Clive had to force himself not to stare at her toned legs. What he wouldn't give to start kissing her ankles and work his way up... He took a deep breath, inhaling her pleasant perfume. "Now that is an enchanting fragrance."

"Thank you." She stared at him. "It's called *Unique*."

There was something in her crystal green eyes, accentuated by the mascara she wore, that simply mesmerized him. And her exquisite turquoise dress would, on occasion, thanks to the ocean breeze, provide him with an eyeful of her tantalizing thighs. He simply couldn't wait to get home and finish fucking Annora. "It's very nice—"

"I'm sure you didn't ask me out here to talk about my perfume."

"Don't be so sure about that." Clive tried not to stare at her legs or her beckoning cleavage. "You didn't have that perfume on earlier...when I walked in."

"You're quite observant, Chief. I sprayed some on to calm my husband. When he's cool, I'm cool."

"I understand." Clive had said it, his voice deeper than before, but he didn't mean it. *Calm? That perfume does a lot of things to a man, but* calm *isn't one of them.*

He cleared his throat, aware he was getting off point. A sexy woman could do that to a man, perfume or not. “Tell me how you got to know Mrs. Valdis.”

“Our room is just down the hall from hers...and Rebecca’s.”

“Rebecca?”

“Her assistant’s name is Rebecca, but Maya insisted that, on this trip, Rebecca was her friend.”

“Where is this Rebecca now?”

“I haven’t seen her this morning.”

He made a mental note to ask Adrian to find Rebecca. “So you all became friends?”

“We did.” Her cheeks colored. “In fact, we got very friendly. I hope this doesn’t make you uncomfortable.”

Clive shrugged. “This is paradise. Lots of friendly things happen to friendly folks here. Go on.”

Portia smiled. “They were both so cool, and Cole had a crush on Rebecca, while I—”

“Had a thing for Maya?” Clive guessed.

She smiled. “But we never did anything.”

“Shy?”

“You’re very observant.”

“I’m the Chief of Police. I get paid to be observant.”

“So...” She sat forward in her chair. “You’re the boss?”

“Let’s just say I am one of them on this island.”

She gazed at him slyly. “I wonder...does the Chief, *chief*?”

He grinned, familiar with the American slang for smoking ganja. “When I am not at work, yes.”

“How delightful.” She clapped her hands. “I would love to chief with you and your wife.”

“And your husband...is he okay with that?”

“Aw...he’s shared me before.”

“Now, that is not a bad idea, but first, can you tell me what happened last night?”

Portia smiled. “Sex, sex and more sex. Cole and I have decided to make our honeymoon one filled with memories we will forever talk about. Living out our fantasies is so much fun. Do you and your wife fulfill each other’s fantasies?”

“As long as I don’t have to put on a pair of women’s panties, I’m all for it.” He laughed. “But please continue about last night. Was Maya as friendly as the rest of you?”

Portia giggled and glanced down at the growing bulge between his legs. She licked her lips. “About last night...all I know is, Maya stayed behind at the restaurant while the rest of us came back here and frolicked freely.”

Clive smiled. “Frolicked? I like that. But why was her panties behind the love seat?”

She shrugged. “I don’t know.”

“Was Rebecca with you all the whole time?”

“Come to think of it, when I woke up this morning, she wasn’t in the room.”

Clive nodded. “Anyone else missing?”

“No, just her.”

“Funny, she wasn’t reported missing.” Clive wondered if she had something to do with the kidnapping.

“Did Maya say why her husband didn’t come along?”

Portia shook her head. “All Maya said was this wasn’t the first time he’d stood her up. I don’t know much else about their marriage. Maya didn’t talk about it. Rebecca was insistent that Maya fuck someone new while she was here, which seemed weird to me.” Portia leaned over, giving Clive a bird’s eye view of her breasts. “I would never encourage my friend to cheat on her husband.”

Clive heard her, but his mind drifted to a bedroom where Portia and Annora were frolicking with him.

“Are you listening to me, or just staring at my tits?” She discreetly brushed her hand against his right knee.

Damn. Clive couldn’t help but stare into her eyes as she winked at him. “Now I—”

"And don't say you weren't looking at my tits."

Just as Clive laughed a shot rang out and stopped him, followed by a scream. Instinctively, he put himself between Portia and the door, his gun already in his hand. "Everybody down." He knocked the patio table over and shoved Portia behind it. "Stay here until I say it's safe. Understand?"

She trembled with fear.

He crouched down, his gun cocked as he crabbed into the room.

Two more shots followed by another scream.

He saw the males sprawled on the floor. "Anybody hit?"

"No," Cole said.

Clive shouted to Larry. "Call the front desk. Tell them we have a shooter on the third floor."

The kid nodded and crawled to the house phone. His shaking hand had a hard time grasping the receiver.

Clive shuffled duck-like on his haunches, easing his way to the door just as a bullet whizzed by his head. He dove to the floor, and Cole gasped. Clive turned to face the males on the floor. His eyes met Cole's. Blood slowly pooled around his body.

"Cole."

He could only stare as Cole's eyes lost their gleam when life passed from his body. "God, damnit." He checked to see Portia's shadow still ducked behind the table. "Fuck."

The skinny black college kid crawled to Cole. "Oh shit, man. Oh shit."

"Yes," the blonde kid shouted into the phone. "And we need medical help up here right away."

Clive shook thoughts of Portia and Cole out of his mind as he crept into the hallway. Adrian had ducked behind an ornate column to reload her gun. She looked at him. "Two," she mouthed carefully. Another shot rang out, forcing Clive to duck. Adrian returned fire then jumped back behind the column.

"This is the Chief of Police," Clive yelled. "Odds are I know you or someone in your family. Put down your weapons so we can all go home. Don't make me tell someone you love that you are dead."

A series of shots rang out in reply.

"This is not good for business," Clive shouted. "Now how many folks do you think are going to keep coming here when fools like you shoot up the place?"

Another shot rang out, and Clive heard a click. He rose up and let off a volley of bullets. Adrian followed his lead. They heard the ding of the elevator and a man cry out. "Okay, mon, don't shoot. Don't shoot. I am out of bullets."

Clive heard a stairwell door open. Backup had arrived to help secure the scene.

Clive got up with Adrian right behind him.

"Chief. Chief." Jackie screamed.

They both ran to the concierge's desk. Jackie was on the floor behind the counter, cradling George's head in her lap. "He has something to tell ya, Chief."

Clive knelt down. The short man seemed even smaller as blood flowed freely from two wounds in his stomach. "What do you want to tell me, George?"

"I...took money from...Bossman..." He gasped. "...paid me to tell him where she was...and what she was doing...her friend knows..." His voice grew faint. "Rebecca..." He stared out at nothing and breathed his last breath.

"George." Clive jostled the man he had known since childhood. "Aww, damn, damn, damn." He stood up and hung his head. "Journey in peace, my friend."

Adrian ran up to him. "We killed one." She gestured to the paramedics who were covering the culprit with a sheet. "And the other is being cuffed as we speak."

"Fuck." Clive holstered his gun.

"I hate to say this," Adrian went on. "Third floor cameras were turned off last night."

"Nicholas works security. I wonder if he had access..." Clive shuddered. "Take the prisoner to our special spot." Clive looked down at George's body. "Don't be gentle when you question him about last night."

"Got it, Chief." She rushed away.

Clive hurried back to the room. Officers and paramedics were kneeling next to Cole. The two college boys were weeping over the body. Clive walked out to the patio where Portia was still crouched behind the upset table as instructed, completely unaware that she was now alone on her honeymoon.

"Portia." Clive really didn't know how to say what he had to say.

Her head popped up, revealing emerald eyes filled with terror. "Is it safe now, Chief?"

Sadly, Clive looked away from her and at the paramedics as they draped a sheet over her husband's body. "It is, but I'm afraid your honeymoon..." his voice fell, and he held out a hand. "I need to tell you something."

She looked up at him, and his face told her all she needed to know. She placed her right hand over her heart, between her full breasts, and her eyes filled with tears. "Not my Cole." She bowed her head, still kneeled on the floor. "No," she whimpered. "No." She screamed and crumpled over.

Clive looked out at the horizon, his own pain for the woman gnawing at his heart. George had mentioned Bossman, and as Clive thought about the notorious gangster, the dark clouds seemed closer, and he knew another kind of storm was already upon him.

And who the fuck is Rebecca?

Chapter Twenty-Four

MAYA RUBBED HER EYES. The world around her slowly came into focus. *I'm in a different room.* She looked around the immaculate white walls surrounding her. The carpet was a light brown and deep. An open door revealed a bathroom. The only other door was closed and probably locked. A crystal chandelier hung from the high ceiling over the bed. She sat up enough to brace herself on her elbows and felt silken material on her soft brown skin.

Who the hell dressed me?

She bolted upright in the bed, swept her gaze left to right and back, and quickly realized she was alone. But was she safe? Where was Nick? Where was Albert?

What the hell happened?

She rubbed her arms then looked down at the black lacy kimono robe she wore. Where did that come from? Fighting panic, she opened the robe to see lacy panties that matched the robe's color and ornate lattice pattern.

Her feet and toes felt soft and clean, and her fingernails and toenails were a different hue than she had painted them before. She moved her jaw and felt some soreness then remembered Rebecca ramming a needle into her thigh. The bruise was further proof of her betrayal, along with the burn spots on her ribs from the cattle prod. "What the fuck? First they kidnap me, beat me, drug me, fuck me...and now they pamper me?" She ran both hands through her silky, fragrant hair. "They even washed my hair?"

Heart racing, she scrambled out of bed and stood, but a wave of dizziness forced her back onto the bed. "Uh, oh, slow down, Maya, slow down." She shook her head, trying to clear the cobwebs. It wasn't too long after the dizziness subsided that her stomach growled with hunger. Made sense. How could they feed her while she was unconscious?

This time, she took her time getting upright, and once she was reasonably sure she had her feet under her, she slowly walked to the bathroom. She peered at herself in the mirror, noticing whoever pampered her did not apply makeup. The bruise under her eye needed makeup badly. In spite of this, she smiled, feeling relieved to be alive when she knew she shouldn't be. Reaching out to the mirror, she rubbed the face she saw as her mind whispered a lie. "I'll find a way out of here."

***

"Where the fuck are you, Albert?" Rebecca shouted into the phone. She was walking along the perimeter wall of Bossman's mansion and didn't care if anyone heard her shouting. "You better fucking answer me." She jabbed her phone to hang up and then went back to texting him the same question for the tenth time.

Where are you?

The phone rang, startling her. Albert's handsome face appeared in the window. *You fucker.* She managed a smile then answered the phone. "I was just about to text you again."

"Now that would be stupid, considering the multiple times you texted did not speed up my response."

"Where the fuck are you? You got me sneaking around here calling you. Bossman says since I'm here, I'm supposed to be entertaining his horny-ass clients, as usual, but I'm not supposed to be here and I damn sure am not supposed to be fucking for Bossman anymore because you're supposed to be here to buy my freedom from this fucking place."

"Now, Rebecca...why in the world would I do that?"

Rebecca looked at the phone, her entire being frozen in astonishment. "W-what are you saying?" was all her broken voice could whisper.

"See, my dear sweet wife is missing. *Kidnapped.* That means she can still be found. Now do we want her found, Rebecca?"

"No."

"No we don't. That would mean life as we know it will continue as is. More sneaking around and more lies behind the bitch's back. Is that what we want, Rebecca?"

"No."

"Once again, the correct answer. So how do we deal with a missing wife?"

Rebecca looked at the ocean waves. "You can't be serious."

"I might be more inclined to fulfill my end of our deal if my dear sweet wife is found dead. Got it?"

"No. I'm not going to do that. I'm not killing someone who was good to me. Yeah maybe she's a spoiled bitch. And sure, she's out of touch, but I'm not fucking killing her. This place...Bossman's whore house, this place is hell on earth. This is what she deserves. Besides, Bossman wants her pussy on the menu. Thinks he can get a million out of her before she's all used up. And I ain't fucking with Bossman. So if you want her dead, do the shit yourself."

"In other words you want to stay there with Maya and keep working for Bossman."

"Fuck no."

"Then you know what you have to do. The plane is already fueled and ready to fly. Just be sure to text me when you've made the right choice."

Rebecca twisted the hem of her dress. "I can't. He'll kill me for killing his new top-tier girl."

"Then be wise about what you do and how you do it.

Now if there is nothing new to talk about, I have a funeral to arrange." He hung up.

Rebecca looked at the phone. The reality of her situation bitch-slapped her in the chest. Not only was Valdis acting as if she was just another whore, he was demanding that she kill his wife, the woman who would allow her to be free of Bossman. Without Maya alive and fucking, she'd never get out of this hellhole.

She closed her eyes, her heart heavy with the weight of her predicament. Killing Maya was an option Rebecca did not want to face. Tears rolled down her cheeks as she opened her eyes and scrolled to her text messages. She took a long and deep breath before typing a two-letter text to Valdis. She hesitated to hit the SEND key.

It's Maya, a voice deep within her cried. *It's Maya. Annoying and naïve sometimes, yes. A slut when she wanted sex, maybe so. And take my place as a whore, sure, why not? But dead? Dead? It's Maya.*

Rebecca looked at the palatial mansion which had been her all-too-comfortable prison for six years before Valdis got her a job with his wife. Rebecca had tasted freedom, and it tasted good. And the thought of just one more hour here was too much to bear. So her thumb fell upon the SEND key.

"Ok."

***

Despite the clean feel of her body and the satisfying scent of perfume, Maya checked her pussy after the drug-induced orgy she had experienced. Her sensitive valley was sore, her lips were slightly bruised, and her clitoris ached. There wasn't a stubble of hair to be found; someone had shaved her good, but all the bathing in the world could never clean the dirty feeling off her skin left by the fucking she'd gotten.

Not just since Nick. She remembered Rebecca kissing her lips, finger-fucking her pussy, and the needle jabbed in the neck. Knocked her the fuck out. Then came the cattle prod and the needle in the arm. *Some kind of hallucinogen maybe*? She'd imagined fucking Nick and Albert, both at the same time, but that wasn't real. The men were complete strangers.

My husband would never let another man fuck me.

Just the thought of his betrayal made her body quake with sorrow.

And why did Rebecca turn against me?

Maya's thoughts shut down when she heard a sound outside. As she crept to the bathroom door to ensure it was locked, she kept the water running as a ruse. Leaning an eager ear against the door, she faintly heard voices. One said, "She must be in the shower."

She heard a loud *clang* followed by more talking, and then the outer room door closed again, followed by a click, the last sound.

She unlocked the bathroom door as carefully as she could before cautiously cracking it open to peer out into the room. Right way she noticed a silver dome on a tray set on a table that wasn't there before.

She tiptoed out into the room, peeked beneath the bed and into a wall closet where her clothes hung neat and clean from plastic hangers. Assured she was alone, she inspected the outer door, and sure enough, it was locked. She then strode to the table and slid the dome open to reveal a plate of baked chicken and asparagus on a bed of brown rice. A glass of wine and what looked like cranberry juice stood on either side of the plate, while a rolled up cloth napkin kept the silverware in a tight embrace. Maya sniffed the food. Her stomach growled. She was hungry, but was this a trap? Was the food poisoned?

Then she remembered the fact they had cleaned her, clothed her, and manicured her nails. In no way did they want her dead.

She unwrapped the utensils and sat down.

***

The prisoner began to find his way back to consciousness. He heard a click, and then the loud whine of rusty hinges echoed in the dark damp room. A door opened then shut. He took a deep breath, smelled the ocean nearby and the piss in his pants. He looked around the dim basement and saw the female cop, Adrian, walk down the cement staircase. Only a chair, a table, and a hose sat on the floor not far from the chair he was tied to. She turned on a single-bulb lamp that hung above his head, causing him to wince under its bright cone of light.

The cop-woman sat in front of him, her full chest teasing him as he wallowed in his own urine. He tested the knots that held his hands behind him. They didn't give. "What the fuck, bitch?"

She took out a small cigar and lit it. The sweet smell of ganja rose in the air. She took a drag then smiled as she held it up to his face. "You want some?"

He spat and kicked at her. "Fuck you, mon."

"Interesting. Seems we have two things in common." She took another drag.

"I got nothing in common with no stinkin' cop."

"Now see, that's where you are wrong. You killed somebody today, and so have I. That's one. Two, neither of us likes to share." She picked up the hose and aimed the nozzle at him. "But I need you to share some information." She swiveled the handle on the nozzle. A cold fast spray of water hit him straight in the face. No matter how he turned his head, he couldn't catch a breath. If he opened his mouth, the seemingly endless torrent would certainly fill his lungs and drown him where he sat.

Then as suddenly as it began, it ended.

He coughed and spat.

Adrian smoked, the nozzle now in her lap. "So. You now know the situation. I am going to ask you questions. Depending on your answer, you will either get the hose, or not. Totally up to you."

"Fuck you, bitch. I ain't talking."

"Wrong answer." She aimed the nozzle.

He flinched, but she didn't hose him. When he relaxed and exhaled, she hit the handle, and the water exploded out again. He didn't have enough air in his lungs to scream. All he could do was writhe in the chair and hope for mercy.

Adrian shut off the water and set the hose on the floor beside her chair. She took one more drag then put the half smoked cigar on the table. "I can do this all fucking night." She folded her hands in her lap and glared at him. "I don't give a fuck about you. I only care about a missing wife. I think you know something about her, and you are going to tell me, 'cause this hose is going to get old quick, and then..." She reached behind her back and produced a semi automatic handgun. "...the big dog comes out. I'll let it bite off a finger, a kneecap, and a couple of balls, if need be." She set Big Dog on the table then reached down for the hose and aimed it at him. "So, shall we continue?" She yanked the handle and let him have it again.

"No more," he shouted over the deluge. "No more, please."

"Sorry. I can't hear you."

"Okay, I'll talk." He choked. "Please stop. I'll talk."

Adrian shut off the hose. "Why did you shoot up the resort?"

Water dripped from his face. "We-we were hired keep folks quiet. Anyone who talked to da police, we supposed to send a message."

"Which is..?"

He looked up at her defiantly. "Don't talk to da fucking cops."

"Then why did you shoot at us?"

He shook water out of his hair. "Not me.

"Your partner did."

"Him stupid...not right in da head."

"Oh, now that is a shame." Adrian scoffed. "Well, his head isn't his problem anymore because I shot it full of holes."

The prisoner dropped his chin to his chest. "Oh no, oh no."

"The time to mourn is later. Right now you're supposed to be talking." She aimed the high pressure nozzle at him. "Who hired you?"

"Gilbert."

Adrian knew the name. Everybody knew Bossman's right hand man.

"He give us five to send message, and when we done we get other half."

"Ten dollars?"

"A thousand American."

Adrian snorted. "That's all? You're some cheap ass labor. Where's the money?"

"What do you care?"

"The money, fool."

He swallowed. "Please, I know how much Chief like the peace. Tourists don't come if we shootin', but I got kids, you know."

Adrian sighed, set aside the hose, and reached for the cigar. She put it to her luscious lips and lit it. "Where is the fucking money?"

"With me wife. Feeding me wife and kids."

"Tell me where they live."

"W-why?"

"We'll need that money back for evidence."

"Okay. The old plantation road...by the windmill. But please, don't hurt them." His body shook out of fear and from the cold water.

Adrian took a deep drag on the cigar. “We don’t hurt women and children.” She picked up the hose. “Now who tampered with the resort’s cameras?”

“Nicholas. Gilbert tells him. He does what he’s told.”

“Where’s the American woman?”

“I don’t know.”

“Then you’re no good to me.” She grabbed the gun and shot him in the neck. The bang ricocheted around the basement. His head fell forward. Blood gushed from the wound.

She smoked until the blood flow ceased then used the hose to wash the gore down the drain. Cell phone in hand, she dialed the Chief. It took two rings before he answered. “Talk to me.”

“The attack has Bossman written all over it. Our friend here said Gilbert paid him half a grand up front to keep the hotel staff silent. Paid Nicholas too.”

“Why did they kill George?”

“He didn’t say. In fact, I didn’t ask.”

Clive sighed. “So it’s Bossman for sure, huh?”

“Yup.” She knew Bossman was someone Clive didn’t want to deal with.

“Guess we’ll have to pay him a visit.” He hung up.

Adrian looked at the phone. Her feelings for Clive surfaced as she looked at his contact photo. The big man was smiling. His dark brown skin shined bright as he looked to his left at his wife, whom Adrian had cut out of the picture.

“Lucky bitch.”

***

Maya looked at the now empty plate with some satisfaction. At least the food around here was good. She burped and covered her mouth. “Excuse me.” Then she realized she was still alone in the room.

A brown object caught her eye. She pushed the plate aside to reveal a nicely rolled cigar. "Dessert?" She picked it up and sniffed the finest weed in the world. "Shit, these motherfuckers ain't all bad." But she didn't see any matches to light it.

There was a lighter in her purse... She glanced around... If she could find it. Where would they have put it? She decided to look in the nightstand drawer to the left of the bed. Yup. Her purse lay inside. She felt around in the purse, and a surge of glee rushed through her when she found the lighter. "Well, well, well." Maya put the cigar to her full lips. "If I'm in hell, might as well be high." She flicked the flint and the lighter came ablaze. A bright flame kissed the end of the cigar, and she twisted it around, allowing the fire to ignite the weed evenly. A deep toke came next, and she closed her eyes to fight the burn in her lungs.

She had no plan to escape in her head, yet the need to do so was paramount. And now as she exhaled the smoke, she felt calmer, better prepared to find out all she could about where she was and why her husband wasn't coming for her.

More importantly, she had to find out why the woman she knew for a year had betrayed her all along.

"Bitch got some payback comin'." She took a second hit. "That for damn sure, mon." Island lingo fit her mood.

***

Rebecca cracked open the door. The moon's pale glow from the barred window and a single dim lamp in the corner lit the room and revealed Maya asleep in the bed. Ganja smoke lingered in the air like an evening fog; its overpowering musk greeted her nostrils as she stepped inside. She left the door ajar, just a crack, then turned to the bed.

Wouldn't want to wake her up now, would I?

Barefoot, she stalked toward the bed, her purse in one hand, her Minolos clutched in the other, which she set on the carpeted floor. Quietly, she sat on the bed, and with her purse on her lap, just looked at her beautiful ex-boss. Even in the dim light, Maya was radiant. She lay on her back, her hair splayed perfectly across her pillow, framing a truly exquisite face. She wore a black kimono robe, open down the front, which revealed her light brown skin and luscious curves of cleavage. Rebecca felt envy and admiration flow through her veins. She reached out and caressed the left side of Maya's face.

What a shame it has to end this way.

She leaned over and kissed Maya's cheek then got down to business. Opening the purse, she searched for the black case. In it was a syringe she'd stolen from the only veterinary clinic on the island. The dog doctor was a fan of her blowjobs, and after she'd delivered the goods and he'd fallen asleep with visions of her lips sucking his dick, she'd rummaged through his backroom for a vile of pentobarbital and the syringe. She'd loaded it with enough of the euthanizing drug to kill a horse in thirty seconds.

And now she couldn't find the fucking thing in her not-so-small purse. She had to wonder if fate was making sure she wouldn't become a killer.

Maya frowned and grunted, a subconscious reaction to Rebecca's movements on the bed.

Rebecca waited to allow Maya to settle back in her slumber then resumed rummaging through the purse. Finally, she found the case and pulled it out while her eyes watched Maya to make sure she wasn't waking up.

Then she never would...

She opened the case and removed the loaded syringe. Death would come easy for Maya, just soft snoring, a gasp or two, then silence. Nothing to explain: no screams to hear, no angry eyes cursing Rebecca's soul.

She took a deep breath, her eyes closed as she looked inwardly for strength.

And with a heavy sigh, she placed the needle to Maya's arm. "I'm sorry." She placed her thumb on the plunger. "I love you, I really do, but damn...I've got to get away from here. Your husband promised me. I'm helping us both. We can both be free." She wiped away a tear running down her left cheek. A trail formed on her right cheek, as well. "Please forgive me."

Chapter Twenty-Five

AT DUSK, CLIVE DROVE the patrol car down a familiar winding road that hugged the rugged coastal mountain curves. The road was no more than a jeep trail, seldom used on the Atlantic side of the island where the beaches were nothing but jagged rock, and the waves, undertows, and riptides kept visitors away.

Adrian sat beside him, her eyes fighting to stay open. Clive looked at his number-one cop and object of his adulterous lust. “You should get some shut eye.”

She shook her head and sat upright in her seat. “No,” she breathed. “I’m frosty.”

Clive just smiled as he deftly took another bumpy curve. It had been a long day and the sunlight was fading. He wanted to get done before dark.

Ten minutes later, he parked the car in a secluded clearing by the ocean. His grin grew anew as he looked over to see Adrian sleeping peacefully in the passenger seat.

That’s cool. She’s done enough dirt for one day.

His stare lingered on her closed eyes, and then it traveled from her face down her throat to her chest. A black t-shirt clung to her ample breasts, a pair he was quite familiar with. His eyes slid down to her crotch, a place he wasn’t familiar with, yet. She wore jeans that tenaciously hugged her supple hips.

And for the umpteenth time, he wished he didn’t sneak around on Annora. He should have come clean about what had happened in the office, but he didn’t tell her, mostly because not a damn thing really happened.

They had come close to fucking on that occasion, but fate tossed a curve ball at just the wrong moment. He had shoved his hand down her pants while smothering one of her bountiful breasts in his mouth. They were just moments from christening his desk when his wife called to say she was outside, there to surprise him for lunch. He'd looked regretfully at Adrian and forced his hand to stop massaging her delicacy. Adrian had pouted and stomped out the back door, left to bring herself to fulfillment at home later that day. He was left with another bout of blue balls.

In all, he supposed it was for the best. He was grateful he had a beautiful wife and partner. Yet Annora and Adrian shared a lot in common, from their figures to their mannerisms to their first initials. He couldn't fathom a life without either of them in it, and he would forever wish he could have them both in all ways without any guilt.

With a sigh, he got out of the car and closed the door gently so as not to disturb Adrian. He walked to the back of the sedan, slid the key into the trunk, and popped the lid. There lay the blood-soaked body of Gilbert's hired henchman.

Clive went to work. He pushed the bag of lye aside, and with much effort stripped off the man's bloody clothes, underpants and all. The body would quickly decay; the clothes wouldn't. He felt sorry that the dead man's shriveled up cock would never again get any pussy. He hauled the naked body out of the trunk, flung it on his shoulder, and trudged across the rocks to a familiar deep crevice that would be the gunman's final resting place. Without ceremony or final words, he dropped the carcass into the abyss. Wiping his hands together, he strolled back to the car and got the 20-pound bag of lye out of the trunk.

Clive was familiar with the area, having spent many a youthful evening fucking or smoking or both under a bright shiny moon. Cops and tourists never came out this way, so there was no fear of getting busted. Disposing of a body here was also nothing new to him. And while some folks would frown on his chosen method of island justice, he felt his way was pure, a surefire way to punish those who'd committed heinous crimes and keep the resort out of the news. This island, *his island*, depended on tourism to survive. So gunfights and missing wives were not good for business, and as he poured the lye down the crevice and over the criminal at the bottom, he felt no shame. Island justice wasn't pretty, but it was necessary.

Back at the trunk, he removed the bad guy's clothes and carried them to rocky outcrop where a nasty riptide sucked everything in its clutches out to sea. He tossed the clothes into the froth and watched the sea swallow them.

After washing his hands in a tidal pool, he got back into the car.

Adrian awoke with a start. She looked at him, still groggy. "We there yet?"

He laughed as he started the car. "We're all done here, heading back to the office."

She sighed. "Will you look at that sunset?"

"Yeah." The sun had dropped below the horizon, leaving the cloudy sky ablaze in color. His island was safe and peaceful, for now.

***

Rebecca looked at the needle poised to pierce Maya's arm.

Just one jab...one little push of the plunger. It would all be over.

Valdis would have his dead vacationing wife and Rebecca would have her freedom from Bossman. She was the reason Albert's affections had drifted from Maya. For a while, Rebecca would fuck him two, maybe three times a week, and lying to Maya every day after fucking her husband was something of a thrill.

Now all she had to do was *jab and push* and take possession of the life Maya led and the husband Maya loved.

With her thumb on the plunger, Rebecca looked at Maya's face. Her smile and laugh flashed through Rebecca's mind. The lunches, the shopping sprees, the friendship they'd shared, all gone with one *jab* and one *push*. But she couldn't do it. It was supposed to be easy. *Jab and push.* All Bossman would know was that Maya had died peacefully in her sleep.

So she tried again to push, and still her thumb didn't move as her mind reminisced about the way Maya had kissed and touched her and brought her to an intense and quick climax. Rebecca enjoyed Maya, as well, especially the way her soft skin felt against her lips, and the way she moved as she and Nick fucked on the sheets.

Not to mention the free gym membership and paid days off. Rebecca shook her head. *No time to get sentimental. Jab and push* would change her life. Maya had to be sacrificed.

Then Rebecca remembered the first time she met Maya, and how Maya offered a complete stranger a much-needed job. Well, the referral from her husband helped, but escaping a dangerous island pimp was not easy, and even in the states, Bossman's callused hand could have snatched her back into captivity at any moment.

From morning coffee, to pastries, to lunch, Maya had treated her well. Rebecca looked at the needle that refused to plunge the poison into Maya's arm.

Then she saw Maya's husband in her fucked up mind. He'd walked into Bossman's office, looking for a special whore. Of course, she was the best, so Valdis became her favorite customer. He could fuck all night, and he didn't like a lot of chit chat, something Rebecca identified with. But their fucking spoke volumes. He thought the scenic island was paradise, while Rebecca hated the place, but his world, his city, what he said of it intrigued her, as she'd only been off the island once to go to Miami. So after she sucked and fucked him for a few months, he'd opened up to her. She listened to him talk about his hometown and she asked questions. Their conversations began to grow in length and depth as each let their walls down brick by brick.

She wanted out and he wanted her pussy every night.

So Valdis made a deal with Bossman and brought her stateside, where they played it cool. He just smiled as Maya gushed over her new employee. Rebecca did a good job of hiding her feelings, but when he walked by her, the mere smell of his cologne sent shivers down her spine. One time at their mansion, Rebecca excused herself from a conversation by gesturing to the bathroom where she freshened up. Then she discreetly snuck about the lavish house until she found Albert in his den, already naked. He tossed the door key to her, and she smiled as she turned the lock then dropped her dress on top of his pile of clothes on the floor.

That was the first time she ever had sex with a customer without a cash transaction. It was also the first time in a long time a man sent her to the highest of heights twice. That was the night he'd asked her to become his next bride.

Now she just had to do one more thing.

Jab and push.

Why in God's name was she hesitating?

The floor creaked just outside the door. Who was there?

She quickly put the syringe back into its case and stuffed it into her purse just as Taite entered the room. "Bossman want cha now, girly."

Rebecca stood up and stormed toward Taite, who was backing out of the room and into the hallway.

"Bitch, how dare you just walk into my fucking

room?" She pulled the door closed behind her as she stepped out into the hall.

"This ain't cha room no more." Taite pointed to the door and smiled. "She got you hot and bothered, no? Bossman thinkin' of replacin' you. Thinkin' you done and over, so he be making this Maya's room now."

"Well, I'm still fucking here, and my pussy is worth as much as gold. And just know that while you keep turning tricks on limp dicks, me and my golden pussy will be sitting in the lap of luxury. But until then, bitch, I'm still the motherfucking queen around here."

"Bitch," Taite shouted. "Bring your ass to Bossman now. Since you still here, he wants you to use that golden pussy you got, your majesty. Got men waiting." She bowed and walked away with a laugh.

"Fuck you," Rebecca snarled under her breath before she tiptoed back into the room and shut the door. She turned around just as Maya's right fist slammed into her jaw. Rebecca dropped to the floor.

Maya dumped out Rebecca's purse, which she'd left on the bed, and kneeled down to pick up the cell phone that fell out.

Rebecca groaned.

Maya kicked her in the face. "Shut up, whore." She kicked her in the stomach then rushed back to the bed, and started to dial 9-1-1, but right away she noticed the last call Rebecca received from a familiar number...her husband's number.

Holy shit! What the fuck?

"That motherfucker called her just an hour ago?" She blinked.

What the fuck?

Still in shock by the reality of betrayal creeping into her heart, Maya didn't hear Rebecca get up, and she could only cry out as Rebecca tackled her from behind and knocked her onto the bed.

"Bitch." She grabbed a handful of Maya's thick black hair. "This how you want it? Okay. This is how you get it."

Maya looked up as Rebecca's open right hand slammed into her face, sending a shockwave through her body. Then Rebecca reared back and hit her with a backhand, which dropped her to the floor. Her eyes glazed over as the onslaught continued.

"I found a peaceful way for you to die, but you go and sucker-punch me, you pampered bitch." Rebecca's breath came out in spurts. "You got soft...from the rich life...it gets them all at some point."

Maya struggled to her feet but Rebecca slugged her in the jaw and knocked her back down. "You get used to being spoiled, getting whatever you want whenever you want it. The old you...the streetwise you...the you who would not be in the shit you're in now if you had open eyes. You should have seen me coming, but you didn't, because all that time around money made you weak and ripe for the taking. And taken you were."

She kicked Maya in the ribs.

A huff of air burst out of her.

"See, I don't want to kill you, but I have to get off this island. I have to be free. I have to be pampered. I have to have the finest foods. I have to go shopping and not pay for a fucking thing. So it came down to you living this life for me, here with Bossman, so I get to live the good life in your place."

Rebecca punched her in the nose. "But now for that to happen, you've got to die." Rebecca delivered a pair of vicious kicks, which sent Maya reeling. Rebecca yanked Maya's head up by the hair. "Everything you love, everything you own, everything you are is now mine. Just know, as you smile down on us from your rightful place in heaven, next to all the other genuinely nice people who once walked this world...just know, I'm going to enjoy fucking your husband in your bed."

Another vicious blow caused Maya to see two Rebecca's before her head slammed into the floor. Rebecca reached for her purse, only to find it empty. "Shit." She looked around for the needle case. She found it quickly, the cold brown leather standing out against the rich carpet.

"You'll still die painlessly." She picked up the case and opened it. "That's the least I can do for all you've done for me."

"Fuck you." Maya groaned on the floor.

Rebecca laughed. "Damn, Maya, that's the best offer I've had all day." She took out the needle, walked over to Maya, and snatched her head off the floor then aimed the needle at a nice vein in her exposed neck.

Maya whipped her head backward and rammed it into Rebecca's nose. She let go of Maya's hair and dropped the needle to cup her hands around her bleeding face. "You fucking—"

As the needle fell toward the floor, Maya reached out and snatched it in midair then slammed it into Rebecca's foot and injected the contents into her bloodstream.

Rebecca cried out in agony, now reaching for her foot, before a fist slammed into her temple.

Rebecca hit the floor. She tried to curse Maya, but only managed a cough as her heart seized and bucked. Struggling to breathe, she reached for Maya's throat, but her arms started shaking and her face contorted into a horrible mask of terror. Maya slapped Rebecca's hands away. A second later, she took her last breath. Even dead, her body shuddered as if in the throes of a grand mal orgasm.

Maya rocked back and forth on her knees. Tears streamed down her face. She picked up Rebecca's head and placed it on her lap. "I thought...you were...my friend."

Rebecca's cell phone rang, jarring Maya out of her shock and grief. Its display light radiated from under the bed. She set Rebecca's head down on the carpet, kissed her forehead, and smoothed back her hair. The phone kept ringing, so Maya crawled across the room and reached under the bed to get it. As it rang in her hand, her eyes widened in amazement at the caller ID. *What the fuck*? It was her husband. She slid her finger across the screen to pick up the call, but she remained silent.

"Rebecca? Is she dead?" he said calmly. "What did Bossman say about you killing her? Did you tell him you saved him from a smart, sexy, but persistent headache?"

Maya slumped against the foot of the bed, still as death, her mouth agape, devoid of any words. Her heart slammed against her chest; tears silently rolled down her face, and her hand trembled as it clutched the phone.

"Rebecca, say something. Is the bitch dead?"

The door flew open. Maya jumped and dropped the phone as Gilbert stalked in. Maya screamed, and channeling her rage, she punched him in the jaw, but Bossman rushed in, picked her up, and slammed onto the bed.

"My, my, my." the big man laughed. "You are one feisty bi..." His voice trailed off when his attention fell on Rebecca's body. He whipped his head around to Maya. "What happened to her?"

Maya tried to sit up, held down by the big man's heavy hand. "Your fucking two cent whore tried to kill me, fat boy."

Bossman slapped her. "No. I told her not to hurt you. She always listens." He slapped her again and again and again, until her face burned red and consciousness flickered out. "She was free. All he had to do was pay me for her." He growled as he dropped her unconscious body on the bed. Then he heard a sound down at his feet and saw the cell phone display aglow.

A tinny voice said, "What the fuck is going on? Rebecca. Rebecca."

Gilbert held out the black case. "Look, boss."

Bossman saw the needle in Rebecca's foot. He was about to let loose a volley of expletives when he suddenly had a better idea. Snatching the phone off the floor, he took a deep breath and spoke. "Rebecca can't come to the phone right now. I'm afraid she is busy entertaining and has a dick in her mouth."

Valdis sighed. "That's not part of our deal."

"Nor was your wife dying part of the deal, but Rebecca tells me that is what you wanted her to do." Bossman smiled at his own cunningness. "So you decided to change our arrangement and fuck me out of my new girl."

"Bossman, I did what I thought was best, saved you a shitload of trouble."

The big man laughed. "So not only will I keep Rebecca as my personal fuck bitch, I will let your wife go home to you. How you like that shitload of trouble?"

"Fuck you, Bossman."

"She does have one pre-paid john to fuck, but afterwards, she's all yours. Of course, I can't be held accountable for what she might have overheard about how her husband arranged her death, just for a piece of Rebecca's ass." He looked down at her still body on the carpeted floor. "A nice piece of ass, but one which has seen better days."

"You know I have connections," Valdis warned. "I can have them come by and put a fucking bullet in your head. You need to accept your place in the world, Bossman, and while you might be a big fucking deal on that island, I can have you wiped off the face of the planet."

"Really now?" Bossman laughed while walking about the room. "I guess you don't know the power of social media, my friend. One picture of your happy wife, suddenly found and free to talk about how her lousy husband planned to kill her and how a kind man helped her gain her freedom. Not to mention the miraculous fact she will obtain solid proof to back up what she says. Recordings, pictures, and witnesses. Shit, by the time your wife gets done with you, I think your connections might come undone. And that's when you and *my* connections will get to know one another, albeit a painfully brief encounter."

Valdis slammed his fist on his desk. "Okay, man, what do you want?"

"Be here within eight hours or your precious wife will go viral." He stepped into the bathroom, which made his voice sound deep with an echo. "I want triple our originally agreed upon price, since you thought you could change the fucking deal, I can change it, as well." He slammed the phone to the floor then stomped on it. "Gilbert, take this feisty little whore to Taite. Get her ready and pretty so she can entertain her first client until her husband gets here with the money. Then we throw them both into the fucking ocean."

Chapter Twenty-Six

ANNORA STOOD IN the bathroom doorway, staring lustfully at her husband. He was in the shower, and despite the steam covered glass, she could see the outline of his cock as it hung loosely, beckoning her to touch it.

She didn't hear him come in last night. When she woke up in the middle of the night to an empty bed, she searched the house for Clive whom she found in his favorite easy chair, a drink cradled precariously in his hand as he slumbered.

She had decided to leave him to sleep, took the drink from his hand, and kissed him on the forehead. Then as the sun's morning rays streamed through the house, and the kids started getting ready for the day, Clive awoke just in time for breakfast and to see them off to school.

Annora could tell by the slump in his broad shoulders that he was tired, so sex might be out of the question for now. As she walked toward the shower, he saw her, and she saw her phallic friend stir as well. "Tired, my love?"

Clive nodded and shut off the water. He opened the door, and she handed him a towel. "Thank you, baby." As he toweled off: "I got a lead on our missing wife."

The long pause as he wrapped the towel around him spoke volumes. He walked to the bed and fell on the sheets face first without another word. She wanted to press the issue, but she'd learned from her mother that a man of the law will often hide his burdens from his wife in order to keep her out of the darkness of his professional life.

She also observed that not talking about his day was the best way for Clive to come back to his family. "Out there, stays out there," he once said to her. "When I come home, I come to peace." Then one of the kids cried and she replied, "Unfortunately, that peace does not come with quiet." Then he planted a sweet kiss on her lips.

So now, as he snored, Annora picked up her cup of herbal tea, complete with a splash of Gran Marnier, and at peace with her world, she was glad her husband made it home safely. Every morning, while she loved to watch him get dressed, she hated to see him go, all too cognitive of the fact that the kiss they just shared might be their last. So each night he came home was a celebration, even if it was a silent one.

She walked over to a radio and turned down the volume before turning it on. Her sleeping husband would approve of the smooth strains of Courtney Pine's saxophone that floated from the speakers.

Annora's mind drifted with the music as she walked to the balcony and stood. Their home faced inland with the ocean to the right. She closed her eyes, basked in the sun, and swayed to the music.

She felt his arms embrace her waist, and his rigid cock pressed into her rounded backside. Annora sighed. "Did I wake you."

"The sun," he whispered, fondling her breasts through her white dress. He loved the feel of the silky garment against her nipple as it rose beneath the material. "It shone through your dress and allowed me to see what's underneath."

She set her tea down on a nearby table. "Then I should take it off."

"Allow me." He gently drew the straps from her shoulders and let the dress fall. Now she was almost naked. He pushed aside her thin panties and, from behind, slid his erection into her already wet pussy, making her sigh with pleasure. As she leaned on the banister, he massaged her chocolate nipples and slowly rotated his hips to and fro. His cock throbbed madly inside her.

"Clive..." She giggled as he kissed a sweet spot on her neck then picked her up off his raging dick and cradled her in his arms. They kissed as he carried her to the bed where he tenderly placed her on top of the sheets then straddled her and slipped himself back inside.

Annora leaned up on her elbows, her lips begging for a kiss. He enveloped her mouth with his and wrapped his arms around her as they became one. Their slow movements soon became frenzied. Annora flung her legs around his butt and called out, "Oh, Clive, fuck me like you mean it."

He nibbled on the crook of her neck as a climax rushed though her trembling body. Her searing pussy forced Clive to moan into her shoulder as he exploded inside her.

Annora caught her breath first. "I think we're gonna have twins."

Clive nodded. "Snip snip."

"Well we could have had twins...it was that good."

Silence passed comfortably between them. Clive rolled off her onto his back, and she laid her head on his chest and rubbed her left foot up and down his left leg. "What's troubling you, Clive?"

"I had to do it again." He sighed. "Dump another body. He killed two people, George and an American man on his honeymoon. It's going to be all over the US news, hell, it probably is already. To save the island from the bad publicity of a trial, I had to get rid of the killer, but Adrian and I still have more to do."

Annora ran her fingers through the fine hair on his chest. "I know it doesn't sit well with you to do that."

"Can't afford for folks to get out of hand. We need these tourists to come year after year. Otherwise, what the fuck would we have?"

"Very little, my love. That is why you have to do what

you must. Did your other wife help you?"

He ignored the jab. "Yes."

"I think she deserves her own post. I hear they need a chief in Montego Bay."

"And lose my best cop? Nah. She's not going anywhere."

Annora sat up. "Why you keeping her around, Clive?"

"She knows her shit. The stuff she learned in the states has been invaluable."

"You got trained in the states too. You could train a replacement."

Clive looked at her. "Why are you so eager to get rid of Adrian?"

"I'm not stupid." She got off the bed, her magnificent backside tempting him with its vertical smile. She turned back around. "A dog knows when another dog is after its bone. And she is after my bone."

"Oh come on, baby. Not this again."

"This again, and again, and again. Until you get rid of her."

"Annora, please, you are my one and only."

"Maybe so. But I'd feel a whole lot better if she was in one place, and we were in another."

"The woman doesn't want me like that," he lied. "Besides, I've seen her with the Governor's son."

"The Governor's son is gay, and she is just eye candy to hide his proclivities. And if you think your little partner doesn't want you, you are either lying to me, to yourself, or you're just plain dumb. I seen the way she looks at you. We both know you are far from stupid, Clive Battersby."

He watched her slam the bathroom door, ending the conversation. Leaning back, he folded his hands behind his head. "Fucking women," he mumbled. "Can't live with 'em, can't live without 'em, can't kill 'em..."

Chapter Twenty-Seven

AS CONSCIOUSNESS FLOODED her mind, Maya took a deep breath. For a moment she thought what happened was all a dream, some weed-induced nightmare she would forget about as the day stretched on. Her right hand ached, and when she tried to ball her fist, streaks of pain shot up her arm. Looking at her hand, she saw it was bruised around the knuckles. She'd definitely been in a fist fight.

So it wasn't a dream.

Only a single lamp by the window provided light in the dimly lit room. Slowly, she sat up, her naked body sore from head to toe. She placed her bare feet on the soft brown carpet and stagger-stepped to the door and then the window, logic telling her to expect them both to be locked. Her instincts were right about the door, however, the window opened, and she looked out through the iron bars at the ocean and a fifty-foot drop to the jagged rocks below.

Chilled by the ocean breeze, she decided to get dressed.

The closet revealed several dresses of various styles and colors she would normally see in high-end clothing stores, hanging next to her own clothes. Three pairs of black heels were lined up next to a pair of tennis shoes, which she snatched off the floor before closing the door and heading to the dresser. She set down the tennis shoes and sifted through the top drawer where she found her jeans and a grey t-shirt, traveling clothes if she could ever get out of here. She shut the drawer and opened the next one. There she found another black kimono robe.

She slipped into it and admired its ornate lattice pattern over her rich brown skin. For a moment, her fears subsided as her mind drifted to the first time she wore a kimono robe for her husband, and how he licked and fucked her pussy to the point of no return.

Then, as quickly as the memory materialized, it disappeared in a pool of agony. He was a fucking traitor, a lying fuckin' pig.

She felt a cool breeze blow in and jiggle the purple lamp shade ever so slightly. The diffused light danced across the room. She looked at herself in the vanity mirror, and leaning closer, her steady stare focused on her eyes. There was something different in them. Anger. Fear. Regret. Turning her head left and right, she examined the bruises. Instead of the high-maintenance woman she usually saw, prim and proper, she looked like she'd been in a war zone. "I'm different... All because of my fucking husband." She closed her mouth and her eyes.

Anger fixes nothing. Despair is no option. Figure a way out of here, girl.

Yet she felt angry and sad.

What the fuck? Five years. Five fucking years, and here I am a prisoner because my husband would rather fuck Rebecca. All the love I gave him...and for what?

She sighed as she opened her eyes to stare at the stranger in the mirror. "Get it together, girl. One monkey don't stop no show."

It was at that moment she decided she had to know why he'd done her wrong. "When the fuck did I become the other woman?" she said out loud to her reflection. "When the fuck did I stop being good enough for you, Albert?" She slammed her palm on the dresser top. "You fucking asshole." She fell to her knees. "I loved you. Damn it, I loved you."

And this is getting you where? A voice eerily reminiscent of her dad's echoed from the recesses of her mind. *Get up, get strong and get the fuck out of here.*

Maya stood and wiped away her tears. “I just have to know why. Then I’ll kill that son of a bitch.”

Or at the very least, beat him like he owed her money.

She walked back to the window as the sun touched the ocean’s horizon. Despair reared its head again, but she would have none of it, choosing to pray for the first time since she’d met her husband.

And then she thought of Nick.

Where the fuck is he? Was he a part of this conspiracy too?

Before she could further muse about his whereabouts, a quick knock rattled the door.

***

Clive walked onto the bedroom balcony where Annora watched the sunset. “Hey. You still upset?”

“Yeah...” She sipped from a cup of tea. “But I’ll get over it. I always do.” She turned to him and scowled. “Why you dressed like that?”

Clive walked toward her. “Look, I’m afraid I’ve got to deal with the vacationing wife.”

A patrol car drove up and the driver’s door opened. “Boss.”

“Upstairs, Adrian,” Clive called down to her.

Annora looked at him like he’d invited the plague inside.

“What?” he asked, perplexed.

The door opened downstairs, and the kids made a fuss over Adrian. She said her pleasantries and excused herself before she raced up the stairs and into the bedroom. “I found Nicholas.” She was slightly out of breath. “The address the resort had for him was wrong. He’d moved.”

“Where is he?”

“Hotel Blair, far side of town.” She felt Annora’s cold

gaze and instantly regretted the tight black t-shirt and jeans she wore.

Annora looked at Clive's similar attire. "Why are you dressed alike? Where are your uniforms?"

"Well, we gotta sneak into Bossman's place."

Annora dropped her cup, which shattered on the ground below the balcony. "My crazy brother? When were you going to tell me?"

"I don't know the whole story yet, babe."

"We're still investigating," Adrian put in.

Annora looked at her. "My husband and I are discussing a family matter. Please go downstairs."

Adrian stepped toward Clive, but Annora jumped in front of him. "He might be your boss, but this is my house, and I say get the fuck out my bedroom, so you better get the fuck out my bedroom."

"Honey, the kids."

"They heard cussin' before. We got that bloody satellite TV."

"Okay," Adrian said sheepishly. "I don't want any trouble." She walked out the door and closed it behind her.

"Woman, you just—"

Annora wrapped her arms around him. "My brother is crazy," she said into his chest. "Must you deal with him?"

"I think he has the American wife. This guy Nicholas was with her last. We've got to talk to him before we approach Bossman."

"Please be careful." Annora hugged him.

"I will. But can you please stop tripping about Adrian? There is nothing going on."

Annora looked up into his eyes. "I'll trust you on that, but why must you be the one to deal with my brother? Send Adrian and some other officers."

"I have to handle him. Me and Adrian be heading that way then I'll come back to you as soon as possible."

Annora frowned. "You can't wait until the morning?"

"We can't wait, and we have to be sneaky. He's throwin' a party tonight. The wife is there, George told me, hopefully alive, and we have to get her out before she is dead. A dead American woman, especially a rich one, will hurt our island's reputation for years and years to come. We're going to worm our way in, snatch her out, and leave without causin' a fuss."

"You don't have to sneak in. Just talk to him."

"No, not this time. I have to do this on the down low, get the wife to safety, then confront him in the morning."

Annora took a deep breath. "If he has the wife, baby, please be careful. Watch your temper, and whatever you do, don't hurt him...or get yourself hurt."

He studied the lovely brown skinned beauty standing before him. "You are so beautiful. Your grace blooms even under a night sky. You don't deserve my worries."

"That is sweet. Corny, but sweet."

"When I get back. I will take a long hot shower, and then make love to you again."

She covered his hand with her own. "I'll be here, as always. You make sure you come back, healthy and able."

He leaned down and kissed her softly, appreciating the sweet taste of coconut tea on her lips. "Don't worry about me."

"It's my job." She kissed him once more.

"I love you." He stepped back, stared at her a moment, and then headed out.

Moments later, she watched as he drove away to rescue a damsel in distress. Her husband was a careful man, but she always dreaded when he left. This time, more than ever.

Her brother was a dangerous man.

Chapter Twenty-Eight

TAITE ENTERED MAYA'S ROOM and looked around. "Ah, there you are."

Maya turned from the window.

"Come get your supper." Taite held the door open.

Maya watched a man clad in a green blazer and black pants push a lavish gold cart into the room. She appraised the expensive-looking apparatus, noticing it came complete with a warmer at the base of the cart.

Taite flipped a switch on the wall. The spectacular crystal chandelier illuminated the room.

Maya squinted.

"Now that better, no?"

The man slid the cart's dome back and left the room.

Taite said, "You have jerk chicken, mash potatoes, and asparagus. We wasn't sure about carbs, so we just gave you one roll."

"I'm not hungry."

"Then I guess the boys outside will eat it for you."

Maya decided a stubborn attitude would do her stomach no good. "Never mind. I'll eat."

"Oh, I almost forgot." She pointed to a glass. "Some wine to wash away your sorrows."

Maya walked toward her, and Taite immediately went on the defensive and took two steps toward the door. Maya stopped. "I'm not going to hit you. I just need to know if it's true what Bossman wants me to do."

"You do what Rebecca done. Be the best fuck here."

"I'm not a whore."

Taite grinned. "You be one now."

***

Clive arrived at the resort and parked the patrol car.

Adrian looked at him. "Uh, this isn't Nicholas's hotel."

"I know." Clive shut off the engine. "I gotta talk to Dillard."

"Why?"

"Think about it. Last time we were here, about the way he stared at Jackie. The fact those shooters knew where Georgie was, and they hit right after Dillard's skinny pompous ass left. He is in on this, but how, I don't know."

"You know he and the Governor are best friends."

Clive shrugged. "Governor will give me a fucking medal when I clean this shit up. Best friend or not. Besides, I can't stand that asshole."

"The Governor or Dillard?

Clive grinned as he got out of the car and walked to the resort with Adrian in tow.

***

"Yes," Dillard replied into the phone. "I know the deal, but you gave me your word that violence would not find its way into my establishment." He heard someone at his office door and watched the handle jiggle. "It's locked, you moron."

This time the handle moved violently and the moron pounded on the door.

"Do you want to fuck her or not?" came through the phone.

"I'll call you back... No, better yet, I'll see you in a bit. And of course I want to fuck her bloody beautiful ass. No matter what the price."

More pounding.

"You want to get fired?" he shouted at the door.

"Stupid workers. When do I get to fuck her?"

"She is claimed until midnight. Come inside the usual way with three grand."

"Three..." Dillard spat. "What happened to my discount?"

"No discount for this sweet, sweet American pussy. Three or pay the usual amount and get the usual hairy snatch."

The door handle kept jerking up and down. "For the love of God. The fucking door is locked."

"We got a deal?"

Dillard shook his head. "Is there no honor amongst men anymore? Very well. Three it is. Just know I'm going to bugger her sweet ass something fierce. She won't be worth a dime when I'm done with her. Then you and I will need to renegotiate our arrangement." He slammed the receiver into the cradle and shot out of his chair. As he stormed toward the door, he straightened his tuxedo shirt. "I hope you enjoy being poor. Today is the last day—"

As he opened the door, all he saw was a brown blur fill his vision before a fist struck him in the nose. He cried out, stumbled backward, and reached for his face. Another blow hit him in the chest and knocked him to the floor. "What the fuck?" His nose spilled blood on his expensive carpet.

Clive closed the door behind him and slid the lock back into place. He knelt next to Dillard as he cradled his bleeding nose. "Now you gonna tell me what you know about the missing wife."

***

"Fuck," Maya said. "Who am I supposed to fuck?"

Taite sat down on the bed. "The top customers. Word has traveled through very, very rich circles that an American is here. Sweet, sexy and new. That's you.

Bossman says he gonna charge three grand a pop for you."

Maya sat on the bed next to Taite. "That much to fuck me?"

"Two hours is all they get. If a man want you longer, all night, that price be negotiable."

"So my husband traded me for a whore, so I could become a whore, so he could sleep with a whore?"

"Ironic, but don't get high and mighty with me, bitch." Taite scowled. "We all is a whore at some point. Whatcha think a man buy you dinner for? Movie? Drinks? For conversation? For company? No. We both know what a man want when they pamper you. He want the pussy. Only now, you don't have to pretend to laugh at his boring jokes, you just fuck him and be done with him."

"And you're cool with that? You spend the day fucking complete strangers for money?"

"Girly, this is the life I dealt. I find peace, or I wallow in hell. I choose peace. And I like to fuck, so why not? Besides, most old men can't fuck much, or can't last when they do fuck. Some guys are cute and smell nice. Some have big dicks, some packin' a wee-wee. I just try to make the best of the shit I am in. We all do."

Maya's mind raced. Whores made good money, she guessed. "How much do I get?"

Taite laughed. "Girly, all you get is the dick, three squares, and a roof over yer head. And the dick is questionable. Guys with big dicks, guys with long dicks. Some dicks are just downright ugly. All shriveled up with the balls, if they have any, hanging down to the knees. And they still expect you to suck it. Yuch. Bossman make them pay extra. Sometimes you get a guy with some good dick. Normal looking, big *and* he knows how to use it. But them few and far between. Most of the time dicks be limp, from nerves they say, but a few can still manage a good hard one. Oh, and look out if they take that little blue pill." Taite sighed. "Them the ones you got to fear. That pill makes 'em think they Superman and just pound and pound away. No finesse. Just bang, bang, bang. Girl, after one of them, my throat, my pussy and my ass be hurtin' for days."

Maya felt vomit fight its way up to her throat. "I...I'm gonna be sick."

Taite saw the alarm in Maya's eyes before she ran into the bathroom and hurled what was left in her stomach into the pristine bleach-smelling toilet. Taite followed and rubbed Maya's back. "That be okay now. You gonna be okay. I threw up my first night too. But after a while, you get used to being a whore."

Gilbert showed up in the doorway wearing a green polo top and black slacks, accentuated by his machinegun in plain sight, hanging from a strap across his right shoulder. "She ready?"

"She will be."

The dark lean man stared at Maya bent over the stool, unconvinced. "She better not smell like puke."

"She be okay, Gilbert. I clean her up good, so go on now."

"Bossman is waiting," he snapped at Taite before leaving the door cracked open.

Taite sighed as she continued to rub Maya's back. "Now I have to go."

Maya spit into the toilet bowl.

"I got my own customers to prepare for. Now you eat, and everything will be fine. Just relax." She leaned to Maya's ear and whispered. "I gave you a thick cigar. It is right under your plate. Ganja always helps me. Makes fucking these men easier when you don't give a damn."

Maya heard the door open and close. She set her butt on the cold floor, felt more bile rise, but fought to keep it down.

Fuck or death, some choice I have.

Maybe death would be welcome after she fucked someone she didn't care for or even know.

And my husband arranged it all so he could have Rebecca.

Surely he had more women than Rebecca on the side.

What if he did? What if he never loved me?

She got up off the floor and stormed to the table. Under her plate she found the fat, well-rolled cigar. It was about half a foot in length and about three inches wide, stuffed full of the best weed on earth. Maya was glad Taite thought enough of her to give her something to help her deal with the humiliation to come.

***

Clive searched Dillard's desk for any documents or notes that could implicate the Brit in the American woman's disappearance.

"Your days as Chief are numbered," Dillard shouted through his cupped hand. "Oh yes, you will be out on your ass. Poor, jobless, and disgraced." He rubbed his bleeding nose, which added to the already annoying whine in his voice. "For Pete's sake, give me a tissue."

Clive looked at the man, whose once pristine tuxedo shirt was now peppered with drops of his own blood. "You just insulted and threatened me. I ain't doin' you no favors. Use your damn shirtsleeve."

"Oh, you are a true bastard." Dillard crawled to the desk and got his own tissue. "And if you think that pretty wife of yours will stick around after I ruin you, think again. I plan on taking everything from you. And be assured I will have her pussy too." Dillard cackled like an old wet hen. "I'll fuck her far better than you—"

"Shut the fuck up before I break your ribs. Take my wife? White boy, please. You can't handle my wife. She throws a better punch and is far too bootylicious for your scrawny ass." He spotted a crumpled up white piece of paper on the floor. "Well now..." He unfolded it and noticed Dillard's intense stare. "What have we here?"

"You have no right to search my belongings." Dillard's voice lacked its usual bluster.

Clive held it out at arm's length, refusing to reach for his reading glasses, which were, now as he thought about it, in the car. "Exotic A W. Three grand for an hour and all night negotiable." He glared at Dillard. "What's this?"

"None of your fucking business."

Clive shrugged. "Wrong answer."

"Fuck you," was all Dillard could mutter as Clive tossed him his tuxedo jacket, which hit him in his face, then unceremoniously snatched him off the floor. Clive held Dillard's arm in a tight grip as he wrested him out of the office and into the lobby.

"Call the police," Dillard yelled to his employee behind the counter.

"I am the police, you idiot."

Clive dragged him outside.

Adrian followed. "What are we gonna charge him with, Chief?"

"Aiding and abetting a criminal enterprise."

"How about racketeering," she suggested. "That'll get him life without parole."

"Are you people out of your minds?" Dillard screamed as Clive shoved him toward the cop car. "Let me go, you brute. You can't make those charges stick."

Clive yanked him close, their faces inches apart. "I know you had something to do with the American woman's kidnapping. At the very least, you know where she is kept. So you can go to jail where I can arrange for you to be another man's entertainment every night, or you can help us crash Bossman's party tonight."

Adrian opened the trunk.

"So, Dillard, old boy..." Clive wrenched the bastard's hands behind his back and cuffed him. "...what will it be, hmm?"

"Fuck you." the Brit spat into Clive's face. "Fuck you both."

Clive wiped spittle from his chin. "Sorry you feel that way." He slugged Dillard's jaw and shoved him face-first into the trunk.

He looked up, his mouth poised for protest, but the trunk lid slammed down and finally shut him up.

"Hope you didn't hurt him too bad," Adrian said. "Now to see Nicholas, then we'll go to Bossman's party?"

"Yup." Clive looked her over. "I like the way you are dressed for night opps."

"Did it for you, Chief."

"Black is not my favorite color."

"Maybe not, but you have to admit, it sure does make my ass look good."

"Get in the car."

Chapter Twenty-Nine

IT TOOK ONLY TWO puffs for Maya to feel the effects of the long brown cigar, which just happened to remind her of Nick's phallic battering ram.

This was only the second time she consciously thought of her illicit lover. She thought about how his hands held her, and his lips kissed her, while his hips repeatedly drove her through a fog of delirious bliss. She remembered holding his glorious length in her hand, then in her mouth, and finally between her legs. It filled her completely. She smiled ruefully in the dark room, choosing to bask under the dim moonlight that crept in through the window as opposed to the bright chandelier above. And as the smoke spilled slowly from her lungs, Maya couldn't help but wonder once again what Nick's role was in her capture and imprisonment.

Plus, where the fuck was he? He was supposed to protect her. "Fucking mall cop."

Maya had to escape as soon as possible. Fucking men for money was not a dream she held dear. "To each his own." Maya giggled as the weed tickled her sense of humor. "Far be it for me to say fucking for a living is fucked up. Porn stars, the women at the Bunny spot cable TV, housewives, all women, according to Taite, fucked for money or favors or a home and security. But this shit. This brothel..." She looked up at the ceiling. "This gig ain't for me, and if you love me, Dad, can you send a little help, you know, to help your daughter out?" She looked at the smoky cigar. "Damn, this shit got me talking to my daddy's ghost." She stared at it for a moment longer before shrugging and taking another puff.

Right now, her mind could think of only two things, revenge and escape. Yet in order to do the former, she would have to achieve the latter.

And she couldn't be too high if any plan was going to work. *But if there ever was a time for me to get higher than high*, she took another hit, *now would fit the bill.*

Escape was an idea, an idea which thrived on knowledge. And since she had no idea where she was, or how the house was laid out, how could she escape? Odds were she was going to have to fuck someone she didn't know tonight.

Maya took another hit.

If I have to fuck a stranger, I need to be high. Maybe, if I fucked him good enough, I might convince him to buy me out of this mess...like my husband bought Rebecca.

She bit her bottom lip as an idea formed in her head. Men were easy, gullible, and egotistic, driven by the will of their dicks. That could work to her advantage. She breathed the smoke out and enjoyed the nirvana as she seemingly floated above the bed.

"Hmm..." She looked around. A plan came to her so easily. *How can I convince a man to let me tie him up?* The curtains each had a gold sash tied around them, and there were pillowcases to blindfold him, and the cloth napkin the utensils were wrapped in to gag his mouth. She grinned wickedly.

"So there it is, my master plan. I'm going to use a little BDSM and fuck some gullible man and get the hell out of here." She took another drag and remembered how Taite had said she'd tried that and failed. If Maya failed, she'd get the *hole, as in piss hole.* She shuddered. Rebecca used her white pussy to get out, *but nobody fucks as good as me.* "I just hope he ain't too fat, or too skinny, or too smelly." She giggled. "I might be asking for too much, but one thing's for sure. He'll be rich." She raised the cigar and made smoke swirls in the air. "Just make sure I stay high during this ordeal, Daddy. Real high...and forgive me because for one night, I'm gonna be the best damn whore on this island."

Knuckles rapped against her door.

She sighed, slowly breathing out the smoke that filled her lungs. *It's time to make a man scream my name.* She glanced at the chair by the cart. *And then the real fun begins.*

She giggled as the door angled open.

***

"Coming, coming." Nicholas sighed, his head heavy with weed and guilt. The banging on his thin door continued as he got off bed, clad only in jeans, and stumbled more than walked to the noisy door and opened it. "What the fuck do you want?"

"Hey, Nick." Clive punched him in the nose.

Nicholas clutched his face as Clive and Adrian pushed into the small hotel room and closed the door behind them. He saw stars as he fell backward on his bed. "Fuck." He shook his head and flared his nose as a small amount of blood trickled out his left nostril.

"How you feeling now?" Clive asked.

Nicholas blinked in an attempt to get his eyes to focus. "What the fuck?"

"You're a hard man to find," Clive said. "But find you we did. And now you're going to help us find the missing American woman."

"What woman? I don't know anything about that woman."

"Really now. Well shit, Adrian." Clive grabbed a chair and slammed it down on the floor in front of Nick's bed then leaned forward on the back of the chair, his face just a foot from Nick's. "Looks like we been lied to."

"What are you talking about?"

"Really." Adrian leaned against the wall across from the bed. "A beautiful woman and a handsome man. You sure your paths..." she took her right index finger and placed it through a hole made by her left thumb and finger, "...didn't cross?"

Nicholas was finally able to focus on the big man who now sat in front of him. "I seen her. How could you miss her? But I didn't know her."

"We got a witness, asshole."

"What witness?"

"Nick. Are we married?"

"What do you mean?"

Clive's hand shot out and slapped Nick upside the head.

He looked at Clive, stung by the speed of the slap. "What did you do that for?"

Clive pointed a meaty finger at him. "Don't say *what* again. Now I asked you, are we married? See, I lie to my wife. She asks me how she looks in an ugly dress. I lie and say, 'Great, dear.' She asks me how I liked a meal she'd burnt, which mind you is rare, I lie and say, 'Great, dear.' Now I asked you to help me find the American woman, and you lie and say, 'I don't know, dear.' So either we are married or you are scared of something, or someone and claim denial."

Nick said nothing.

"I know about Bossman. I know he is in on this. I figure he paid you to get her alone and vulnerable. I mean, you are the perfect guy, big strong strapping and sexy, right, Adrian?"

"Hmm, hmm." She agreed from across the room.

"Yeah, you are a sexy beast, aren't you, Nicholas? So you helped Bossman get her. Now, you can help us get her back. Or do you want option B?"

"Option B?"

Clive pulled his gun and waved it in Nick's face. "Enough said?"

Nick noticed Clive's all-black clothes then glanced at Adrian, who looked a hell of a lot better in similar garb. "You two dressed to rob the place?"

Adrian leaned her back against the wall like she was at a cocktail party. "We're dressed like this so we can sneak into Bossman's mansion to save the vacationing wife."

"But why you gotta sneak in?" Nicholas asked. "Yer the cops—"

"Come on, Nick." Clive huffed and put the gun away. "Don't try to act naïve. We all know Bossman don't like cops...not even me."

"But he's got cops on his payroll."

"So we gotta be discreet," Adrian added. "We don't want to bite the hand that feeds us. We just want to get the girl."

"Tell Bossman to give her up or he goes to jail," Nicholas offered. "That's what I would do."

Clive shook his head. "You can't really think he'll go for that."

Nick stared at Clive. "You know I want him to go down for this...but he's nobody to fuck with."

"I know you were a solider boy like me. Marines, right?"

"Rangers."

"So why you so scared?"

"I ain't scared," Nick replied slowly, trying not to antagonize the Chief, whose short fuse was well known. "I was just wondering why you need *me* to sneak in."

Adrian snapped her fingers. "Because you gotta carry her when we sneak her out."

"Bossman...he never let her go easy."

"We know that. She is exotic." Clive harrumphed. "Hell, you fucked her, and it didn't cost you a dime. Now imagine how much these lifelong billionaire bachelors and married men would *pay* to fuck her. I mean, I'm just on the outside lookin' in, but she seems like she has some top shelf pussy."

"Hmm," Adrian asserted. "I hear she's a bad mamma jamma."

"Ain't that the truth," Clive said. "We know Bossman ain't gonna let some top notch, top shelf, bad mamma jamma pussy go without a fight."

"Or some kind of compensation," Adrian chimed in.

Clive looked at her then at Nick. "Think we could trade this one..." he tipped his head to Adrian, "...for the American girl?"

"I heard that," Adrian replied, playing along. "Just know my kitty is seven-figure kitty."

"Oooh weee." Clive clapped his hands. "Now that sounds like some good pussy." He scowled at Nick. "Maya was some good pussy, wasn't she, Nick?"

"Not good enough to die for, mon." Nick looked at him while images of Maya's body flashed through his mind. "But fucking her meant more to me than just getting some pussy. I mean, her smile, man, her smile was something else. Something wonderful, like she really loved my cock." He sniffed and winced then rubbed the bridge of his nose. "You almost broke it, mon."

"Damn. I hate it when I fall short of a goal."

Nicholas glowered at him. "Fuck you."

The gun was the next thing in Nick's line of sight.

"I would not talk shit to a man with anger issues and a gun." Clive held the gun steady. "Now, you gonna quit whining and help us rescue this vacationing wife with the killer pussy and award winning smile?" He cocked the hammer back. "Or take option B?"

"Just know Bossman hates being wronged." Nick looked past the gun at Adrian who was inspecting her fingernails, and then back at Clive whose steady gun barrel was even closer to Nick's left eyeball. "We get caught, he kill us for sure." There was a deafening silence as the gun remained in Nick's face. "That is why I won't help you, mon."

Clive frowned, un-cocked the hammer, and as quickly as it appeared, the gun disappeared. "Wish you were on our side. But oh well." Clive's frown morphed to a sneer. "Yet, there are a few things I need to know before we go."

"Like what?"

"Who set up the American woman and why?"

Nick felt the air in his lungs freeze.

Adrian glared at him, her well manicured right eyebrow arched. "Answer him."

The heat of anguish spread over his face as he pondered his next words. His fright-filled eyes darted back and forth between the two cops. They had him bent over the proverbial barrel. One wrong word and he'd go to jail for a very long time. "I plead the fifth, mon."

Clive sniffed like he'd smelled a shit pile. "This ain't the USA, mon. We got no fifth. However, tell us what we want to know, and we'll give you immunity. Was it Dillard set her up? How about Gilbert? He's a snake. Or maybe it was you. You set her up?"

"Me?"

"You won't do jail time." Adrian clicked her nails.

Clive spread his arms like Jesus Christ. "No jail time. I mean why waste a good cell on a dead man?"

"Wha-whatcha mean a dead man?"

"The way we see it, you sold the wife off to Bossman, who decided to double-cross you and not pay. So he shoots you, and a few days from now we find your body in the jungle and mourn your untimely death."

"That's if the animals don't eat you up," Adrian put in.

"What-what the fuck? Clive, mon, whatcha doing to me?"

"Explaining how option B works."

"You won't kill me. You're a cop."

"Island justice, mon." The gun was once again in Nick's face. "I will kill you if you do not tell me. So let's begin again. Who set up the wife and why?"

Nick looked at Adrian. "You already know it's Bossman."

"Tell me, motherfucker...how did he know you two shacked up in the Presidential Suite?"

Nick's face showed the anguish of the choice he'd been presented. Finally he looked down, took a deep breath, and confessed like a man facing the gallows. "Rebecca tells me she's fucking the woman's husband, and that he paid for their trip to the island. And Rebecca said the husband gonna pay Bossman and trade in his wife so Rebecca could be his whore back in the states. Rebecca tells Bossman about the wife's fantasy for a big black dick."

"Now ain't that some shit," Clive said.

"It is what it is, ugly, mon, but what it is, is the truth."

"So...where do you come in?"

"You were right. Gilbert paid me to get her into the Presidential Suite... Look, if I had it to do all over again, I would have put her on a plane and got her the fuck out of here."

"Hindsight is always 20/20, Nick. That time has passed. The question is...are you willing to help us rescue her? Be a real hero and not just some American bitch's fantasy fuck toy."

Nick didn't hesitate to answer. "You are the cops. I won't risk my neck to help you do your job. If I steal his new girl, Bossman will kill me."

"It's your fault she's in this mess."

"For that I am sorry, mon."

"Your apology means shit to me," Clive snapped. "You know where she is?"

"I know she's taking Rebecca place. So maybe she's

in Rebecca's room. But I don't know where that is in that big ass mansion."

"That's cool." Clive grinned. "I have someone in the trunk who does."

Nick frowned.

"And you're going to meet him." Clive cold-cocked him with the butt of his gun.

***

Abel Syrus stood outside the door to Maya's bedroom as Gilbert slid the key into place. Sounds of jubilation faintly rang from the party downstairs, slowly replaced by the pounding roar that slammed against his chest. He wiped his palms on his tux as the lock slid away, and Gilbert cracked open the door. "She's all yours, mon."

Abel hesitated to step inside. "It's pretty dark in there," he said with a slight quiver to his voice.

Gilbert grinned. "No need to worry, mon." He took a deep sniff of the air. "She been smoking the best ganja and is more than ready to please you in every way you can imagine."

"I'm not worried," Abel snapped.

Gilbert's grin remained. "Then you should get in there. Two hours is not as long as you think."

"Yeah, you're right." He clapped Gilbert on the shoulder. "And I have waited long enough." He slipped past Gilbert and in through the doorway.

The room was almost dark, the only light from moonbeams peeking between curtains on the far side of the room. Abel coughed on the pungent aroma of weed that permeated the air. A thin sea of smoke hovered above the bed and the woman's silhouette sitting on it.

The door close behind him and the lock slid into place.

"Maya," he said, his voice cracking.

She just sat there.

"Maya, are you all right?"

He heard a faint giggle and then the sound of a match striking to light.

"I heard you the first time, baby." An orange hue illuminated Maya's angelic face. "Forgive me for not being talkative. I'm a little high."

He saw her carefully twist a cigar around between her succulent lips, evenly lighting all sides. Her brown eyes remained on the flame, only looking at him as she blew it out. Shadows again enveloped her beauty.

"I gather you...you are my first customer."

"Maya, how I've waited so long for this."

"Uh, are you cute?"

Abel knew she couldn't see his face in the dim light. "So I've been told."

"That's nice."

Abel heard surprise and delight in her voice, and she seemingly forgot her initial query.

"Now, if you are so cute, why do you pay for sex? Never mind." She waved her hand. "To each his own. Well my name is...wait a minute...you already know my name." She tilted her pretty head to the left. "Silly me. Do I know you?"

"Yes...we've met before." Abel was hesitant to move forward in the unfamiliar confines of the dark room.

"Hmm. And that accent, let me guess...Boston, maybe upstate New York."

"You got me. Syracuse born, raised, and graduated." Stepping forward, he bumped into a food cart and heard her giggle, then the cigar tip grew bright.

"You want some of this fine ganja? Might ease your nerves."

"No thank you. I would however like some more light in here."

He heard her moving, the sheets rustle, but he

couldn't see her in the room's shadows. Then he smelled a sweet fragrance merging with the marijuana.

"Why would you wish to ruin a good time?" Her voice came from directly in front of him, but he could barely see her outline. "Besides, I don't know about you, but fucking in the dark is so, so much more intriguing."

Abel swallowed hard. "Perhaps, but a face like yours deserves to be seen. I have wanted you for a long, long time, and I wish to see you in all your glory—"

He stopped in mid-sentence as Maya's arms wrapped around his neck and her soft lips covered his. He fell into the kiss, and quicker than he'd expected, felt his cock swell within his slacks. She tasted of wine and weed, which he enjoyed as her tongue met his.

She felt his erection press against her, so she reached down to gently brush her right hand over it, making him shiver. She leaned back, and he leaned forward, almost falling. "My, you really do want me."

Abel contained himself as she slipped something into his hand.

"You do look cute up close." She stepped back. "And familiar."

He felt a book of matches in his hand.

"The candles are to your left." She turned and walked away from him.

He could faintly see her hourglass shape swaying as she walked back to the bed.

"My name is Abel Syrus, in case you're interested."

"I'm not."

He coughed as nerves momentarily got the better of him. His eyes had adjusted enough to see the candelabrum with three candles set on a nearby dresser. He pinched a match, struck it, and deftly lit all three candles. He set down the book of matches and lifted the candelabrum.

"No. Leave it there and come here."

"I want to see you," he insisted. "And since I paid for

this pleasure, I get what I want."

"That may be true with a whore, but I'm not a whore." She patted a nearby spot on the bed. "Now come sit next to me and leave the candles there."

Abel shrugged as he paced toward her.

"First, take off your jacket and shoes."

Abel stopped, caught off guard. "Okay." Once he was finished he took another step.

"Do you have the matches?"

"Uh, they're on the dresser."

"Well...go get them."

"For what?"

"So I can light my cigar again, silly." She giggled like a school girl.

Abel walked back to the dresser and retrieved the book of matches. He started toward her again.

"Now take off that tie and shirt."

He stopped. "How about I just get naked?"

"Now, Abel, baby, how about you stop thinking this is your usual jaunt with some whore and realize you're standing at the precipice of a dream come true. Believe me, I'm worth every penny you paid, but how this dream turns out is all on you, baby."

He could see the candlelight sparkle in her eyes.

"Now be a good boy and just do what I say."

Abel realized, not only was she in complete control, but he didn't mind her being in complete control.

Deftly, he draped his shirt and tie over his jacket, which he'd hung on the back of the only chair in the room. Clad in a wife-beater T, black slacks, and matching socks, he walked toward the bed while pulling his undershirt out of his pants to hang loosely about his waist.

Maya looked at him in the candlelight. "Wait a minute. You're the guy from the gym...in my husband's building."

"Yes."

Maya exhaled smoke. “How long have you wanted to fuck me?”

He basked in the glow of her presence. “The first time I saw you, about three years ago at the country club.”

“Small world.”

“Then at the gym in my building. And of course, our delightful conversation at the country club a few weeks back.”

Maya gasped. “So you were stalking me.”

“Just admiring you from afar.”

“Oh?”

“Your shoes were silver and your nail polish matched the dress. I took a picture of you on my phone as did more than half the people at the party. Women envied you, and men lusted for you. I lusted for you. Your beauty took my breath away, just as much then as it does now, yet your husband neglected you. He had such a vibrant beauty on his arm, but he didn’t care.”

“You are perceptive, and let that be the last time we mention my husband...or this night will not end well for you. After all, you paid to fuck me, not piss me off.”

“That’s fair enough.”

She appraised the tanned white man before her. He had graying temples that accentuated his dark brown hair. His lean muscular frame was a far cry from what she had imagined a brothel customer would look like: fat, hairy, and smelling of beer.

“I must admit, I never expected *you* to be my first customer. I mean from the gym, to the club. We have crossed paths so often for so long, I gotta ask, is our meeting here by chance or on purpose?”

“Fate is how I see it. I see this as a blessing.”

She glanced at his bulging crotch. “You blessed with anything else?”

“Let’s find out.” Abel leaned forward to kiss her.

“No, not yet.” She placed the flat of her hand against

his chest. "How did you know I was here?"

He stood there, the bulge in his pants growing. "I got a text. All the VIPs did."

"How much did you pay to fuck me?"

"A gentleman never tells."

"That much huh?"

Abel shook his head. "No amount would be too great for you and now that your husband has foolishly discarded you, I plan to claim you."

"I'm not yours to claim. I belong to Bossman now."

"I'll offer him a million dollars for your freedom."

"You're sexy when you talk money." She pulled him down to sit on the bed, leaned forward, her face inches from his. "You would do that for me?"

"I want you to be my queen."

She sighed. "I've been placed on a high pedestal before, only to fall." She pointed around the room. "It's a long way down."

"I'll never let you fall."

"To place me in such high regard might be a mistake I can't live with."

"No other man will have the privilege of paying for your pussy ever again. Can you live with that?"

She sat back, the candlelight dancing on the cleavage revealed in the gap of her open kimono. "And if I refuse to be your queen?"

"Why would you run from a man who loves you?"

"Because a man who once proclaimed his love just tried to kill me."

"I will do no such thing," Abel insisted.

"How do I know that?" She rested her hand on his knee. "How do I know I'm not going out of the motherfucking frying pan and into the motherfucking fire?"

"Because once we get back home, you and I will start a life anew. One where you will be the object of all my focus and desire." He placed his hand on top of hers. "At least you'll be out of that terrible marriage."

"Wouldn't it be cheaper just to fuck me and forget me?"

"I love you."

"Stop it."

"I'll worship you, but not enshrine you. Your happiness is my joy." His grin returned stronger than ever. "Just know I plan on winning your heart and never letting go."

She gazed into his baby blues, his last four words echoing in her ears. "You're full of shit. All the romantic dribble you just spat, and all the promises you just made, you don't need to say these things to get a blowjob."

"I know, but I'm a romantic, a horny romantic, and while I paid to fuck you, this will mean more than just a fuck to me. Everything I said is the truth, and I think when people share the truth, the sex is a lot better."

She dragged on the cigar before the ash went out. "Do you woo all your whores?"

"You're no whore. You're a walking, talking dream."

Her hand began to finger walk toward his crotch. "Then tonight, all your dreams come true." Her watery eyes reflected the blaze of candle fire. "Tonight I'm yours, bought and paid for. So tell me, Abel, my king, will you make love to your queen or fuck her like a whore?" Her hand reached his engorged dick.

Abel swallowed hard, his throat dry. "You're not a whore, so I'll make love to you."

She leaned into him and softly kissed him. "Give it your best shot." She unzipped his pants and released a very lovely cock that seemed stretched to its limits. Pretending he loved her had its advantages.

Her mind raced with the possibility of him buying her freedom.

Then she'd kill that no good fuckin' husband of hers.

***

"You got a plan, I take it," Adrian said from the passenger seat of Clive's speeding patrol car. She was loading up her pump shotgun as he drove toward Bossman's estate down the shore.

"I don't."

"Then how are we going to play this?"

"I have no fucking clue."

"You trust either of them to help us?" A shell clicked into the load slot. "After all, you stuffed them both in the trunk."

Clive shrugged and jabbed his thumb at the back of the car. "Fuck 'em."

Adrian pumped a shell into the chamber. "Agreed."

"Look, we just need them to get us in. Once inside, we search the house quietly as possible, find the vacationing wife, and sneak her ass out of there."

"Why are you so dead set against asking him outright?"

"Bossman speaks the language of currency and bullets. I don't have the currency and damn sure don't have enough bullets to take on Bossman's henchmen. We don't have a warrant for a no-knock raid, so sneaking her out is the only option."

"You really thought this through," Adrian chided. "I think we need more men."

"I can't trust anybody but you."

She showed him a proud smile. "Then why don't we ever fuck? I mean, if you trust me, then you know I won't say shit to Annora."

Bossman's estate came into view.

"What Annora don't know won't hurt her," she added.

"But I would know." Clive looked at her. "I'm a married man. A happily married man."

"So why do I see your eyes wander around my body

all the time?"

"I'm married, not blind."

"I still remember that delightfully freaky rendezvous in your office. I want you, Chief. I respect your marriage, but damn it, I want you."

"My wife isn't stupid. She knows we got a thing for each other. In fact, she wants you out of the picture, says I should transfer you to another jurisdiction."

"Clive, please, you wouldn't." She pouted.

He steered the car close to a cracked grey perimeter wall, switched off the headlights, and stared at the lighted mansion before him. "Focus," he said, looking at Adrian.

Her eyes met his. "Yeah, easy for you to say. You don't have drippy drawers."

Silence sat between them as they stared at one another, unknowingly drawing closer and closer until their lips touched and passion swept through their bodies. Clive took her face into his hands while Adrian scrambled out of her seatbelt and climbed onto his lap. He held her round buttocks as thoughts of Annora were swept away by the lust filling his loins for Adrian.

"Oh God," she breathed when his right hand found her sensitive nipple. She reached down for his cock. "I've wanted your dick for so fucking long," she cried into his hungry mouth and rubbed the bulge in his pants. "So, so, so fucking long."

"I want to eat your pussy," he stole a breath, "and fuck it 'til you can't walk."

Banging reverberated from the trunk. "Hey, we can hear you."

"Shit."

Then a light shined from in front of the car, forcing her to turn around on his lap. The car was suddenly bathed in a dozen flashlight halos. Men rushed out of the shadows.

All Clive thought about was *Annora*...a grieving widow.

“Well, well, well,” a voice bellowed. A dozen weapons clicked and cocked. “Mr. Chief, why don’t cha come inside, get a room, and fuck that woman properly?”

Adrian and Clive shared a *we’re-fucked* look as the bulge between his legs swiftly deflated like a punctured balloon.

Chapter Thirty

THE DOOR TO VALDIS' private jet popped open and he ambled down the steps. The cool night air helped wake him up from the nap he'd taken while en route to the island.

This is some bullshit. He never wanted to pay for Rebecca in the first place.

Now I gotta pay more to get her back. Fuck. If not, I'd have to take my wife back, and that's the last thing I want.

Carrying a duffle bag full of cash, he saw a black Rolls Royce idling on the tarmac; the driver, wearing black, leaned lazily against the driver's door. "Sir," he said as Valdis walked his way. "No luggage?"

"Fast turnaround." Valdis thought about his secretary, Nikki, and the way she trembled when he licked the nub on her pussy. He had to leave her hot and bothered, and the frustrated look in her eye when he closed the bedroom door almost broke his heart.

Not.

The driver reached for the duffle bag, but Valdis yanked it out of his reach. "I got this. You just get in the car and take me to that fat fuck Bossman." He got into the backseat and slammed the door shut.

The driver nearly said something about the disrespectful way Valdis spoke of Bossman, but he remembered what happened to the previous driver who failed to properly handle an asshole customer. *The customer is always right.* So he took a deep breath, opened the driver's door, and got in behind the wheel.

Valdis looked out at his black and gold jet. His name

was emblazoned on the fuselage. He recalled a time when he had no home and had to sleep in his car, then on a friend's couch when his car got repossessed. *Now I'm a fucking billionaire*. "And a bad motherfucker."

"Sir?" The driver looked at Valdis via the rearview. "You say something?"

Valdis glared at him. "Fuck off and drive."

"No problem, sir, will do."

The car drove away and the jet faded from view.

***

Clive felt like an utter fool as he and Adrian were shoved through the servant's entryway into Bossman's mansion. Dillard and Nick walked behind them, unshackled, yet still herded along at gunpoint. Clive looked at Adrian who just gave him a wan smile.

How the fuck am I going to get out of this? Worse, what if Annora finds out about his near miss with Adrian's pussy?

He was sure Nick and Dillard would love nothing more than to blab what they'd heard from the trunk. His concerns came to an abrupt halt when they arrived at Bossman's office.

"Sit." He and Adrian were pushed into a pair of high back leather chairs beside a hand-carved mahogany desk. Right away, strong hands yanked their arms behind the chairs, and heavy duty zip ties were applied to their wrists.

"Unhand me," Dillard shouted. "I'm a VIP guest here." He straightened his blood-soaked shirt. "Is the Chief restrained?" he asked one of the captors who nodded. Dillard smiled as he stood in front of Clive. "I told you your days as Chief were numbered. Now your life has mere minutes remaining." His smile grew as he reared back and punched Clive in the face. "See how you like it."

Clive's head snapped to the right. He spat on the

carpet. "Your fist is soft like a feather, bitch." He shook blood from his lip and glowered at Dillard. "That all you got?"

"Fuck you." Dillard reared back, but Nick caught his arm. "No, mon. Please allow me. The cop made me ride in the damn trunk with *your* fuckin' ass."

"Yes please," Clive said flippantly. "Allow him. He doesn't hit like a three-year-old girl."

"Why you son of a bitch..." Dillard struggled against Nick as the double doors to the office flew open.

"Now this is truly a surprise." Bossman was clad in a white tuxedo with black piping and accessorized with a thick black cane adorned with an ivory handle. He took off his black and white fedora as he charged into the room. "I was expecting Dillard's pompous ass." He twirled the hat around his right hand. "But not our illustrious Chief of Police, nor my favorite lady cop, and..." He gestured to Nick. "...the head of resort security. Got an all-star cast tonight." Bossman walked behind the desk, set his hat on the corner, and sat in a comfortable leather chair. The big man leaned back while flashing a cynical smile at the two cops. "Adrian, my dear, have you finally considered my very generous job offer?" He winked at her.

"I'm not ready for a career change," she replied sweetly. "Yet, I think we both know I would make you a fortune with this booty."

"Are you bloody flirting?" Dillard stepped in Bossman's field of view. "They are here to get the American wife, you ass. They kidnapped me and my head of security. They threatened our lives."

Bossman spread his hands "Very heroic, I'd say."

"Heroes die all the time. I say we kill this son of a bitch." Dillard kicked Clive in the shin. "He's overstepped his bounds by not adhering to the rules. Hell, the brute nearly broke my fucking nose."

"Hush, fool," Bossman ordered. "This is my house,

my party. And no one will die here without my say-so. Especially if they were seen coming here." He grinned at Clive. "Besides, my dear sweet sister would be upset if I killed him."

"Annora would cut off your balls and wear them for earrings." Clive didn't laugh. "All the more reason for you to give me the woman and let us all go. No questions asked."

"Clive..." Bossman stroked his beard. "Now you know handing over the American would go against the very fiber of my nature. However, I am open to negotiation." He pointed at Adrian. "How about a fair trade, one gorgeous woman for another. That would make explaining to Annora how we found you with your hands all over Adrian's sweet ass a whole lot more unnecessary."

"He called my ass sweet." Adrian grinned at Clive.

"Hello." Dillard waved at Bossman. "Yoo whoo. I was talking here."

Bossman looked at him, far from amused. "And you're done."

"I want him dead."

"I am not sure why I have to say no twice. Besides, killing the Chief in the middle of the investigation of a missing American woman would be poor judgment and hard to get past the Governor." Bossman shifted in his chair. "Besides, my sister would never forgive me, and I'd rather keep the family jewels in my pants where they are, thank you very much."

"You own the fucking island," Dillard persisted.

"Yes, yes I do. In fact, the Governor is upstairs with two of my finest women. How do you think he would feel if I killed the Chief right under his nose?"

"Who gives a bloomin' fuck? Kill this man."

Bossman leaned forward. "That sounds like an order. Are you giving me orders, Dillard?"

"It was an order, you fat bastard. I pay you good

money, and when I want something, I get it. And what I want is this man dead. Now you do as I say, or you will force my hand, and I will have you replaced."

Bossman pursed his lips. "Why, Mr. Dillard, I was unaware your balls had dropped." He laughed.

Dillard straightened his shirt and pointed down at the desk phone. "Are you going to acquiesce to my demand, or shall I make a single phone call and end your life as you know it?"

"Okay then..." Bossman scowled cunningly. "So I have two choices. I just want to be clear that you have given me two choices. I can kill Clive or you'll have someone replace me."

"You bearded fuck, I have given you—"

Bang.

A single bullet pierced Dillard's skull, creating a hole just above the bridge of his nose.

Clive watched the man teeter before he crumpled to the floor in a lifeless heap. Blood gushed from the wound that would never heal. A look of surprise and bewilderment plastered the now dead man's face, and for a moment, Clive felt sorry for the bastard.

"Make that three choices." Bossman returned the smoking gun to his desk drawer. "Anyone else want to tell me what the fuck to do in my own damn house?"

***

Albert Valdis strolled confidently down the hallway toward Bossman's office. The driver was leading the way. He heard the house party revelry all around him, and for a moment he felt envious. Normally he would be one of the partiers, his face deep between the thighs of some wanton woman screaming his name because he'd paid her to scream his name. However, today was about finishing a business transaction, where everything was clear to see, and all questions asked were answered.

Except one: what was he going to do with Rebecca? If he brought her home, Nikki would have a fit.

He and Nikki already had a thing, and Rebecca's role in this con was done. While he enjoyed fucking her, he enjoyed fucking Nikki a whole lot more. She was classy, intelligent, and the only woman he felt he could trust. Nikki wasn't money hungry like Rebecca, nor was she in need of cuddle time like Maya. Nikki was content with her place in his world, and that made her special.

So he couldn't just take Rebecca back with him. She had to stay here...he smiled as a plan formulated. He would pay Bossman for his trouble and then just let him keep her and Maya. He'd have two top-shelf pussies to peddle.

Two jean clad guards armed with Uzis stood outside Bossman's double doors. "He's here to see Bossman," the driver said.

"Bossman busy," one of them said, watching Valdis with some disdain.

"He'll see me." Valdis used the duffle bag of money to shove his way past the driver and the armed guards, and then barged into Bossman's office. He looked around the room, his eyes first falling on Dillard's body. A blade of fear stabbed his chest. "Ah...Perhaps I should come back another time."

The door slammed shut behind him, and several guns were now pointed in his direction.

"Mr. Valdis." Bossman stood from the chair behind his desk. "I see you are your usual disrespectful self." The big man looked at Clive who was shaking his head. "See how men with money think their affluence buys them reverence?"

"I can buy whatever I want, and I want to resolve things with you concerning Rebecca and my wife. I don't want either one of them back, and I'm prepared to pay you for your trouble."

Bossman laughed. “How ironic.”

Valdis frowned. “You get both women *and* the money. What’s ironic about that?”

“Well for one, this man here, this is our illustrious Chief of Police Clive Battersby, and she is his right hand cop, Adrian O’Hare. And this,” he gestured to Nick, “is the man who thoroughly fucked your wife, Maya.”

“Still not sure how this is ironic.” Valdis glanced at Nick.

The bitch just had to fuck a black man.

“See, Clive is here to rescue Maya from my evil clutches, and you are here to buy Rebecca’s freedom.” Bossman leaned toward Clive. “Only thing is...you are missing one very important fact.”

“What fact?” Valdis sounded annoyed.

Bossman laughed. “Maya killed Rebecca.”

Valdis dropped the duffle bag of money on the floor. “What...how..?”

“Clive, I have a confession. This man...” he pointed to Valdis, “...paid me to exchange his wife for Rebecca, essentially making Maya disappear, but he also wanted me to kill his wife so she would never reappear. I, of course, declined to kill such a fine asset to my business, so he told Rebecca to kill Maya. However, that didn’t work out so well for Rebecca. I, being a businessman who sees opportunity everywhere, decided to take his money and rent out his wife for top dollar. Hell, tonight I pimped her to a man for three grand.” He looked at Valdis. “She is being fucked as we speak. There are men willing to pay ten times that amount to fuck your wife, my friend, yet you won’t take her pussy for free. No. You want her dead.” Bossman indicated the duffle bag. “I see you brought my money. Too bad you’re out the girl it buys. Not my fault, mon.”

“How did she kill Rebecca, you fat—?”

“Easy,” Clive chimed in. “I would not talk about his weight. The last man got the bullet—”

Valdis silenced him with a fist to the jaw. "I did not tell you to speak."

Bossman shouted, "Do not assault my guests in my house."

Valdis pulled a gun and rushed him, the muzzle now pressed against the big man's hairy chin. "How did Rebecca die?"

Bossman's men cocked their weapons.

"Easy, easy," Bossman said to his men as well as Valdis. "No need for such rudeness. It's an easy question to answer."

"So enlighten me."

"Your wife stabbed her with her own poison needle."

Valdis bared his front teeth. "Maya has more dumb luck, that fuckin' whore."

Nick shouted, "Maya is not a whore."

"Motherfucker!" He swung the gun around and shot Nick twice in the chest, propelling him into the wall, and then thrust the hot end of the barrel into the hanging beard beneath Bossman's rounded chin, keeping the guards at bay. "Now you bring that whore to me," Valdis ordered. "I will kill her myself."

Nick slid to the floor, gasping for air.

Clive and Adrian shared a look, as if deciding that when their chance came they would act. Then sadly, Clive looked at Nick as he lay motionless on the floor, his life ebbing from his body with every passing second.

"Go get her," Bossman ordered the guard nearest to the office door. "Make sure she is dressed appropriately."

The man nodded to Bossman before he rushed away.

"I want your wife to remain alive," Bossman growled. "She is payment for Rebecca's loss."

"Maya fucked up this whole deal. She deserves to die for that."

Bossman strained against the gun barrel. "I don't take kindly to being ripped off."

"Then I'll kill you too."

"Easy to say," Clive said. "Might not be as easy to do."

"Did I say for you to speak? I just killed the man who fucked my wife. You think I won't kill your black ass?"

"If you do, you won't make it off this island alive."

"Just what the fuck do you know?" Valdis scoffed. "Money goes a long way. It gave my needy, clingy, soon to be dead wife everything she ever fucking wanted. So let me ask you again, what the fuck makes you think I won't shoot you and this fat fucking lowdown dirty pimp dead?"

Clive coughed. "I 'spose your money buys many things, but it can't guarantee your safe passage. Your money won't get you out of this house, because it is loyalty to this fat fucking dirty pimp that'll get you killed."

"Don't forget *lowdown*, Chief," Adrian added.

"Oh yes, lowdown dirty pimp. Your money won't stop his employees' bullets."

Valdis snorted. "As soon as my wife comes through that door, I'll kill her, and you, and maybe this fat fucking lowdown dirty pimp, too, even though I kind of like the guy."

Bossman smiled. "Thank you."

Clive struggled against his ties. "I would just like to know what Maya did to warrant her death. What is so bad about her?"

"I don't have to explain myself to you."

Clive shrugged. "Okay, you're just a punk ass bitch who wants to kill a woman. Tough guy, huh?"

For a moment, Clive could tell Valdis wanted to point the gun at him, but the steely eyes of shotgun-wielding Gilbert and the other three guards in the room must've made him think twice about killing their Chief of Police.

Instead, Valdis took a deep long breath and exhaled. "When I shoot you, I'll be sure to aim for the big balls you have, which seem to make you think you're in charge of this situation."

"Where you gonna shoot me?" Adrian asked. "My pussy is much too sweet to be shot." She spread her legs and smiled wide. "You should try some."

Adrian's alluring answer caught Valdis off guard, and the henchman closest to him decided to take advantage. The man lunged forward, but Valdis caught him making the move, swiveled the gun from beneath Bossman's hairy chin, and fired at the would-be hero.

***

With his luscious cock in her mouth, Maya admired the ruggedly handsome man beneath her. Her hand glided in time with her mouth as she stroked and sucked his iron shaft. She watched his face contort with pleasure as she licked the contours of his bulging head, causing a trickle of pre-cum to dribble onto her tongue. "Mmm," she groaned as his hips began to move in synch with her mouth.

"Oh my God." He groaned. "You're going to make me come too soon." He ran his hands down the contours of her beautiful face and lifted her head up, freeing his dick from her mouth.

Maya crawled up his body and soon they were kissing again as she began to grind her pussy against his hardness. "I have an idea." She licked the edge of his lips. "We can make you last longer if we play a little game. Do you trust me?"

"Of course."

"Get naked."

"You first." Abel slipped her robe off her shoulders. His eyes danced across her firm full breasts as his hands caressed her silky skin. A groan escaped her throat as he gently massaged her nipples.

Maya took his hard erection in her hands. "Promise me something," she said, allowing his hand to wander down between her legs.

"Yes," he breathed as his fingers probed her folds. "Anything, anything for you, Maya."

"Promise me you'll make me come. Promise me you won't just get your rocks off and call it good. Don't leave me hanging like my husband did."

"I'll take you to the moon and beyond, baby."

Abel leaned in to kiss her, but she held up her hand. "Sit down in that chair."

"Why?"

"I told you I have an idea."

"Okay." Unfolding from her embrace, he stood, dropped his pants, and yanked off his underwear.

She grabbed his protruding cock and led him to the chair where she shoved his other clothes off the chair-back and onto the floor. "Sit."

He sat and watched her stroll back to the bed and bend over, displaying her sensational ass as she freed a pillow from a pillowcase. He admired the curves of her deliciously shaped body as she strode to the window and took a sash from around a curtain. Twirling it, she walked back to him, smiling broadly as her naked body sent warm surges of desire through his loins.

"Now close your eyes."

Abel nodded, excited about the possibilities of game-play with Maya.

She looked at the naked man sitting in front of her. His rock hard dick stuck straight up. "You have a great cock." She rolled the pillow case lengthwise. "Long and thick, but not too much of either." She placed the pillowcase over his eyes, but he jerked back. "Don't be afraid." She knotted the pillowcase behind his head. "Your cock is just right for me, just how I love it."

"Good." He breathed. "My cock loves you, too."

Gently, she took his right hand and drew it around to the back of the chair. "I can't wait to ride it...or do you want me to suck it some more? Hmm?" She put his left hand behind him and tied the sash around his wrists.

"I want both," he said breathlessly. "I want you to bring me to the edge and when I'm hard as steel—"

"Like you are now?" She swung her leg over his thighs and placed her pussy on the head of his granite dick. "Do you feel me, baby?"

"Oh, yes..."

She slipped just the head of his shaft inside her wet opening. God knew she wanted to take it all in with one mighty plunge, but she hovered there, her legs trembling as she straddled him. *Focus girl. Focus*. However, he twitched his hips and she succumbed to her desires with a gasp as her honey pot swallowed more and more of his throbbing cock. "Damn." She groaned as his dick filled her completely. Her eyes rolled back and her lashes fluttered.

"Oh, Maya." He moaned, loving the feel of his member as it worked its way into her deep, wet snatch.

"Oh damn..." Her body trembled. "Oh my God, you feel so fucking good."

"Are you sure it's me and not that weed you've been smoking?"

"It's all you, baby."

Despite the blindfold, his wanton mouth found her right breast and his tongue circled her nipple a few times before he came up for air. "This is what it's like to be loved." He rotated his hips and thrust upward at the same time. "Untie me so I can wrap my arms around you."

She moaned in his ear. "Just fuck me, baby. Fuck me like the whore that I am." Maya closed her eyes and bucked her hips, totally entwined in the arms of bliss.

Abel felt her vaginal walls clutch his shaft then drown his hardness in a flood of her juicy euphoria.

She looked at him speechless, surprised by how quickly he'd brought her to a climax.

Abel grinned "I told you I'd make you come."

"You did." Maya continued to slide up and down his now cum covered erection. "Now it's your turn."

"May I look at you?" he asked while throbbing inside her.

She looked at the blindfolded man she was fucking. "Uh, no." She reached for the cloth napkin on the cart. "No, baby. Not until you come." She twisted her hips as she gripped the back of the chair, a clandestine move to hang the napkin, as his clothes once were. "But not yet. I wanna cum all over this good dick one more time."

Abel imagined her face glowing with rapture in the candlelight. "Please let me see you. Hold you. I've waited a long time to pleasure you, and I want to see the passion in your eyes. I want to feel your body in my arms."

She rubbed her hands across his fevered skin, making him shiver. "You feel me, don't cha, baby?" She twisted his nipples in her fingertips and sent new shockwaves through his body.

"Oh yes," he said as his cock begged to be fucked. "I feel you."

Maya's back arched. His rigid shaft fit her perfectly, stretching her walls and finding the right spots to rub, and soon she started bouncing up and down, her legs trembling with each stroke as another explosion began to build inside her. "Oh shit," she cried as her abs tightened. Her thighs shuddered and pulsating spasms rippled deep inside her vagina.

He laughed with joy as he felt a flood of her cum rain down his hardness while his own climax was rapidly building.

Then without a word, Maya stood up.

"What?" His head twisted to and fro in bewilderment. "Maya, darling, where are you?"

"Gotta pee," she said from the bathroom.

He heard a toilet flush, and then the sound of running water. "Please come back." His shiny slick cock throbbed up and down in total abandonment. "I'm almost there."

Maya snuck out of the bathroom and slinked to the dresser. Quietly, she opened the drawer and donned her blue jeans and gray t-shirt.

"What are you doing, Maya?"

"Just getting something to end this just right." She stared at his rock hard member begging for her body as it twitched in sexual agony. She had to force herself to look away as she slipped into her tennis shoes.

"Oh, darling, please." Abel whined like a child.

Maya pursed her lips and walked around the chair then leaned down and licked his neck. "You ready to come for me, baby?"

Abel nodded rapidly. "Yes. Yes."

Maya's grin grew as she took his hardness in her hand and began to stroke him. "Oh, I'm gonna make you come like you made me come."

His hips moved in union with her hand, and Maya felt it throb as a single stream of cum spat out and landed on the floor by the dresser. "Oh my," she whispered in his ear. "You're coming, baby."

Abel's face contorted with pleasure as a second stream flowed from his tip. She stopped stroking him and squeezed the shaft, making his pink head swell as his rigid cock pulsated twice then released five thick streams of cum with five mighty throbs. He screamed in ecstasy then Maya stuffed the napkin in his mouth.

A sudden and hard series of knocks crashed at the door, jarring her abruptly from his rapture. Abel's head twisted in the door's direction and he mumbled something that sounded like *help* around the napkin.

Maya pulled on his cock and added a painful twist. "Shut the fuck up. Nice cock or not, I'll break the motherfucker off if you even think about making another sound."

She turned back to the door. "Who is it?"

"Bossman need ya," a male voice shouted. "I'm coming in."

"We're busy in here."

The lock clicked.

Maya grabbed the dome from the tray and raced to the door. It opened just as she got there. A lean man with dreadlocks stepped in. He wore a machinegun over his shoulder and a revolver on his belt. His eyes went straight to the naked man tied up in the chair then his forehead met the metal dome.

Bang. Lights out.

He hit the floor like a sack of weed.

She looked down at him while Abel fought to free his hands.

The man stared blankly at Maya, the bridge of his nose shattered and bleeding. She quickly relieved him of the machinegun and revolver.

Abel was grunting something, and making the chair bounce as his struggles grew more fervent. She raced to him and placed the gun against his head. "Enough."

Instantly he stopped fighting, and his once proud erection began to wane under the weapon's threat.

"You got a great cock, but I'm not your whore. I'll never be your queen and I'm not available for purchase. Now, I'm walking out of here, and I need you to stay calm and cool."

He grunted something unintelligible.

"You're welcome for the pussy, and by the way, thank you for the great dick."

Abel twisted in his chair and called her name from around the napkin but only heard the door open and shut.

Maya stooped in the hallway to tie her sneakers.

Elgin strode around a corner. The big man was unarmed, and his eyes grew in surprise as she aimed the machinegun at him.

"Take me to Bossman," she ordered.

"Okay. Don't shoot me, mon. You know I ain't against cha. But you not getting out of here alone. Let me help you."

Maya looked at him uneasily. "I don't trust you."

"I hate Bossman just like you. I stuck here 'til my sista be free. Please." He gestured with his hand. "Give me the machinegun."

Maya looked into his eyes and knew he was right. If she was going to get out of here alive, she needed his help. "Okay." She held out the machinegun.

Elgin took it. "Put the other gun out of sight and walk ahead of me. I'll tell you where to go."

"Not a chance." She wasn't giving up her back to him. "You lead the way." She brandished the handgun. "One wrong move and I'll put a bullet in your ass."

Elgin laughed. "You a lot harder than you look, princess."

They headed to Bossman's office, neither aware of the firestorm that awaited them.

Chapter Thirty-One

ELGIN GUIDED MAYA down a hallway where sounds of revelry and ecstasy mixed together in a chorus of party and pleasure. Maya felt her heart pounding in her chest as the idea of confronting Bossman grew closer to becoming reality.

She had no idea if Elgin was a man of his word, yet, only he and Taite had showed her any compassion while the others treated her like a piece of meat. He glanced back at her, and she gave him a quick nod to let him know she appreciated his concern.

They stopped at the double set of doors. "That's weird," Elgin said. "No guards outside his office. He always has men out here during a party."

Angry voices emanated faintly from inside.

"Sounds like trouble. Keep your gun hidden and stay close behind me."

Maya stuffed the gun behind her waistband and drew the t-shirt over it.

As Elgin opened the door and stepped in, a shot rang out. He crouched to a combat position. Two more shots rang out.

Elgin flew backward and crashed into her. The back of her head slammed to the floor and the room began to spin. She heard a familiar voice scream, "Is the bitch dead?"

The words echoed in her head as she tried to get her bearings.

Is the bitch dead?

Maya moved her head. A sharp jolt of pain ripped

through her neck. She froze. Something wet, warm, and sticky dripped on her face, and she tried to wipe it away, but something heavy was on top of her and she couldn't move her arms. As her eyes revealed the truth of her situation, horror filled her mind.

Elgin's body was on top her. His blood dripped on her face.

No, no, no.

She looked past Elgin, and her eyes met her husband's. She knew he wasn't here to rescue her...but probably finish what Rebecca started.

He blinked in astonishment. "She's alive. No fucking way." He squeezed the trigger of his silver handgun only to hear a dull click in the dead silent room.

Bossman grinned. "Uh oh."

Clive laughed. "No amount of money is going to help you now."

Bossman gestured to his men, but before they could surround the now dumbfounded billionaire, Maya freed her right hand, snatched the machinegun that had fallen beside her and fired wildly at the man she once would have died for. Three rounds spat from the gun, and Albert fell to the floor, writhing in agony.

She dropped the gun and struggled to get out from under Elgin's dead weight. A guard rushed over and helped her, while Gilbert trained his sawed-off shotgun on Valdis. She knelt beside Elgin as his chest heaved, but the air rushed from his lungs through the unwanted hole. His eyes danced wildly as he struggled to breathe, then one last fall of his chest came before he lay still. She squeezed the man's hand. "I'm so sorry you got involved in my fucked up life."

"Do I shoot him now, boss?" Gilbert asked, his eyes gleaming with anticipation.

Maya looked at her husband who was moaning hoarsely. A bullet had ripped through his collar bone.

“Motherfucker.” Maya grabbed the gun from her waistband and waved it at Gilbert. “You need to move aside,” she told the shotgun-toting guard. “*I’m* gonna kill him.”

Bossman laughed. “Hell hath no fury.”

“You’re right, you bastard.” She shot Bossman in his left arm. “That’s for making me your whore.”

Gilbert swung his shotgun on Maya, but Bossman raised his hand. “No.”

“But boss...you’re bleeding.”

“I had that coming. She’s no whore.” He chuckled despite the pain.

“Now tell your man to step aside. This is between me and my husband.”

“Don’t shoot him,” Clive shouted. “He ain’t worth the paperwork.”

She looked his way, then at Bossman. “Why are they tied up?”

“They crashed my party.”

Clive said, “We came to rescue you.”

“Some great fucking rescue.” Maya’s eyes darted around the room and fell on two bodies. The one in a blood-soaked tux, she didn’t know, but Nick’s body she knew. It lay still against the wall in a pool of tarry goo. “What happened to Nick?”

“Valdis shot him.” Clive stared at her intensely. “He died defending your honor.”

Rage burned a hole in her chest. She stalked toward her husband. Gilbert let her get to him. She pointed the gun at his head. “Must you destroy everything good in my life?”

“Maya, baby, please—”

“I’m not your baby.”

“Now, Maya—”

She fired off a shot that zipped past his right ear and splintered the wall behind him.

He pissed himself. "I need a doctor."

"I just want to know one thing before I blow your fucking brains out."

"No, please—"

"Why do you want me dead?"

"Don't be silly, woman."

"I loved you while you and Rebecca were fucking behind my back, and I'm sure Nikki's in on the fun too. Why did you do this to me?"

"For money...what else?" He grabbed an agonizing breath and sat up on the floor. "Plain and simple. Your company is making a lot of money, and since you refused to sell it to me, I knew I'd get it anyway, if you died, so, yeah, I set you up. I used Rebecca to get you here, but I didn't expect Bossman wouldn't have the balls to kill you." He laughed a haunting kind of cackle. "Rebecca did though...I made her an offer she couldn't refuse. It's always been about the money for me. Now put that gun down and get me a doctor."

"He's an asshole," Clive said. "But he's right about the gun. Put it down."

"Don't shoot him," Adrian put in. "You think this whore house is bad, it's heaven compared to a Jamaican jail."

She blew out a long breath, "Fuck it," and dropped the gun to her side. "They're right. You're not worth my time."

"Maya, baby—"

"Shut the fuck up. I was so damn stupid, blinded by love and the need to be loved, but to you I was just window dressing. Your trophy wife, a woman worth more dead than alive." She took a deep breath. "You broke my heart, but you know, I'm already over you."

Valdis looked at her as he struggled to his feet. "You don't mean that. My money is too good to walk away from."

"I've got my own money."

Gilbert drew close to him, shotgun pointed at his midsection, but his eyes drifted to Maya as she stepped over Dillard and walked to Nick's body. She kneeled down next to him and brushed her hands over his eyes, closing them. "You foolish man."

Valdis snatched the shotgun from Gilbert and struck the butt against his chin. He dropped like a dead mule.

"Bitch."

She turned to Valdis, and their eyes locked.

Shotgun at his hip and aimed at Maya, he stepped forward, only to be tripped up by Clive's suddenly extended foot. As Valdis hit the carpet, the shotgun discharged. The blast tore away the right side of his face.

Another gun banged. A bullet zipped through his skull. Maya looked up at Bossman. His desk drawer was open. A gun smoked in his only good hand.

"Fuck," was all Clive could say.

Chapter Thirty-Two

CLIVE PARKED THE patrol car in the familiar clearing just as the sun's rays began to peak over the horizon. He looked to the passenger seat at Maya. "It's the only way. Bad publicity will kill tourism on our island for many years to come."

She sighed. "I love this place, Clive. I'd hate to know that my husband tarnished its image."

He got out of the car. She did the same and followed him to the trunk. "You can carry the lye." He popped the lid.

Maya looked in at the bag of lye set next to her naked husband and his duffle bag. She hefted out the lye. It wasn't light, but she bent her legs and hoisted it up on her shoulder.

Clive smiled, impressed at her effort, then dragged Valdis out and draped him over his right shoulder.

Carefully, he led her across the rocky beachfront toward his dumping ground. Stopping at the edge of the abyss, he asked her, "Got anything you want to say?"

"I hope he rots in hell."

"Amen." He tossed Valdis in. The body thudded down the rocky gorge and landed at the unseen bottom with a solid thump. He looked at Maya. "Give me the lye and step back."

She did as she was told and watched Clive rip open the bag and pour it down into the crevice, sure to cover Valdis' body and mask any stink he made in death.

Maya peered down the crevice and saw nothing. "What did Bossman tell the coroner and the Governor's investigators?"

Clive folded the bag. "He's my brother in law."

"So?"

"He owns most of us in one way or another. They'll buy his story that Dillard did the killings before Bossman killed him in self defense. As far as the world knows, Albert Valdis simply disappeared with three million dollars."

"And I'm the grieving wife."

"You're free, Maya." They made it back to the car. He tossed the empty bag in the trunk and looked at the duffle bag stuffed with three million dollars. "Watcha gonna do with all that money?"

"It's blood money. I don't want it."

Clive sighed. "To be truthful, I could use it. My wife, Annora, she'd appreciate a good payday."

Maya nodded. "It's all yours, Clive."

He slammed the lid shut.

"Don't spend it all in one place."

"I'll keep that in mind." He dusted off his hands and got in to drive.

***

A gentle breeze blew Maya's hair into her face as she and Portia stood over Cole's grave. He loved the island, and one time he'd said he wanted to be buried here. The women decided to have him and Nick buried on the same day, with Nick's funeral an hour before Cole's. Nobody knew for sure what became of Rebecca's body, but rumor had it the sharks got her. Dillard's body was shipped back home to Britain, and yesterday, Elgin was buried in his family's plot. Taite refused to speak to Maya, let alone even look at her.

Dressed in black, the women stood alone while Clive, his wife, and other mourners who were kind enough to come walked back to their cars. Adrian was absent, on duty protecting the good of the island.

"Must we go back to the resort?" Portia asked timidly. "I just want to go home...like Larry and Trevor did."

"It's a local tradition to celebrate life instead of death." She linked her hand to Portia's. "Besides, you won't be alone."

Portia nodded weakly as she continued to stare down. "I wonder where Cole is now. Heaven? Maybe hell...after what we did the other night."

Maya smiled. "He's in your heart and by your side until you two unite again."

"So you believe in life after death?"

"I do." Maya laughed. "In fact, Nick and my dad are getting along just fine. I'm sure Cole doesn't want you to be sad for long."

"How do I go on without him?"

Maya was silent as her own pain cradled her heavy heart. "I don't know how. I just know you'll find a way."

"I once read this quote on the Internet. It said something like *those we love don't truly die but live through us each and every day."*

Maya tugged her toward the road and the waiting limousine. "Come on. We have the rest of our lives to mourn good men. I think they would rather we celebrate than cry."

"I wish I had your strength."

Maya smiled at Portia. "And I wish I had the love you two shared."

***

Maya stood on the balcony of her suite and stared at the moon above. She wore a turquoise nightgown and drank rum from a glass shaped like a coconut. Just as a shooting star streaked across the sky, she raised her glass in the air. “Here’s to you, Nick.”

Portia emerged from the shower with only a towel around her midsection. “I never thought I would get high after a funeral.” She sucked on a joint and made her way to Maya’s side.

They’d grown close in the past few days. Portia helped Maya navigate through the endless questions from the press about her disappearance, and then the disappearance of her husband. Maya could only remember that she was taken from the resort by unknown assailants. She was blindfolded, tied up, and drugged until Clive and Adrian rescued her. Maybe it was a kidnapping for money. Maybe her husband fell victim when he came to pay the ransom. He was gone. The money was gone. Rebecca was gone. Maybe they’d run off together with the loot. Who knew?

“It’s a mystery to me,” she’d said and let the tears fall. “I hope it’s solved someday,” she lied.

And Maya helped Portia plan Cole’s burial. She’d talked to his parents who were heartbroken. They invited Portia to stay with them when she got stateside. She hadn’t slept in her own room since Cole passed, and Maya was glad for the company in the king size bed in her suite.

“I think high is the best way to be after a funeral.” Maya accepted the joint and took a toke.

Portia stared out into the night. “But no matter how high I am, I still miss him.”

“Of course you do.” Maya sipped her drink. “I don’t think you will ever stop missing him.”

“I wonder if I will ever love again.”

Maya laughed. “Of course you will, silly. Now stop with all the gloom and doom and just enjoy tonight.”

Portia grew quiet, her buzz still strong.

Maya stared out at the black ocean and enjoyed the sound of the waves crashing against the shore.

Portia sighed. “You’ll have all your husband’s money

now."

Maya looped an arm around Portia's naked shoulders. "I suppose."

"All his money. All his homes. His businesses. Everything. Kind of ironic, don't you think?"

"Yeah, he wanted it all, now I've got it all." She downed the rest of her drink. "Do we still have that bag of weed?"

"I'll go get it. I need to get dressed anyway." She kissed Maya on the cheek and walked inside.

Maya stared out into the night, wondering what lay ahead for her. She'd received a call from Albert's secretary, Nikki, who could barely speak as she confessed to sleeping with her husband. She especially liked giving him head. One day Maya might forgive her, but not today. It wasn't Nikki's fault Albert was a dog, but my how the tables had turned. Now Maya was Nikki's boss.

She thought about the man from the gym, and how they'd met at the country club, and then again in Bossman's lair of sin. She had to chuckle at the thought of Bossman finding Abel tied up in a chair, blindfolded, his dick limp between his legs. She hoped he'd forgive her for the humiliation. Then she thought about Finn at her favorite coffee shop. He'd said he would buy her a cup of coffee when she returned. She liked that idea.

Maya wandered back inside and lay on her bed. The ceiling fan twisted above her head as her mind drifted to Nick, then Rebecca, and finally to her husband. Maya had never known such loss in such a short span of time. "Set adrift on memory's bliss," she whispered. Fucking all three of them was the best time she'd ever had.

She heard Portia call, "Maya."

"I'm on the bed."

Portia slinked out of the bathroom. She wore a short red nightgown that barely covered her sleek legs. Maya even noticed the red panties beneath. "What's with all the red?"

"Island custom." She sat cross-legged beside Maya and lit a freshly rolled cigar. "I'm supposed to wear red so Cole's *duppy* won't mess with me." She breathed in the smoke, held her breath, and closed her eyes.

"His what?"

"*Duppy.*" Portia exhaled. "It means soul." She took another toke before handing the cigar to Maya. "I actually want to mess with him." She slid out of her panties and tossed them beside the bed. "I want him to see how happy I am with you." She snuggled under Maya's right arm.

"I know how you feel." Maya breathed in Portia's freshly showered scent.

"You got what you wanted, a big black dick."

"Yeah, it was great."

"I'm glad you cheated on your husband."

"Maybe Nick's *duppy* will see how happy I am now."

She started to sob.

"It's okay, baby." Maya kissed Portia's forehead and rocked her back and forth until her tears subsided then she stroked her silky black hair. "We have each other now."

"I wouldn't have made it this far without you." Portia looked into Maya's eyes.

Maya smiled at her, now stroking her cheek. "You are much stronger than you give yourself credit for." She leaned forward and kissed Portia's lips.

Portia inhaled then kissed Maya in return. Passion on the rise, their tongues danced while their lips molded into one. Hands roamed every direction, up under nightgowns, over luscious breasts and hard nipples, and between sugar-sweet thighs.

Portia rolled on top of Maya and slid the straps of her nightgown off her dark skin, and then paused to marvel at her naked breasts before leaning over and kissing her lips again.

Maya reached under Portia's short gown and caressed

her flower, which made Portia shiver with delight. Her lips came away from Maya's as she sighed in ecstasy. Maya sat up and wrapped her mouth around Portia's now bare left tit, suckling on her peak and reveling in how quickly it grew rigid in her mouth.

"Ahh," Portia sighed as Maya's hand continued to explore Portia's folds. Her lips spread, and her juices allowed Maya to slide a single finger inside. Portia groaned as the finger coaxed more and more of her honey from her well, and soon her hips began to move in time with Maya's finger, and before long, a second finger slid inside, and Portia cried out.

Maya's mouth kissed and teased its way to Portia's right tit, which like her own, was the more sensitive of the two. Maya smiled as Portia's nipples grew taught and rigid while her pussy tightened around the relentless motions of Maya's hungry fingers.

"Maya, my God..." Portia squealed in ecstasy as she exploded, causing her hips to shudder in exquisite agony.

"Mmm." Maya slid a third finger inside.

Portia whimpered and snatched her pussy off the surging fingers as her yearning mouth desperately sought Maya's parted lips.

Maya giggled as their mouths merged once more. She enjoyed the sweet flavor of Portia's tongue. "Let me taste you," Maya said. "Down there."

"Let's do it together." Portia allowed her gown to form a puddle around her waist then pivoted over Maya's body to gain access to her pussy.

Maya gasped as Portia tenderly kissed her shaved mound before settling her already dripping pussy over Maya's wanton mouth.

Both women chose to take a moment to stare at the beautiful pussies gracing their eyes. As if on cue, they each ran a pair of fingers along the outside of the folds, each trembling as a second pass also slipped over their clits.

Portia's essence dripped into Maya's open mouth, and she couldn't help but suck Portia's clit into her mouth to join with her juices. Softly she dragged her tongue down Portia's valley to her honey pot, and then back up to her pretty pearl. Her pink skin was so soft, so wet, so hot...

Portia could only close here eyes and revel in euphoria as Maya's tongue exquisitely drove her closer to a second climax.

Maya luxuriated in the sugary sweetness that was Portia's pussy, and she moaned in surprise when Portia's tongue began to dance up and down Maya's aching mound.

Both women moved their hips and ground their sexes into the mouths that promised heavenly release. Tongues darted and dove, licked and lapped, and each woman's hot breath titillated each other's sensitive parts, each racing higher and higher to eventually succumb to a screaming orgasm. Like the ebb and flow of ocean waves against the shore, they moaned in unison, each eager to make the other soar into euphoria as they swallowed their juices.

Maya slid a finger inside Portia, making her scream in wild abandon as her mouth clamped down on Maya's tightening pussy, forcing Maya to cry out as well. Her body trembled in breathtaking bliss.

Portia twisted about and found Maya's open mouth again. She kissed her passionately and tasted her own sweetness on her lover's lips. Mouth against mouth, flesh against flesh, breasts against breasts, hips against hips...both bodies shuddered under the sensual onslaught until they finally fell still in exhaustion.

Once the passion waned, they rose up together, and still naked, moved arm in arm to the patio that overlooked the shore. It was just before sunrise. Maya relit the cigar once again. She relished her place in Portia's soft embrace. They were silent as they watched the sun rise over the blue ocean.

"I'm scared," Portia said.

Maya rubbed Portia's hand. "You're going to be okay."

"What about you?" Portia kissed her tenderly on the ear. "Will you be okay?"

Maya thought about Finn's big smile and Abel's perfect cock. The possibilities for love and sex were definitely in her future. Then Portia's big smile made her think that perhaps men weren't the best way to go. She felt her heart beat hard at the thought of another roll in the sheets with Portia.

"I'll be okay." She stared out at the morning sun's reflection on the water and hugged Portia tighter. "We'll be just fine."

About the Author

T. A. Malone kept a journal while attending Saul High School in Philadelphia, and he took several writing courses at Kutztown University of Pennsylvania. He then used his writing skills to develop his professional career in Texas as a corporate manager/trainer and teacher. A good friend once told him to start writing, but he didn't heed her sage advice. However, when he tore his left quadriceps muscle, forcing him to stay at home, he decided to write his first novel.

A proud husband and father of two, Malone hopes to leave an indelible mark on the world of erotic fiction.

Enjoy more erotica from Amore Moon Publishing - an imprint of TWB Press

No Limits by Ashley Adams
www.twbpress.com/nolimits.html

Army Buddy by Ashley Adams
www.twbpress.com/armybuddy.html

My Valentine Cowboy by Ashley Adams
www.twbpress.com/myvalentinecowboy.html

White Stallion by Theda Hudson.
www.twbpress.com/whitestallion.html

Extremophile by Ian McKinley
www.twbpress.com/extremophile.html

My Sweet Entity by Soliel De Bella
www.twbpress.com/mysweetentity.html

Entity Mine by Soliel De Bella
www.twbpress.com/entitymine.html

The Seduction of Lexie Dane by Soliel De Bella
www.twbpress.com/lexiedane.html

Claiming Holly by soliel De Bella
www.twbpress.com/claimingholly.html

Slump Buster by Brian Smith
www.twbpress.com/slumpbuster.html

www.twbpress.com